Tessa stood up. 'Do not mistake one kiss in an alcove for more than it was.

'It does not grant you permission to pry into my life. My business is mine alone. I am capable of taking care of myself and my sisters.'

Peyton Ramsden rose to meet her, his own temper rising with her. Lord, the woman was stubborn beyond all good sense. He knew instinctively that she would argue *ad nauseam*. He could think of nothing else to do except take his friend's advice and kiss her.

'One kiss might not qualify, but perhaps two will.' Tension sparked between them. Thank providence the Ramsden brothers counted kissing among their many accomplishments…

Author Note

I hope you enjoy THE EARL'S FORBIDDEN WARD and watching Peyton fall in love. It was great fun designing a heroine who would challenge him. This story was the perfect chance to do something with Russian history. I had the opportunity to study in Russia, right outside St Petersburg, a few years ago, and I've been wanting to do a story with some Russian history in it ever since. Giving Tessa the background of being a diplomat's daughter was a great opportunity to do that.

It was also interesting and a bit tricky doing some of the research about the location of the Russian embassy in London at that time, since the embassy moved from its original location to Kensington and even went through a non-active period during the Napoleonic wars.

A third point of interest is the scene set at the Academy. The recollection Peyton has about the John Turner painting is all true. I found a short but great article that talked about the Academy art show that year and I just had to use it.

The final challenge with this book was stepping out of the regular *tonnish* neighbourhoods. I knew Tessa wouldn't have a home in Mayfair, so it was fun researching the Bloomsbury population of the 1830s. I had a chance to walk through Bloomsbury on a recent research trip to London, which helped me describe Tessa's neighbourhood more thoroughly.

For more about Bloomsbury, the Academy art show or embassies, check out my website at www.bronwynnscott.com and keep reading!

THE EARL'S FORBIDDEN WARD

Bronwyn Scott

⊚™ MILLS & BOON®
Pure reading pleasure™

All the characters in this book have no existence outside the imagination of the author, and have no relation whatsoever to anyone bearing the same name or names. They are not even distantly inspired by any individual known or unknown to the author, and all the incidents are pure invention.

First published in Great Britain 2009
Harlequin Mills & Boon Limited,
Eton House, 18-24 Paradise Road, Richmond, Surrey TW9 1SR

ISBN: 978 0 263 86783 1

Set in Times Roman 10½ on 13 pt.
04-0609-66924

Printed and bound in Spain
by Litografia Rosés S.A., Barcelona

*For my niece, Rachel, who wanted to know
how wars got started and actually listened
when I explained it to her.*

Bronwyn Scott is a communications instructor at Pierce College in the United States, and is the proud mother of three wonderful children (one boy and two girls). When she's not teaching or writing, she enjoys playing the piano, travelling—especially to Florence, Italy—and studying history and foreign languages.

Readers can stay in touch on Bronwyn's website, www.bronwynnscott.com, or at her blog, www.bronwynswriting.blogspot.com. She loves to hear from readers.

Recent novels from Bronwyn Scott:

PICKPOCKET COUNTESS
NOTORIOUS RAKE, INNOCENT LADY
THE VISCOUNT CLAIMS HIS BRIDE

Chapter One

London—Spring 1832

Peyton Ramsden, fourth Earl of Dursley, was doing what he did best—technically superior, emotionally removed sex with his mistress of two years. Certain of her fulfilment, he gave a final thrust and efficiently withdrew to make a gentleman's finish in the sheets.

His mistress, the elegant Lydia Staunton, raised herself up on one arm, letting the white satin of the sheet slide provocatively down her hip. 'So, you're giving me my *congé*,' she said matter-of-factly.

'Yes, I am,' Peyton answered evenly. There was no need to dress up the conversation, although he'd planned to bring up the issue *after* he'd got out of bed. For a man who liked to keep his life organised into neat compartments, there was something inherently wrong about discussing business so soon after coupling, even if it was the business of sex.

'How did you know?' He hadn't spoken of it or dropped the slightest hint at ending their arrangement since he'd come up to town three days ago, although he'd made it plain at the beginning of their association that he had no intentions of sustaining their relationship beyond two years.

'It was worse than usual tonight.' Lydia could always be counted on to speak her mind.

Peyton fixed her with an arrogant stare, one eyebrow raised in challenge. 'I highly doubt that, *madame.*' If there was one area the Ramsden brothers excelled at, it was in the bedroom arts. They'd been schooled at an early age about how to please a woman, part of their father's training regimen for a gentleman.

Lydia fell back on the pillows, ennui punctuating her words. 'It's not *that.* It's *never* that. You know you're exquisite in the bedroom, Dursley. You don't need me to tell you your skills are unsurpassed.'

Dursley. He hated being a title to everyone, especially someone he'd shared conjugal relations with. Peyton rolled out of bed in a single fluid motion and strode across the room to the chair where his clothes waited. He picked up his shirt to put on. Perhaps he'd demand his next mistress call him 'Peyton'. And perhaps not. Forced intimacy wasn't true intimacy and he required honesty above all else.

'Well, thank goodness. For a moment I was

starting to doubt.' His tone conveyed the exact opposite. There was no misunderstanding the real message. The Earl of Dursley did not doubt himself in the least, in any aspect of his life.

Lydia sighed. 'Skills aren't everything, Dursley. It takes more than prowess in bed to be a good lover. Some day, you're going to have to feel something.'

This was an old discussion. Lydia had accused him of being detached more than once during their association. Tonight, Peyton chose to ignore the comment. Arguing at the end of their association would resolve nothing. He pulled on his trousers and shrugged into his coat. He walked to Lydia's dressing table and pulled a slim box from the inside pocket of his coat. He didn't need to tell Lydia what it was. She was experienced enough in these dealings to know the box contained an expensive parting gift; something she could choose to flaunt or sell, depending on her circumstances. He placed a calling card on top of the box.

'Peter Pennington, Viscount Wyndham, has suggested he is in the market. I offered him the lease to this house if you're amenable.' Lydia would know exactly what that meant. He'd found her another protector. Her financial security would not lapse in the wake of his exit.

'Bravo, very nice, Dursley. You've wrapped up all the loose ends in two sentences.' Lydia got out of bed and slipped her long arms into a silk robe, one of his many gifts to her over the years. She belted it at the waist. 'Tell me, do you ever get tired of being in control?' The words were not kind.

Ah, the usually unflappable Lydia was piqued. Peyton sensed it was time to make an expedient exit before a quarrel cast a pall over their parting. He understood her discontent. For all the physical pleasure he gave her, Lydia wanted something more from him, something he was unwilling to give. 'I know what you want, Lydia. Wyndham is better suited to give you the illusion of romance than I am.' He made a short bow in her direction. 'I wish you the best. Goodnight, my dear. I have other business to attend to before my evening is through. I will show myself out.'

Once outside in the cold evening, Peyton sent his coach home, choosing to walk instead. The night air was bracing and he suddenly found himself in possession of a burst of energy begging to be spent. It was just as well—a walk would give him time to think and there was plenty to think about. Giving Lydia her *congé* was only one of the situations he'd come up to town to resolve. The other item involved a summons from an old friend at Whitehall regarding a colleague who had recently passed away.

Peyton reached for his pocket watch and flipped it open. Nine a.m. That gave him a half an hour to make his nine-thirty meeting with Lord Brimley. It was Whitehall business they were to discuss. Brimley had made that clear in his letter. But they would discuss it at White's in a private room.

He had plenty of time to travel the few streets to St James's and White's Gentlemen's Club, but his pace increased none the less. There was a certain excitement in the prospect of the upcoming meeting and he'd acknowledged weeks ago he needed something to keep him occupied.

His youngest brother, Paine, and Paine's wife, Julia, had taken up residence at the family seat, deep in the idyllic heart of the Cotswolds, to await the birth of their first child not quite a year after their marriage. He was, of course, thrilled to have his brother under his roof. But the birth of Paine's son four weeks ago had made Peyton restless in a most uncomfortable way.

He adored his new nephew without question, having been shamelessly caught on numerous occasions in the nursery with the infant in his arms—a sight most of London would have been shocked to see, given his reputation towards sombre decorum. Yet, watching Paine and Julia together with their new son had filled him with disquiet and a sense that his life, for all his accomplishments, was incomplete in his thirty-eighth year.

Logically, the assumption that his life lacked something was ludicrous. He'd come into his title at the young age of twenty-three when he had years ahead of him to maximise the earldom's prosperity and take advantage of all the technological advances open to agriculture. Maximise them he had. While others struggled with outmoded notions of estate management and agricultural depression, Dursley thrived. It was no small thing to accept responsibility for the Dursley holdings and the people attached to them. His successes were their successes.

Additionally, he did his duty in Parliament, coming up to town when sessions needed him to lend his voice on weighty matters. And his devotion to country and king didn't end there. During the years following the Napoleonic Wars, he'd done his duty as a discreet diplomatic courier to Vienna when tensions over the future of the Balkans arose. He'd become a regular face in the drawing rooms of the New Europe in those days as nations negotiated new political boundaries and privileges.

Oh, no, although he was not one to need public acclaim for his efforts, he could personally acknowledge that his efforts had borne worthwhile fruits. His life had not been spent in idle pursuits of no account, but in the pursuit of building an empire that would far outlast his years on earth. A man could take pride in such achievement. Indeed, a man *should* take pride in such a life.

Which was why the internal unrest he'd suffered from lately was so distressing. It had sprung from nowhere and for no reason. Such an appearance was all the more disconcerting for a man of his ilk, who exerted control over all aspects of his life—demanded it, in fact. Imbalance was not a common or tolerated occurrence within his domain.

The façade of White's loomed across the street. Redemption waited inside. Soon, he'd appease the errant devils that plagued him and get his life back to normal.

He was expected. A footman whisked away his hat and outerwear while another one smartly led him upstairs to the private rooms. Brimley was already there. Peyton's anticipation grew. Brimley's early arrival suggested the man was anxious about the meeting.

Such concern seemed out of character for the context of the meeting. In his note to Peyton, Brimley had indicated simply that there were a few details to wrap up with Branscombe's passing. The only oddity was that Brimley had summoned him at all. He could count the times he'd met Sir Ralph Branscombe on one hand and still have fingers left over. If he remembered correctly, Branscombe had primarily been stationed in St Petersburg.

The footman opened the door to the luxuriously appointed room with its thick carpet and carved marble mantelpiece. The room would have done any grand home in Mayfair proud. But Peyton had scarcely a glance for the stately elegance of the décor.

Brimley rose from his chair by the fire and came

forward to greet him. 'Dursley, so good of you to come. What's it been? Two years, now?'

Peyton nodded. Brimley looked tired and careworn beyond his fifty years, but his memory was clearly still sharp if he could recall the last time Peyton had worked for him. 'Nearly two years,' Peyton affirmed, taking time to carefully study Brimley's features, searching for a reason for the weariness that plagued him.

Brimley seemed to sense Peyton's scrutiny. He waved a hand. 'Come and sit, Dursley. You're a lucky man to have missed the last two years, after all.'

Brimley pushed a hand through his greying hair. 'I was disappointed to see you go, but I understood you had estates to run. You couldn't be hotfooting it off to Vienna or wherever else at my beck and call. Now, I wonder if I shouldn't have bowed out, too. The Balkans and the Eastern Question are enough to drive any man insane. One wonders what we really won when Napoleon was defeated—a pile of war debt here at home and a handful of cocksure pocket-tyrants in the Far East stealing access to waterways.'

Peyton gave a short laugh. 'You don't fool me for a minute, Brimley. You love the intrigue of this new world.' He settled in his chair, relaxing into its depths. Ahhh. White's knew the value of a comfortable chair.

Brimley opened the humidor on the table next to him and selected a cheroot. He offered the cherry-wood box to Peyton. Peyton declined with a mild wave. 'Well, I suppose I do like some of the game,'

Brimley admitted, taking a long draw on the cheroot. 'But I don't like loose ends and that's what I've got with Branscombe's fiasco.'

'Fiasco?' Peyton felt his body tense. He certainly hadn't got that impression from Brimley's note. But then, Brimley was a master diplomat, never letting out more than he wanted anyone to know before he wanted them to know it.

'Branscombe had the bad taste to die while in possession of a list of Russian insurgents deemed dangerous by the Czar. Unfortunately, since his death, the list has not come to light. Our sources in St Petersburg are certain that the Russians have not found it. There's been no report of arrests or suspicious disappearances. However, we have not found it either.' Brimley gave a heavy sigh.

Peyton steepled his hands and studied the fire, digesting Brimley's news. He'd always known there was a fine line between espionage and diplomacy. Not every diplomat was a spy, of course. But some were. It seemed the mild-mannered Branscombe had crossed that line.

And why not? Diplomats had very little accountability to any authority once they were at their posts. Accounts of their deeds or decisions would take months to reach England, if at all. Often there was no time to waste in waiting for responses from home regarding how to proceed. One simply had to rely on instinct and do what one felt was best.

Peyton certainly understood the ease with which diplomacy and espionage could be mixed. What he didn't understand was why this particular list had Brimley edgy. He doubted Brimley was all that concerned about preserving the identity of Russian revolutionaries.

'What makes the list so important to us?' Peyton asked.

Brimley eyed him for a while. Peyton knew the man was weighing him up, assessing what could be told and what could be left out. 'This is strictly confidential, Dursley.'

Peyton smiled. Most of their conversations over the years had included that phrase. 'I assumed it would be.'

Brimley grimaced. 'An unstable Russia weakens Russia's power to influence Turkey and that's good for us. We need the waterway for our Indian trade routes.'

He was talking about the Dardanelle Straits, which Turkey controlled. A conquered Turkey, a Russian-controlled Turkey, would be an intolerable situation for Britain. Passage through the Dardanelles made it possible to cut weeks off the trip between London and Bombay, making passage around the dangerous African Horn unnecessary.

But this explanation would be commonplace to a man who'd been keeping up on current events. There was nothing confidential here. Such information was bandied about the House of Lords daily. Peyton shook his head. 'That's not good enough,

Brimley. I know all that already. How does the list influence Russia?'

Brimley seemed to concede. 'All right. It has come to my attention that Branscombe compiled the list on behalf of some ambitious and wealthy businessmen who would be glad to fund an internal rebellion to overthrow the Czar. In exchange, they are asking for guarantees from the new government to leave Turkey, and the Dardanelles, especially, alone.'

Peyton let out a low whistle. Foreign involvement in plotting revolution was serious business. He didn't need to be told Branscombe had been well paid by these men to make the necessary connections and compile the list. Even after the disastrous 1825 December uprising in Russia, secret revolutionary societies still abounded. The promise of cash for weapons and munitions probably appealed to the most organised groups.

But where there were secrets, there were traitors. The 1825 Decembrists had been betrayed to the Czar at the last minute and apparently Branscombe's intentions had met with the same fate. A suspicion crossed Peyton's mind. 'How did Branscombe die? I don't think you mentioned it.'

'For all intents and purposes, it was a natural death. He passed quietly in his sleep,' Brimley hedged.

'But you don't believe that, do you, old man?' Peyton pressed, not willing to be fobbed off. He didn't understand yet what his role in all this was to be, but he certainly wasn't going to commit himself without knowing all the details.

'Well, I only know what the doctors tell me. He was a thousand miles away in another country, after all. At this distance, I am heavily dependent on second-hand information,' Brimley prevaricated.

'I don't doubt the doctors told you exactly what you told me. But you suspect otherwise?'

'I only know the Russians knew he had made a list and what he intended to do with it. Which gave them a motive to put their best assassins on the case.'

Peyton recognised he wasn't going to get anything further from Brimley on that account. 'All right. We can leave his demise at that. The more burning question for me is what can I do here? I am not clear at all as to why you've contacted me. I hardly knew the man and I've only met him a few times.'

'The list is not in Russia. It's not at the British embassy in St Petersburg. If it's anywhere, it's in England.'

Peyton raised his eyebrows, encouraging Brimley to be more forthcoming. 'Yes?'

'The list is in England. As of today, a highly alert delegation from Russia is also on British soil.'

'So, we search the man's residences quickly.'

'We've tried that, but we've run into several stumbling blocks.' Brimley seemed discomfited. The man shifted in his chair. 'Precisely, four stumbling blocks in the form of Branscombe's daughters. The biggest stumbling block is his eldest daughter, Miss Tessa Branscombe.'

Peyton found the room had grown hot. His cravat seemed extraordinarily noose-like. Brimley's discomfiture was contagious and for good reason. He had his suspicions about where this conversation was headed.

'I want you to get close to the girls, Miss Branscombe particularly. I've arranged for a codicil to Branscombe's will to be drawn up regarding your ability to act as a guardian for the girls. With the exception of Miss Branscombe, the other three are all under eighteen. But they will all be under your guardianship. Once you've established the girls under your protection, you'll have access to the house. You can search it at will and in broad daylight without arousing their distrust.'

Peyton spread his hands out before him as if he were warding off an unseen blight. 'No, I will not play nursemaid to four silly females. What do I know about young girls in the schoolroom? I raised brothers. The condition of my unwed state alone would make the arrangement unseemly. I am a bachelor.' What Brimley suggested was not diplomacy at all, but babysitting in disguise.

'A bachelor with an impeccable reputation for honour and responsibility,' Brimley reminded him. 'Not to mention a formidable aunt in the Dowager Duchess Bridgerton.' Brimley meant Peyton's father's sister, Lily.

'Lady Bridgerton will be the perfect guide to help Miss Branscombe through the Season,' Brimley said, beaming over his thorough plan. 'And you'll be the perfect escort.'

Peyton gripped the arms of his chair. 'Wait, this is a new development. Why does Miss Branscombe need a Season?' He had no intention of doing the pretty. When he'd come up to London, he hadn't meant to stay longer than was necessary to take care of this 'small' issue with Brimley and settle things with Lydia. He was eager to return to his family in the country and his new nephew.

'Escorting her around town will give you a chance to gain her confidence. The more time you spend together, the more willing she might be to confide in you.' Brimley appeared untroubled about the breach of ethics the scheme demanded.

Peyton did not share the man's detachment. This was becoming more unpalatable all the time—a forged codicil to create an imaginary guardianship, and a veiled request to seduce the father's secrets from the daughter, smacked of dishonesty and double dealing.

Peyton got up from his chair and walked to the sideboard holding an array of brandies. He poured himself a glass and turned back to face Brimley. 'I won't do it merely to support the pockets of self-serving businessmen. You should have known I was the wrong man for the job.' He took a long sip of brandy, spearing Brimley with his eyes, letting him see the disdain in which he held Brimley's proposal.

'You'll be well paid,' Brimley said obtusely. 'I don't ask you to do this without reward.'

Peyton set the heavy tumbler down hard. 'There is no sum of gold that would entice me to flirt with an innocent young girl under false pretences and to betray her sisters at a vulnerable time in their lives.'

Brimley rose. 'I am not offering you gold, Dursley. We all know you've got more blunt than the rest of us. I am offering you lives.'

Brimley took a folded sheet of paper out of his coat pocket. 'Read it. British intelligence reports that the Russian army is preparing to mobilise against Turkey. It will be war by this time next year and British boys will be on the front lines. Internal instability in Mother Russia would be a powerful piece of leverage for our diplomats in St Petersburg to negotiate with. With the right persuasion, our diplomats will be able to halt the war before it begins.'

Peyton scanned the letter, weighing his options. But that was the irony—there were no options to weigh. He could not countenance the discomfort of four young girls against the lives of hundreds of soldiers. Neither could he countenance his own discontentment at escorting Sir Ralph Branscombe's daughter through the Season when it would prevent British soldiers from enduring far worse discomforts on the battlefield.

Peyton Ramsden, fourth Earl of Dursley, lifted his glass in a toast. 'Well, then, here's to king and country.' He drank a large swallow. It had been a hell of a night.

Chapter Two

Tessa Branscombe was doing what she did best: flouting convention intentionally and in some ways unintentionally as she ushered her three sisters through the busy markets of London. A basket hung from her arm full of prizes wrested from merchants who'd been cowed by her shrewd negotiations.

To Tessa's way of thinking, there was nothing inappropriate about the conduct of the outing. All four of them were dressed conservatively in sombre colours, although the period of half-mourning for their father had passed. Furthermore, they were escorted by the gallant Sergei Androvich, newly arrived from the Russian embassy.

If there was a glaring oddity about the outing, it concerned the place she'd chosen to take her sisters. She'd taken them to obtain greens and other food-stuffs that were usually obtained by a cook or house-

keeper in a common marketplace. Tessa acknowledged this was not an errand polite society deemed
appropriate for a lady of her station, and certainly not
an appropriate outing for impressionable young girls.
But while she acknowledged English society's
outlook, she staunchly disagreed with it.

In Tessa's opinion, a tradition that prevented a girl
from learning the intricacies of providing for a household's meals wasn't a very useful tradition and, thus,
not deserving of her attention. So, here she was, a
basket full of vegetables, a string of high-spirited
sisters trailing behind her and the handsome delegate
from the Russian embassy and old friend from St Petersburg, Sergei, beside her.

All in all, the little entourage made a strange
picture in a marketplace not used to seeing a lady of
quality amongst its customers, bargaining over prices
with the tenacity of a fishwife on the docks. If merchants' jaws dropped in amazement as the little group
passed, that was their problem. Tessa had a faultless
escort in Sergei Androvich and that was as far as she
was willing to bend for tradition's sake.

They passed a flower girl selling violets. Sergei
tossed the girl a coin and snatched a bouquet, which
he promptly presented to Tessa. He sketched an
elegant leg in a playful, elaborate fashion that made
her laugh. Her sisters gathered about her, giggling
and clapping. Sergei dug out some more coins and
presented each of them with their own posies of

violets, to their great delight. Tessa pressed her nose to the gay bouquet and smiled. 'Thank you.'

'It is my pleasure. It's been too long since you smiled, Tess,' Sergei said softly in his perfect, but accented, English.

'I know.' Tessa met his blue gaze with her own, exchanging much with him in that moment. It had been a long nine months since her father's death. There had been the enormous effort of leaving St Petersburg, a place that had been their home for fourteen years. She'd grown up there and had left many friends behind. Then there had been the work of setting up a home in her father's little-used residence in London, a place Tessa had not seen since she was eight and her mother had been alive.

'I am so glad you're here, Sergei,' Tessa said sincerely. Sergei had arrived yesterday with the Russian delegation and she was glad of his company. London was foreign to her. She missed the familiar faces and pace of life in St Petersburg. 'How long will you be in London?'

'I am not sure, but at least until September,' Sergei replied. 'My work with the embassy won't be so arduous that I won't have time for you. We'll put a smile back on your face in no time.'

'You already have.' Tessa smiled again, slipping her free hand through the crook of Sergei's arm. She meant it, too. All she knew of London was through the Englishmen who'd been posted to the St Petersburg embassy. But Sergei was a familiar friend. The son of a Russian noble, Sergei had appeared at the Czar's royal court three years ago, looking to make his way in diplomatic circles. He'd been an instant success with his fluency in English, his education and his dashing blond good looks and blue eyes. It hadn't been long before he'd been assigned as a junior liaison between the British embassy and the Russian diplomats.

He'd become a fixture at the Branscombe home, talking over situations with her father and a natural friendship had sprung up between them, which extended to Tessa and the girls.

Tessa looked around at her sisters, busy admiring their posies. The simple gestures had brought them a moment of pleasure in their uncertain world. Seeing how happy the bouquets made them, she privately vowed it was time to start getting out more. London was full of sights to see, and, with Sergei here, it would be a perfect time to take in the attractions. For now, though, it was time to head home.

Sergei offered to hail a cab, but Tessa insisted the walk was good exercise.

Several streets later, they reached the neat row of town houses in Bloomsbury, a neighbourhood preferred by a well-to-do intellectual set. The town houses ringed a well-kept key-garden for the residents' private use and smartly dressed nannies pushed babies in prams up and down the park.

Overall, Tessa found it a pleasing area, quiet and

removed far enough from the hub-bub of the city and busier neighbourhoods for her tastes. She had no desire to call attention to herself. The last thing she wanted was interference in her life. All she wanted these days was to set up house, see to her sisters in her own fashion without society's intrusion and forget about the last tumultuous days in St Petersburg. She preferred remembering how life had been there before her father's death and the quiet terror that had stalked her afterwards.

The girls bounded up the front steps ahead of her, eager to get their violets in water. Sergei laughed at their enthusiasm. 'They're exuberant,' he said.

Tessa nodded. 'It's good for them. Will you come in and have tea? Mrs Hollister was making scones this morning.'

'It will be a perfect end to a perfect afternoon,' Sergei accepted.

Within moments, the perfection Sergei had spoken of evaporated. If Tessa had known what lay beyond the front door of her own home, she might not have gone in. No sooner had she and Sergei entered the hall than they were surrounded by her sisters, all talking excitedly at once. She caught only snatches of nonsensical phrases such as, 'A guest!', 'An earl', 'In the front room'.

Tessa clapped her hands for silence. 'One at a time, please!' She turned to Petra, her junior by five years. 'Petra, what is going on?'

Petra never got a chance to answer.

A masculine voice spoke with clipped, commanding tones from the doorway of the front room. 'I believe what the girls are trying to tell you is that the Earl of Dursley is waiting to be received.'

Tessa turned to her right. All her instincts were on alert at the sight of the imposing, dark-haired man. Her first impression was one of danger. This man was dangerous. Dangerous *and* powerful. His eyes were like cold sapphires. There was no warmth in them as they surveyed her and her sisters.

Her second reaction was to protect. Tessa stepped forward, adopting a cold hauteur of her own, the one she used when she had to inform an importuning guest her father wouldn't receive them. 'I don't believe we've met. Furthermore, I don't believe you have an appointment. I regret you've been waiting. However, I am not receiving today. I must ask you to leave.' She pasted on a polite smile at the last. She'd found in the years acting as her father's hostess that people often accepted bad news better when it came with a smile.

The man stepped forward, quirking a challenging eyebrow at her. 'You must be Miss Tessa Branscombe.'

Tessa's smile disappeared. The arrogance of this man was unprecedented. He'd come to her home unannounced, no doubt intimidated Mrs Hollister into being allowed to wait, and now refused to acknowledge her dismissal. She'd asked him to leave and he was ignoring her. Instead, he was carrying on with his visit as if she'd accepted his presence in her home.

Beside her, Sergei bristled. 'The lady has asked you to leave and come another day.'

The Earl turned his gaze on Sergei, as if noticing him for the first time. Tessa thought the gesture was intentionally done, meant to suggest that the Earl didn't feel Sergei was worthy of his particular notice. She doubted this earl in all his kingly arrogance over-looked anything or anyone.

'And you would be?'

'Count Sergei Androvich,' Sergei said with all the coldness of a Russian winter.

Tessa watched the blue eyes of the Earl become positively glacial. 'Ah, yes, the attaché with the newly arrived Russian delegation.' She was certain he was ignoring Sergei's title on purpose. In one sentence this man had demoted Sergei from Count to a mere attaché. Sergei had gone from a foreign peer worthy of being treated as an equal to nothing more than another man's clerk.

'I see you've heard of me.' Sergei summoned a modicum of aristocratic hauteur of his own.

'It is my business to be apprised of all the people and things related to the Misses Branscombe,' the Earl drawled elegantly.

What audacity! She didn't even know him and the man was arrogantly insinuating he had some claim to the intimacies of their lives. Tessa had had enough. The social temperature in the entrance hall was frigid. She wasn't going to let these two men, not even well-meaning Sergei, squabble over territorial rights when it wasn't even their home. It was hers, and right now her sisters were staring wide-eyed at her, expecting her to act as if it was.

'My lord, I must again request that you leave. This is a highly unexpected visit.' She gestured towards Sergei. 'As you can see, we've already got company.' Sergei gave the Earl a small triumphant half-smile.

'I heard you perfectly the first time, Miss Branscombe. However, I think you'll find time for me, once you hear why I've come.'

Was that a bit of condescension in his voice? Was he so certain of his news? Tessa placed her hands on her hips, her temper getting the better of her. 'Then tell me and get out.'

The Earl chuckled. 'Miss Branscombe, I am here to inform you that I am your guardian. A codicil to your father's will has placed you and your sisters under my protection.'

Like hell it had. Tessa stifled the urge to speak her mind. She was a diplomat's daughter and knew the importance of time and place. There would be nothing gained from erupting over the news. She needed more information before she could decide what to do and this overbearing male seemed to be the most immediate source to hand.

'I stand corrected, my lord. Won't you join us for tea?' Tessa said with great aplomb. She gestured to the drawing room and the group filed in.

He might have forced her to receive him, but she didn't have to like it. Round one to the Earl. She would not readily cede any more ground to him. He could take tea with them, but he wasn't getting a single bite of Mrs Hollister's scones.

Chapter Three

Tessa Branscombe hadn't *looked* like the kind of woman who caused trouble. When she'd come through the town-house door, Peyton's first reaction had been an entirely manly one at the sight of her. Brimley had not mentioned how stunning the eldest Miss Branscombe was. But Brimley was an old man.

Brimley had not mentioned the piles of pure gold curls that shone like a halo on her head, setting off the curve of her delicate jaw, or the cameo-like fragility of her ivory-skinned features. The woman was a walking incarnation of an angel, not to mention a properly dressed one. It would be a pleasure to see this young woman turned out in the more stylish, fashionable gowns of the *ton*.

His second reaction was that Brimley was getting soft if he'd had difficulty getting around this lovely chit with liquid-gold hair. He had every indication that her demeanour would match her beauty. Then she'd opened her mouth, her blue-almost-violet eyes flashing with irritation and Peyton understood with instant clarity what Brimley had implied.

The so-called angel had *dismissed* him, the Earl of Dursley. Out of hand, moreover. Peyton could not recall a time when he'd been so thoroughly given his *congé*. There was little he could have done aside from obliging her, which was out of the question, so he'd ignored her dismissal.

Fortunately, her escort made it easy for him to shift his attentions and now they were having tea— all six of them, including the Count and every one of Miss Branscombe's sisters. Miss Branscombe had made no move to send her sisters up to the school-room or wherever else they were supposed to go.

Peyton thought it was most unorthodox of her to let them sit in on this difficult meeting. To be fair, perhaps she meant to send them out of the room after tea, so he dutifully made small talk over two cups of tea—without cakes, he noted—waiting for an opportunity to continue with his business.

Over the third cup of tea, Peyton began to think Miss Branscombe had used the tea as a rather successful delaying tactic. He was growing thin on the patience a man needed for appreciating the girlish chatter that flowed about him. He now knew a copious amount of information about each of the Branscombe girls.

Petra, who was seventeen, had plied him with a veritable oratory regarding the differences between the horses she'd ridden in St Petersburg and the horses she'd seen here in England. He gathered she was as horse-mad as his brother Crispin had been at her age.

Eva was fifteen and gabbed incessantly about clothes and gowns, and how she liked to design her own dresses. The youngest was Anne, a shy ten-year-old who said nothing, but leaned against Tessa for comfort, staring at him with frightened wide blue eyes the entire time.

Miss Branscombe put down her tea cup during a lull in Eva's dissertation on the different qualities of silks and speared him with a sharp look. 'Well, my lord, we have had three cups of tea and you have not broached the reason behind your visit.'

Peyton set his cup down and met her challenge evenly. 'I've been waiting for you to send the girls out of the room. It is not the English custom to discuss business in front of children.'

Miss Branscombe visibly bristled. 'But it is *my* custom.'

'I do not wish my news to be unsettling to them. Sometimes, children are not mentally equipped to process information the same way adults are,' Peyton explained politely.

Miss Branscombe's fascinating eyes narrowed. 'My sisters are hardly children, as you've had a chance to ascertain. Petra and Eva are of ages where they should have a say in the direction of their destinies, and, while Annie is young, I must inform you that my father's death and all the changes of the past year have been most unsettling to her.'

Peyton's eyes flicked to the Count. 'And Count Androvich? Is he to remain as well?' Brimley had not suggested one of the Russian delegation would attach themselves so intimately to the Branscombe household. This was an unforeseen development and one Peyton didn't like in the least. He wanted Count Androvich dislodged. Hunting for the list would be difficult enough without the Count around. The man's presence begged the question of his motives. Was he here as a friend? He did seem quite protective of Miss Branscombe. Or was he using his association with the family to search for the list?

Thankfully, Miss Branscombe recognised he was giving her a victory by allowing her sisters to remain. She knew what she had to do to secure that victory. She nodded her angel's head at the Count. 'Sergei, we've taken up enough of your time today. I thank you for your escort to the market. I will not take up any more of your time. I can talk with Lord Dursley on my own.' Miss Branscombe rose and offered the Count her hand. Peyton silently congratulated her on the smoothness of her actions. There was no way the Count could refuse her polite invitation to exit the conversation without looking either obtuse or rude.

Miss Branscombe saw the Count to the door

and returned shortly, smoothing her demure skirts about her as she sat. 'Now, my lord, we can discuss your business.'

All four pairs of Branscombe-blue eyes fixed on him, waiting. Peyton brought out the papers and began. 'I have been informed that guardianship has passed to me upon your father's demise. That guardianship will last until each girl marries or turns twenty-five, at which point your trust funds shall be given into your individual care.'

Miss Branscombe assessed him shrewdly. 'You mentioned this permission was granted to you through a codicil to my father's will. But I assure you there was no codicil or mention of one in the will. I was there when it was read, we all were.' Her sisters nodded in affirmation.

Miss Branscombe continued, 'I have no reason to believe you and I certainly will not turn over control of my family and their modest fortunes to a man I do not know simply because he shows up on my doorstep with papers and a title.'

'It is regrettable that the codicil became separated from the other documents. It is fortunate that it's been recovered and placed in the right hands.' Peyton struggled for patience. He told himself he'd have been disappointed if the brassy Miss Branscombe had not been astute enough to see the possible flaws in his claim. He *should* appreciate that she was not easily hoodwinked. But the truth was, he didn't appreciate it in the least. It had been a long time since anyone had countermanded the Earl of Dursley. He'd quite forgotten what it was like.

'I understand your misgivings, Miss Branscombe. I assure you that I am the Earl of Dursley and I am, in the absence of any close living relations in your family, the man assigned to guide you and watch over you all. I have the most honourable of intentions.' And he did have honourable intentions for England— just not necessarily for the girls.

'I've never met you,' Miss Branscombe challenged. 'I am hard pressed to believe my father would have selected a guardian that we've never met. Quite frankly, it seems unlikely that he would have picked a man we didn't even know existed until this afternoon.'

Peyton nodded. 'I met your father on a few occasions in Vienna, but I never had the chance to journey north to St Petersburg.' At least this wasn't a lie, although the implications it hinted at—those of a relationship with Ralph Branscombe—were non-existent.

Peyton pushed the papers towards Miss Branscombe, since she hadn't moved to take them from the table. 'If you look at the papers, Miss Branscombe, you will see that they are in order. There is a letter of introduction that vouches for me. The codicil is there, as well as an outline of how my guardianship is to be managed.'

Forced to acknowledge the papers, Miss Branscombe picked them up and began to read. And read.

A weighty silence fell. Peyton could hear the mantel clock ticking off the minutes. The muffled sound of a passing carriage could be heard from the street and still Miss Branscombe read. At last, she looked up. Peyton thought he saw her hands tremble slightly, but she adroitly folded them and hid them in the lap of her skirt and he couldn't be sure.

'What do the papers say, Tess?' Petra asked in a quiet voice.

Miss Branscombe reached for Petra's hand. She was all calmness; the angel quality Peyton had seen in her earlier had returned. 'There's nothing for you to worry about, dear. Now, I need to speak with the Earl privately. Please take the girls upstairs.'

Anne whimpered next to Miss Branscombe and she bent to whisper reassurances to the little girl, gently nudging her towards Petra's outstretched arms. 'Annie, your dollies will be missing you. Perhaps you and Eva can try on the new dresses she made them,' Miss Branscombe cajoled. 'I'll be up in a while to see how they look and we can have a tea party.'

Peyton watched Miss Branscombe walk the three girls to the door, Petra shooting a last glance at her older sister, clearly worried. The scene was hard to take in. Seeing the sisters together reminded him all too acutely of life after his father had passed away, leaving him an earldom and two brothers to care for. But that was years past and he'd locked the feelings associated with those difficult days away deep inside himself long ago. He didn't want them resurrected. Nothing could come of them. They were best left alone, unexamined and unexplored.

When Miss Branscombe turned back to him, the angel was gone. She was all fire and rage. 'I will not stand for you or anyone splitting up this family. I have worked too hard keeping us together, too hard trying to give them stability.'

Peyton rose, since Miss Branscombe had no intention of sitting down. He strode to the window and drew back a lace panel to view the street below. 'I imagine the life of a diplomat is often trying for a woman. Moving about, making new friends, learning new customs must be an overwhelming task.'

'It is a difficult task for *anyone*,' Miss Branscombe promptly corrected. 'I have done it admirably and now I deserve my reward.'

'Which is what?' Peyton turned from his study of the street to watch Miss Branscombe.

'To be left alone with my sisters, to raise them where they will be safe,' she retorted sharply.

That got Peyton's attention. He veiled his reaction carefully. 'Were they not safe in St Petersburg?' Miss Branscombe seemed to hesitate. Interesting.

'Diplomacy in general is not always the safest of fields,' she answered vaguely.

Peyton nodded. He wondered—did she know about the list? Had something happened in St Petersburg to give her reason to fear for her own personal safety and that of her sisters? He couldn't ask her now. Such probing would seem too nosy. He'd have to file this away and remember to pursue it when the timing was better.

'I assure you, Miss Branscombe, that your fears are understandable and misplaced. I have no intention of swindling your fortunes out from under you. You are welcome to do a financial check on me. My solicitor has been instructed to be at your disposal. Additionally, I am not proposing that the family be split up. The girls are welcome to stay in London with you for the Season.' If he couldn't convince her of his reassurances, he'd be off to an awkward start in gaining her trust.

'We can decide, *together*, at the end of the Season where all of you should go next. I am prepared to make you welcome at Dursley Park until you're settled. My family is there,' Peyton offered. The last bit was spontaneous, perhaps motivated by guilt over the situation. His arrangement with Brimley did not require him to do anything for the girls.

Miss Branscombe appeared to visibly relax at the prospect. She nodded. 'Will your wife be joining us in London?'

'I am not married, Miss Branscombe. When I mentioned my family, I meant my two brothers, my brother's wife, their new child and my Cousin Beth.' Peyton held up a hand to ward off the protest he saw coming. 'I understand your hesitation. My Aunt Lily, the Dowager Duchess of Bridgerton, has agreed to sponsor you for the Season. Everything will be *comme il faut* and above reproach, I assure you.'

Miss Branscombe studied him for a long while. 'I do not desire a Season. Your aunt need not worry and neither need you. I am sure squiring around an unknown girl who is rather too old to be making a début is not high on your list of priorities.'

True, it wasn't. But that would not do. Peyton needed a reason to be in her company, to become a fixture in her life. 'Surely you wish to marry and settle down with a family of your own? A Season will enable you to meet people and get to know England all over again.'

'I've never known England,' Miss Branscombe said sharply.

'Still, if it's to be your home, you'll want to make friends,' Peyton argued. He'd never encountered a more obstinate female. His Aunt Lily was headstrong, but quite capable of seeing reason. His Cousin Beth was pleasantly compliant. But there was nothing reasonable or compliant about Tessa Branscombe. He offered her a Season under the sponsorship of the revered Lady Bridgerton. No young lady he knew of would take such a gift lightly. Yet Miss Branscombe simply refused and kept pacing the carpet, intent on studying the pattern. Perhaps she was unaware of the honour he accorded her with such an offer.

Peyton played his ace. 'If you are unwilling to do it for yourself, I would encourage you to do it for your sisters. Petra should be out next year and Eva won't be far behind.'

That stopped her. She looked up. 'I will speak to them. Perhaps, for their sakes, I will consider it.'

Peyton nodded, knowing that was the closest to an acceptance he would get from her today. He couldn't push for too much too soon. He would have to instil his guardianship in gradual, subtle steps. It was clear from today's meeting that Miss Branscombe wouldn't take kindly to his outright assumption of authority. But there were definitely things that needed doing, starting with curbing inappropriate outings to the market and teas without cakes. It seemed that Tessa Branscombe intended for her sisters to grow up as wayward as she.

That would not play well amongst the *ton*. Her beauty and his reputation would only go so far in making the Branscombes acceptable. He knew how the *ton* worked and the Branscombes were fringe players at best in that world. Any mis-step from Tessa Branscombe would be magnified a hundred times over.

Peyton drew out his pocket watch. It was growing late. The visit had taken longer than he'd anticipated and he'd promised Aunt Lily he'd come for dinner after assessing the Branscombe situation.

'I appreciate your time, Miss Branscombe. I'll let you take the evening to help your sisters adjust to the news, although I want them reassured that all will be well. I do not wish to be wrongly painted as the ogre here. I will call with my aunt tomorrow in the afternoon so you can meet her and begin to make plans. It's early yet and the Season isn't fully underway for another two weeks. You needn't panic on that account.'

'I don't panic on any account, my lord,' Miss Branscombe informed him crisply.

The remark won a smile from him. 'I didn't mean to imply that you would. My apologies.'

Miss Branscombe was more than happy to help him find his way to the door. In the hall, Peyton felt the need to offer her a final assurance. 'All will be well, Miss Branscombe.'

She met his eyes evenly. 'I know it will be. I won't tolerate anything less.'

'Good evening, Miss Branscombe.' Peyton bowed over her hand, choosing to ignore her cold farewell.

Outside felt warm compared to the chill of Miss Branscombe's parting comments. Peyton's mind was already whirring with lists and plans in regards to the Branscombe girls before he got down the town-house steps. They would need additional staff and new gowns. The younger girls would need a governess to help with their studies. He suspected Miss Branscombe was overseeing that herself, but she'd be too busy once the Season started to plan lessons.

He stopped at the bottom of the steps to caution himself. It was best not to make too much of this

guardian role. This was make believe. This was a
role he was playing for his country in order to prevent
a war. This was about recovering a list that could
save the lives of British soldiers. His guardianship
would terminate once the list was recovered. In all
reality, his role wouldn't last past the Season, regardless of his offer to take them to Dursley Park. If Tessa
Branscombe ever fully understood his role in all this,
she would be glad to see him go, a thought that sat
decidedly ill with Peyton for no logical reason.

Peyton tried to shrug off the feeling of disappointment. Most likely, that gladness would be reciprocal.
The next time he saw Brimley, he would ring a peal
over the man's head. The man had left out quite a lot
about Tessa Branscombe when he'd outlined the
mission, starting with her ethereal beauty and ending
with her inconvenient streak of tenacity. Both attributes
made Peyton Ramsden extraordinarily uncomfortable.

Chapter Four

Tessa climbed the stairs to the schoolroom, trying to decide how best to put the news to her sisters. A guardian was a completely unlooked-for development. All her protective instincts were on alert. She didn't like it in the least and not only because it curtailed her own freedom and plans. Such a development simply didn't make sense. Why would a codicil appear now? The Earl had implied she feared a swindle of their trust funds, but he was wrong there. She feared something worse than losing money.

Tessa shivered at the thought. It conjured up the disconcerting incidents that had occurred before they'd left St Petersburg. Their home had been broken into days after the funeral. She'd told Sergei, but even with his protection, she'd known she was being followed whenever she went out. She had hoped that distance would have quelled the subtle danger she'd begun to feel in Russia. The appearance of the Earl today suggested otherwise. They knew no one in England, but he'd certainly known them.

It seemed to be an eerie coincidence that after a month alone, they were beset with visitors. Sergei had arrived and now this unknown Earl was claiming guardianship. These newly developed circumstances begged the question: was this truly an accidental happenstance brought on by a quirk of fate, or were these men after something or someone? If the latter were true, it would be much easier to defend herself if she knew what their objective might be.

Tessa took a deep breath and pushed open the door, taking a moment to appreciate the rare tranquillity of seeing her sisters quietly engaged in activity. Eva sat with her embroidery. Petra pored over a beloved book of horses and Annie played quietly with her dolls. Then they spotted her at the door and questions erupted on all sides.

'Wait! Wait! One at a time,' Tessa said, moving to sit on the floor next to Annie.

Eva and Petra gathered around her. 'Well, is he or isn't he our guardian?' Petra asked pointedly.

Tessa opted for the direct approach. 'He has legal documents that proclaim him as such. Until I can prove otherwise, it seems we must abide by this development. I will meet his solicitor and look through the situation quite thoroughly, I assure you. I won't allow us to be taken advantage of.'

'When will we see him again? Is he going to live in the house with us?' Eva asked.

'Tomorrow and no,' Tessa responded. 'He will keep his own residence. His aunt will come with him tomorrow afternoon.' Tessa paused before adding the next bit of news. 'It seems that I am to have a Season, although I've told him I have no interest in such doings.'

Eva protested immediately. 'Oh, Tess, you *must* have a Season! Think of all the gowns and parties. You'll meet new people. You'll know how it's all done when it's Petra's turn and my turn.'

Tessa smiled thinly, thinking of the Earl's goad that she must be cognisant of her sisters' needs even if she would shun such an opportunity for herself. It was the argument of a traditionalist and it helped alleviate some of her suspicions about his appearance. It was exactly the sort of argument a real guardian would make, wanting to see his charges married off. A man on a different mission would hardly take an interest in such things. 'Of course, dear.' She patted Eva's hand, aware of Petra's gaze on her.

'The Earl is not married?' Petra asked, her natural intuition easily reading between the lines of what had and had not been said. 'Is that why his aunt is calling?'

Tessa nodded.

Eva gushed, 'He'll escort you everywhere, Tess. It will be like a fairy tale. He's what they call an "eligible *parti*".'

Tessa grimaced at the notion. Where had Eva

learned such a thing and so quickly after their arrival? She was growing up far too fast. Tessa tried to tamp down Eva's romantic notions. 'I have Sergei to act as an escort. I needn't rely on the Earl wholly, just because a set of papers made him guardian.'

Eva shook her head. 'Sergei will have to go home eventually. Besides, I thought the Earl was much more handsome than Sergei. He was so dark and mysterious.' That was saying a lot, considering Tessa knew that Eva harboured an adolescent infatuation with Sergei's blond Slavic good looks and courtly manners.

'I thought he was rather pompous and stuffy,' Petra argued.

Eva shot Petra a sly look. 'It's the perfect ones who have the most to hide.'

'Hush, girls,' Tessa scolded. She made a mental note to keep a closer eye on Eva's reading material.

'Will we stay in London with you, Tess?' Petra asked, returning to the subject at hand.

'Yes. I have the Earl's promise we are not to be parted.'

Petra nodded. 'Then perhaps his guardianship won't make that much difference and we'll be allowed to go on as we have been doing.'

Tessa smiled her assurances, hoping to convince her sisters that Petra was right and all would be well. Life would certainly be easier to manage if that was the case. Although she'd protested against the idea of a Season, and although she'd argued that Sergei would be a preferable escort, Tessa couldn't fully deny that the idea of spending an evening or two on the Earl's arm held some appeal. He'd been arrogant today, but beneath that arrogance she'd sensed compassion. He'd offered to keep the girls in London and to let her decide where they went after the Season. Tessa found such a mixture intriguing, and, in Eva's words, slightly mysterious.

Petra's idea of a *laissez-faire* guardian succumbed to reality at precisely eleven o'clock the next morning. The hypothesis that the Earl of Dursley would leave them be had hardly lasted fifteen hours, and they'd been asleep for eight of them.

Mrs Hollister arrived in the modest library Tessa used as her private office, nervous and out of sorts. 'Miss, there's visitors here to see you.'

Tessa looked up from her letters. The Earl wasn't expected to call until the afternoon. 'Did they say what they wanted?' It wasn't like the capable Mrs Hollister to be edgy.

'They say they're from the Earl of Dursley.'

Tessa frowned, trying to make sense of the arrivals. 'His solicitor, perhaps?' she mused out loud. It was the only explanation that made sense.

'No, miss. A maid and a footman,' Mrs Hollister breathed in alarm. 'I have them in the kitchen. I didn't know where to put them.'

'I'll see them at once. Send them up.' Tessa set aside her letters. 'I will see what they want.'

Tessa waited for them to appear, conscious of her choice to receive them in the library. Modest though it was, the room was done in dark woods and carried an aura of authority. Whatever their reason for being here, she wanted the message to be clear that she was mistress of this house. This was not their master's house.

Mrs Hollister returned with the unexpected arrivals and Tessa was immediately glad of her choice to stay in the library. She'd seen servants like these before—well-trained members of an exceptional noble household. In her experience, these types of servants had their own brand of haughtiness. She should have expected no less from Dursley's household.

'What is your business here?' Tessa asked, taking her seat behind the wide desk.

'The Earl of Dursley sent us. He said you were newly come to town and had need of staff, miss.' The maid was dressed as crisply as she spoke. She bobbed a curtsy at the end of her message.

'I appreciate his thoughtfulness, but he is incorrect in his assumptions. I do not require further staff. We keep an informal house here and Mrs Hollister sees ably to our needs.' Tessa took out a sheet of paper and dipped her quill in the inkwell. 'If you wouldn't mind waiting, I will pen a note to the Earl, explaining my position. I am sure Mrs Hollister will be happy to provide you with tea in the interim.'

The maid and footman exchanged anxious glances. The footman cleared his throat. Tessa stifled a sigh. Of course it wouldn't be that easy. She was starting to suspect that nothing regarding the Earl of Dursley would ever be easy.

'Excuse me, miss, I don't mean to be impertinent,' the footman began, 'but the Earl said you might not share his opinion on the issue and that we were to remain until his arrival this afternoon.'

Oh, that was very neatly done, Tessa fumed. She couldn't argue with them because they had no power with which to negotiate. All she could do was let them follow orders until Dursley arrived.

'I understand your predicament,' Tessa said tersely. 'You may make yourselves comfortable in the kitchen.'

They did more than make themselves comfortable. They made themselves *useful*.

When Tessa went down to check on the state of things shortly before Dursley's arrival, she was astonished at the amount of industry taking place. The footman had set about the business of polishing the silver and was now arranging it in the glass-fronted storage cabinet. In another corner of the large room, the maid was assisting Mrs Hollister with the ironing. A pile of freshly laundered sheets already lay folded on a work table in testament to their efforts. What was more, Mrs Hollister had lost the cowed look she'd sported upon their arrival and was chatting amiably with the girl while they worked.

Mrs Hollister spotted her at the doorway and excitedly waved her over. 'Miss Branscombe, Meg here knows a most effective recipe for getting food stains out of tablecloths.' Such first-name familiarity was a bad sign.

Tessa forced a smile. 'Lovely. Really, you didn't have to go to all this effort, Meg.'

Meg beamed, taking Tessa's comment as a compliment. Encouraged, Meg went on, 'Of course we did. You've hardly unpacked. Arthur discovered the silver and the dishes still in their packing crates in the cellar. I have no idea what you've been eating off since your arrival. We decided at once we had to set the kitchen to rights. Mrs Hollister is just one woman. She can't do everything.' Meg smiled again, no doubt convinced she'd said just the right thing to prove her and Arthur's efficiency.

Tessa reined in her temper. It wasn't Meg and Arthur's fault, after all. They were just doing what they'd been ordered to do. It was all Dursley's fault they were here at all. Still, it didn't help things that, while she'd been upstairs going over accounts, they'd been down here inventorying the household goods and deciding on their own she wasn't living grandly enough to suit them.

In the month they'd been in London, she'd made no move to unpack the household goods they'd brought from Russia or the items that were stored in the home for the infrequent times her father had come to London. She'd decided to keep life simple and unpack only the basics.

After all, she and her sisters had spent the prior months in mourning, travelling and living plainly during the journey. They knew no one in London and had no intention at this time of formal entertaining, although the house was big enough to do so. Tessa supposed there would come a time when they might offer salons and dinners, but not yet, not now when they were still adjusting to their circumstances.

Tessa didn't mind the practical nature of their lifestyle. Although, she had to privately admit that the sight of the well-polished silver service in the case looked magnificent and the elegant samovar she'd brought from Russia conjured up nostalgia for days past when they lived among the opulent surroundings of the St Petersburg court.

'The pieces look lovely, Arthur.'

'Thank you, miss. There's plenty more in the cellar. I saw the labels on the crates. I can begin work on them tomorrow.' Arthur rolled down his sleeves and put on his discarded coat bearing the Dursley livery in dark green and silver. 'Since the Earl is due in a few minutes, I'll post myself at the door for his arrival.'

It was said with perfunction and kindness. It was

clear from his tone he didn't mean to be high-handed. He only meant to please. Tessa hadn't the heart to remind Arthur she was sending him and Meg home with Dursley.

Tessa offered a few instructions to Mrs Hollister about serving tea and turned to go. She wanted to be ready in the drawing room when Dursley arrived.

'Miss Branscombe, don't be too hard on the Earl. He did what he thought was best. Meg and Arthur are good folk,' Mrs Hollister called after her. 'It was good to have the extra hands today.'

In all fairness, Tessa supposed it was a boon to Mrs Hollister to have the help. Running the kitchen alone for four girls was work enough for one person, not counting the laundry and other sundry chores that cropped up on most days. Tessa did her part, too.

She wasn't above shopping at the market or greengrocers or dusting furniture or changing sheets. After years of running her father's household, she'd learned how to do for herself. She didn't live an idle life while Mrs Hollister shouldered the lion's share of the chores. She saw to her sisters' lessons; when they weren't studying, she saw to it that they helped out around the house as well. She wanted her sisters to be prepared for whatever circumstances life threw at them.

Diplomats' daughters lived in an interesting half-world, not truly peers, but definitely a cut above the world of assistants, clerks and military officers. Some of her acquaintances married well, perhaps to a baron or a knight, and grabbed the bottom rungs of the peerage ladder. Others married merchants who'd engaged in lucrative import/export businesses. Others married clerks and assistants who had little in the way of money or family connections, but hoped to make their way in the diplomatic circles through hard work.

Now that she and her sisters were not part of that circle any longer, it was hard to know what kind of suitors they might encounter. Without their father, they were nothing more than four girls with only modest trust funds to recommend them and a respectable house in Bloomsbury. Tessa knew such dowries would limit suitors to the gentry. Dashing men with titles like Sergei Androvich would disappear from their palette of choices when the time came.

Tessa knew she should thank providence for the Earl of Dursley. His presence in their lives would provide a buffer from falling directly into obscurity. If she chose, she could use her Season to secure a match from among the *ton* and give her sisters a chance to make more advantageous matches than they could hope for otherwise.

Perhaps that was the very reason her father had chosen such a man to act as guardian. Such a rationale would explain much in regards to her father's actions in choosing Dursley. Maybe her father had seen a chance to give his daughters a leg up in the world in case of his untimely demise. That sparked another thought. The date on the codicil of the will had been six months before her father's death. A shiver went through Tessa. Maybe his demise hadn't been so untimely after all.

She was contemplating these new thoughts when Arthur announced Dursley's arrival with his aunt and ushered them into the drawing room.

The Earl nodded a dismissal to the footman with a proprietary ease that sat poorly with Tessa. Her earlier resentment over the Earl's high-handed assumptions flared.

'I hope Arthur and Meg have made themselves useful,' the Earl said after introductions, taking a seat in one of the chairs across from the sofa. Dursley looked immaculate and handsome in buff breeches and a blue coat. His presence filled the room, masculine and powerful. Tessa thought another kind of woman would be quite intimidated. As it was, she was merely annoyed.

'Yes, we must speak about that, my lord,' Tessa began bluntly. 'I do not recall asking for your assistance with my housekeeping needs.'

'None the less, I ascertained those needs during my visit yesterday and hastened to address them,' the Earl said easily, refusing to rise to an argument.

Tessa bristled at his smooth arrogance. He was quite sure of himself. He must walk over people's feelings on a regular basis to have acquired such a superior skill.

'I don't want them here.'

The Earl favoured her with a chilly smile. 'Ah, but, Miss Branscombe, it is my pleasure to have them here.'

'The pleasure is not shared,' Tessa shot back, momentarily forgetting the presence of the Earl's Aunt Lily in the other chair. The regally coiffed woman gave a discreet cough at the hot rejoinder. Tessa had the good sense to apologise. 'Pardon me, your Grace,' she said swiftly to the Dowager Duchess, sure to imply that the Earl was not included in the apology.

'Miss Branscombe, I think it would be wise to accept the offer of additional staff,' the Dowager offered. 'Life during the Season becomes hectic. One cannot see to all the little things as one usually might. The only way to survive is through competent staff. Additionally, it lends you an air of respectability, which, I dare say, you will need. Peyton tells me you went to the market on your own the other day. Those kinds of errands will have to stop or tongues will start to wag.'

Tessa studied the older woman. The Dowager Duchess was an attractive woman of middle years, blessed with stately height and a regal bearing. Her dark hair was streaked with the beginnings of grey, but it was unmistakably the same dark hair the Earl sported. The family resemblance ran strong between them. Tessa suspected the family tendency towards firmness ran strong as well. Aunt Lily showed all the signs of matching the Earl in forceful personality.

What the Earl's aunt said made sense and it was

hard to argue with the practical need for more staff, even if she had plenty to say about curbing outings to the market. Perhaps she could allow her pride to give way in this one matter. It served no purpose to turn away something she needed simply to spite the Earl. 'Perhaps you're right, your Grace. I will need the extra help in weeks to come.' Tessa turned to the Earl. 'I would prefer that you consult with me in the future before making decisions about my household.'

'I shall do my utmost to remember that.' The Earl nodded.

The rest of the visit passed more smoothly. The Earl's aunt was formidable, but likeable, with her straightforward opinions, and Tessa found her easy to get along with over tea. They talked about the upcoming Season and Lily's plans to get Tessa to a dressmaker post-haste the next afternoon. After tea, Tessa gave them a tour of the house, at Lily's request, including an introduction of her sisters. Lily wrung a gasp of sheer delight from Eva by announcing a visit to the dressmaker was in order for them as well as Tessa.

The Earl was silent, trailing the two women through the house without a word or comment. Tessa had half-expected him to be articulating lists of changes as they went. But he didn't have to say anything in order to make himself heard. Tessa's nerves were fully primed by the time she showed them the last room in the house, the small music room. It had seen little use and by the time they'd arrived there, she had begun to see the house through the Earl's eyes.

He didn't have to run a finger across the top of the pianoforte for her to be keenly aware of the thick layer of dust the instrument sported. He hadn't had to comment on the state of the faded striped curtains in the dining room for her to realise they might be outmoded. In her urge to settle into a quiet life, she had not noticed such things. To her, the house had been respectable, and for a middle-class family of some means, it probably was. Still, she found herself making subtle apologies as they returned to the sitting room.

'We've only been in town a month. We are still settling in,' she said. 'A good dusting will set quite a lot of it to rights.'

Lily smiled in sympathy. 'Whatever dusting and beeswax can't mend, Dursley's purse can. I can suggest several decorators to you.'

'My purse, you say?' The Earl cocked a challenging eyebrow at his aunt, who merely grinned.

'You're the guardian responsible for this house and its occupants, are you not, Dursley?' Lily had the audacity to wink at Tessa. The Earl's features clouded and Tessa fought back a laugh. She saw Lily's ploy in all its glory.

The scolding Lily had sent him was a subtle slap

on the wrists. If he was going to play lord of the manor by placing servants here without Tessa's approval and lay claim for the responsibility of the house, he would have to do so on all levels. Lily wasn't going to let him pick and choose which responsibilities he shouldered. He would shoulder them all or none of them.

'Aunt, make your plans with Miss Branscombe about tomorrow's outing. I need a word with Arthur before I go,' Dursley deftly excused himself.

'Thank you,' Tessa said after the Earl had left.

Lily waved such thanks away with her hand. 'It was nothing. My nephew can be stiff-necked at times, but he means well. Often, he has reasons for what he does that aren't always clear to us at the time. I have learned to trust him and you will too. Between us, we'll see you married and settled into a good situation by autumn. Dursley knows who would suit and who would not. He won't let you be snatched up by the wrong sorts.'

'I don't intend to marry,' Tessa said quickly. The sooner her new chaperon had that idea fixed in her mind, the better.

Lily patted her hand, dismissing the statement. 'That's what you say now. Wait and see. You can always change your mind.'

Dursley returned to escort his aunt to the carriage waiting at the kerb. As she was leaving, the Dowager Duchess said, 'Until tomorrow, Miss Branscombe. Thank you for a delightful afternoon.'

The Earl added his thanks. 'Good day, Miss Branscombe.'

'Good day, Lord Dursley,' Tessa said, trying out his name for the first time. It seemed silly to keep thinking him as 'the Earl'. He was going to be a fixture in their lives. She might as well give the fixture a name.

Chapter Five

Peyton sat with Brimley at White's, more relaxed than he had been the evening before. He felt much better now that Arthur was stationed at the Branscombe house. Anyone contemplating a break-in would think twice with a strapping man like Arthur on the premises. He told Brimley as much as they drank evening brandies in a quiet corner. The club was nearly empty; most people had headed out for the evening entertainments.

'I'll have a chance to look around tomorrow,' Peyton said. 'Aunt Lily is taking Miss Branscombe to the modiste's and the girls go to the park with Mrs Hollister in the afternoons.'

'Do you really think the list is here?' Brimley asked.

Peyton nodded. 'I think the sudden presence of certain Russians in the city confirms it. What other reason could there be for a diplomat of Count Androvich's background to be in London? Who better than a family friend to ferret out family secrets? After all, we're doing precisely the same thing, only we had to fabricate the family friend in me. The Czar had a legitimate one to send.'

'Maybe he could not bear to be parted from Miss Branscombe,' Brimley hypothesised. 'They are old friends.'

The idea that Count Androvich might carry a *tendre* for Miss Branscombe sat awkwardly with Peyton. 'It's hardly practical to wait until the object of one's affections journeys a thousand miles before declaring one's intentions.'

Brimley shrugged, enjoying the debate. 'Love isn't practical.'

Peyton laughed. 'Love isn't, but Miss Branscombe is, I assure you. I can't believe Miss Branscombe would waste her time on a trans-European romance. She would have settled the matter before she left St Petersburg.' The surety of his own declaration gave him pause. He'd thought as much about Tessa Branscombe as he had the location of the list lately, a sure testimony that she'd started to get under his skin. Such a feat was a novelty all of its own. He seldom allowed himself to be attracted to anyone so quickly. In this case, he wasn't convinced he'd 'allowed' anything to happen at all, it simply had.

He'd only known Tessa Branscombe for a couple of days, but he felt certain his analysis of her situation was correct. This transition point in her life would have been the perfect time to accept an offer from Androvich. She could have settled down with a wealthy count and avoided the turmoil of her recent upheaval.

But she had implied she hadn't felt safe in St Petersburg. His mind had chased that one elusive remark around his head after their first meeting, resulting in sending Arthur and Meg to the house as soon as possible in the morning. It had also resulted in drawing another conclusion—if Miss Branscombe didn't feel safe, she probably had a justifiable reason for it. Did she know about the list? More importantly, did the Russians think she knew about it? If they thought she was in personal possession of the list, the amount of danger she was in had just escalated exponentially.

The shopping expedition had turned out surprisingly pleasant. In spite of her original misgivings, Tessa had enjoyed herself greatly. Dursley's Aunt Lily was an intelligent and delightful companion. The two of them were loaded down with packages and chatting amiably when they entered the hall of Tessa's town house. Tessa set her purchases and her reticule on a small table in the hall and stilled suddenly.

'What is it, dear?' Lily asked, noting her distress.

Tessa shook her head, her panic starting to rise. It was happening again, the old fear she'd felt in Russia. 'I don't know. The house feels different. It feels unsettled, as if something isn't right.'

Lily smiled fondly. 'It's probably all the changes. Arthur and Meg have done a substantial amount of work in a short time. I can even see differences from before we left. I dare say the house is improved greatly.'

Tessa had to agree. Meg and Arthur had tirelessly devoted themselves to unpacking some of the crates from the cellar as well as the crates she'd brought from St Petersburg. She had not realised how incomplete the house had been until she'd seen the family's personal effects spread throughout the home and the rooms filled with furniture brought down from the attics.

There had certainly been a lot of changes, but those weren't what contributed to her sense of disquiet. The house felt disrupted from another's presence. Someone was here.

Tessa felt the gnawing fear start again in her stomach. She'd hoped to be done with such worry. Would the need to be constantly on guard ever be gone? She'd thought she'd beaten such fear since their arrival in London, but over the last few days the sense that she was being watched had returned, and now this. She reached for her reticule. She had her small gun inside. She went nowhere without it.

'Lily, if you would just wait for me in the drawing room, I'll have a look around.'

Lily looked at her strangely, but Tessa didn't care. At least her fears weren't misplaced. In St Petersburg she'd been right.

Tessa started upstairs slowly, her back against the

curving wall of the staircase as she went, making herself less visible if anyone was looking down. If there was an intruder, he would be upstairs. Anyone else would have heard them come in.

Tessa slipped the small gun from her reticule. She cocked the weapon, not doubting her instincts once. It was the perfect time to break in. Her sisters were on an outing to a nearby park with Mrs Hollister and Meg and Arthur were spending their afternoon off at Dursley House. There was no one around to notice the comings and goings of a stranger in the house.

She was five stairs from the top when she heard it: the sound of booted feet on the hardwood floor. She'd done a good job of hiding herself against the natural curvature of the staircase, but, reciprocally, she was blind to all else that moved above her. She could no more see who was coming down the stairs than they could see her.

Tessa had only seconds to think before the intruder was upon her. Her mind raced over her options. There was no chance someone coming down the stairs wouldn't see her as they passed. Her only choice was to seize the advantage.

Tessa boldly stepped out into the centre of the stairs, gun ready to fire. 'Stay where you are.'

She was not prepared for what happened next. Instead of obeying her command, the intruder flung himself at her, propelling them against the stair wall as opposed to tumbling down the steps. Tessa found herself most indecently pressed between the wall and the hard body of her attacker. Breasts met chest, her skirts met with the hard muscles of his thighs. She could barely breathe, let alone summon a scream. Her hand holding the gun was shackled against the wall by the intruder's iron grip.

Tessa struggled, but she was too closely imprisoned to land an effective kick. She tore her gaze from her trapped gun hand into the intruder's face. She found her voice. 'Dursley!'

'Miss Branscombe!' His shock was nearly as great as her own. In his amazement, he released her gun arm.

Tessa hadn't been ready for such freedom. The gun slipped from her weakened fingers and clattered down the steps. A misfire rang out. Instantly, Dursley surrounded her again with his body, this time as a protector. His arms bracketed her on either side, his body in full contact with hers, disregarding any compunction for propriety.

Tessa recognised the stance for what it was: the posture of a human shield. No one would be able to get close to her with such a force surrounding her. It was dark and safe in the confines of Dursley's protective circle. For a moment, Tessa let herself savour such a luxury. Then Dursley realised the only danger was the misfire of the gun.

The look he gave her was incredulous. 'The gun was loaded? The gun you pointed at me was *loaded*?'

Tessa looked up at him, his face very near hers. 'Of

course it was. I didn't know it was you. A lot of good an unloaded weapon would have done me.' She'd not noticed what a dark shade of blue his eyes were in their prior encounters. Then again, she'd not had the opportunity to appreciate them at such close proximity.

There were other things she was starting to 'appreciate' at this range, too, like the breadth of his shoulders and the firmness of his thighs, not to mention the supposed intimacy of their position on the stairs.

Any moment his Aunt Lily would determine it was safe to come out of the drawing room. Tessa could only imagine what kind of image she and the Earl would create to the unsuspecting onlooker who happened upon them. Tessa shifted, squirming a bit in the hopes of creating some distance between them. She immediately wished she hadn't moved. Her gyrations caused her hips to brush against Dursley in a highly improper manner. To her great embarrassment, she actually felt that most unmentionable part of him stir at the contact.

Dursley took a step back. 'A thousand pardons, Miss Branscombe,' he said with polite neutrality, as if they'd merely brushed past one another on the stairs at a ball.

Lily appeared at the bottom of the steps. 'Is everyone all right? Heavens, Dursley, is that you?'

'We're all right, Aunt,' Dursley assured her.

'Tessa thought she heard an intruder,' Lily called up.

'Did she?' Dursley shot Tessa a foreboding look. 'Do you have a lot of experience, then, in listening for intruders, Miss Branscombe? I find my curiosity is piqued as to why a young lady would feel it necessary to be armed with a gun in her own home.'

'No more so than my own curiosity, milord, as to why you were skulking about upstairs in my house,' Tessa replied coolly.

'Skulking, is it?' Dursley said in his most high-handed tone.

'Yes. Skulking,' Tessa insisted, moving down the stairs ahead of him, doing her best to match his haughtiness. But her cool exterior was a façade only. Inside, she was so jangled from the encounter that, after picking her gun up from the hall floor, she rang for tea before she realised all the staff was gone for the afternoon.

It wasn't until much later, after her sisters were asleep, that Tessa allowed her mind to consider the scene on the stairs. She sat at the desk in her private office, dwelling on those few moments. The most important concern on her mind was what Peyton—*Dursley*—had been doing upstairs. One of the consequences of the afternoon was that she was finding it difficult to think of him without wanting to use his first name. One could not brush up against a man's groin in such an intimate fashion and continue to think of him as a title. At least she couldn't.

Tessa marshalled her thoughts. She had to stay focused. What had he been doing here? It wasn't out of the realm of possibility that he'd come by to escort his aunt home from their shopping trip. Finding them still out, he'd decided to wait.

But waiting could be done quite nicely in the public rooms downstairs. There was no need to wait upstairs. Upstairs consisted of bedrooms, the school-room and her small office. Peyton—Dursley—had been properly appalled at her sisters' chatter over tea the first day. She doubted her sisters' bedrooms held any interest or allure to him. Never mind that it wasn't proper for gentlemen to go poking around young girls' bedchambers. And propriety mattered greatly to him. The only room that could hold any interest would be her office, and only then if he were looking for something.

Tessa gazed around the room. There was only a chair and a small bookcase, in addition to her desk. On the wall was a portrait of her father, newly hung by Arthur that morning. She couldn't imagine what Peyton thought he might find in here.

She huffed. There it was again—Peyton. She might as well give in. She would call him 'Peyton' in her mind. It could be her little secret. Tessa fiddled with a paperweight, studying the portrait of her father, which had been completed a few months before his death. In the painting he was elegantly posed, standing next to a table that contained a long scrolling document. She supposed the setting was to symbolise his diplomatic career, the scroll representing some kind of treaty or agreement he was so famous for.

She wondered what he might make of this afternoon. Her father had been an expert at reading people. What might he see that she'd missed? Something niggled at her about the encounter. At the actual time of its happening, her mind had been racing too much for the nuance to register. But now as she slowed it down in her head, pieces began to form. Peyton had not recognised her immediately. His instincts had not seen her. His instincts had seen danger. Had he thought she was an intruder? That raised a host of other questions, most prominently— why would he have suspected an intruder at a quiet house in a quiet neighbourhood?

The way he'd reacted indicated he'd expected the worst, for whatever reason. She'd never met a man with such lightning reflexes. He'd been on her before she could have even considered firing the gun. His skill was more than natural talent. That kind of reflex was carefully honed and acquired. She'd seen men with that kind of skill in the Czar's personal guard.

Once he'd recognised her, his demeanour had changed. He'd been all protection when the gun misfired. It was almost as if he'd thought the shot came from somewhere else. It clearly hadn't. But his reaction had been that of a bodyguard. If there had been another shot, his body would have taken the brunt of it. Surely such action was above and beyond a guardian's duty to his ward.

Then there had been that moment of mutual, acute awareness, the searing gaze of his hot eyes. How would she ever face him again without blushing? He and Lily had not stayed long once he'd been assured of her safety in the house. She'd been grateful. Her eyes had developed a fascination for glancing at certain male parts of his anatomy. Luckily, he hadn't seemed to notice. But she'd better get over the penchant for such behaviour quickly. He would be escorting her to the Broughtons' ball in three nights' time. *Where they would dance.* As her escort, he was obliged to dance with her once. The thought of being in such close proximity to Peyton's body again was unaccountably exciting.

Such emotions were unwise. Developing an infatuation over Peyton would cloud the real issue. Could she trust him? His actions suggested both yes and no. He'd been wandering around odd parts of her house while it was empty. He'd entered their lives without warning with only a misplaced codicil to recommend him. Those circumstances were highly suspect. Yet, he'd opted to protect her, which bespoke a message of trustworthiness and honour. Her own reaction to him had been one of security. In those moments on the stairs when she'd been surrounded by his body, she'd thought that here was a man who could share her burden.

She recognised her reaction was based solely on impulse. Tessa shook her head to clear it. No, she would not tell Peyton about her fears. Not yet. Not until she knew more about her situation and him. She'd thought there had been an intruder today, but it had only been Peyton. Her instincts might be off. If no one was following her, if it was all in her head, then there was nothing to tell him. He would ask for proof and right now she didn't have any.

The darker side of her conscience emerged, prodding her to more difficult hypotheses. All this assumed Peyton was on the side of good. Perhaps he was the source of her fears. He was the one new variable in her life these days, along with the arrival of Sergei's Russian delegation. The only difference was that she knew Sergei.

Tessa sighed in exasperation. There was so much she didn't know! What did she have that was worth all the trouble someone was potentially going through? Was Peyton connected to that? What did he know? Anything? Nothing? Everything? The only thing Tessa was sure of was that Peyton Ramsden and his exquisite body was dangerous to her in more than one way.

Aunt Lily had that dangerous look in her eye, Peyton noted over an excellent trifle. He'd agreed to dine with her simply because not to do so would be to immediately admit to hiding something. Damn Tessa Branscombe and her inconvenient gun. He'd hoped to avoid the complicated topic. To that end Peyton had now exhausted every subject of conversation he could think of.

But in the end, it was clear Aunt Lily could not be put off the scent.

Lily set down her spoon and fixed Peyton with her gaze. 'I think it's time you explained to me why Miss Branscombe carries a gun and apparently does not hesitate to use it. If I am to act as a sponsor for her, I want the truth, Nephew.'

Peyton dabbed his mouth with his napkin, gathering his thoughts. 'She's a woman on her own and quite alone. She's entitled to provide herself with protection.'

Lily gave him a long considering look. For a moment Peyton thought he might have succeeded in thwarting her. 'Let's try the question another way. Why were you upstairs in her house?'

Peyton sighed. 'There is concern that the Branscombe girls may have inadvertently brought some sensitive information with them from Russia.'

Lily raised her eyebrows in challenge. 'You're spying on those delightful girls and they know nothing? That is a bit different from what you told me two days ago when you asked me to take up their cause.'

'I'm not spying on them. I am protecting them from themselves and anyone else who might happen along,' Peyton clarified. Leave it to Lily to boil it all down to its simplest form.

'And who's protecting them from you?' she retorted. 'I assume they know nothing about your role or that they're even in the possession of this "sensitive information"?'

'I am of no danger to them, Aunt.'

'They're not really your wards, are they, Peyton?' She gave him a disapproving look that made him feel like a small boy again.

'Perhaps not legally, but I will do right by them. They'll have no reason to suspect otherwise.' He met Lily's gaze with a pointed one of his own. She nodded. The implicit message was clear. No one was to know. It was a compliment of sorts that he'd confessed as much as he had. But Lily had a right to know what she was getting into, at least to some extent. He did mean to see the girls taken care of.

Lily raised her glass. 'A toast, Peyton, to tangled webs and all that.'

Peyton knew it wasn't so much a toast his aunt offered as a warning. She understood the need for such subterfuge, but she didn't approve, not fully.

Chapter Six

'Peyton Ramsden's claim to being a guardian is a fraud,' Sergei Androvich spat angrily. The knife he'd been spinning on its handle clattered to the desk top of a private office in the Russian embassy.

The three men with him exchanged sharp looks with one another. They were older, more seasoned diplomats. Sergei felt the anxious undercurrents of their exchange. 'What?' he barked.

'We have no concrete proof of that,' Gromsky reminded him. 'We know only that he's done some diplomatic work before in Vienna. He hasn't done anything for the diplomatic corps for over two years now. He's a peer of the realm. If we go after him, we'll have to be very sure of ourselves and his level of involvement.'

'I agree. Still, I think what evidence we have suggests it is not a mere coincidence he's arrived in the Branscombe girls' lives. His actions suggest he has an agenda,' Ilanovich put in.

'That agenda is to push himself into their lives and to push you out, Sergei,' Vasilov said baldly. 'The whole reason you've been assigned to this mission is your connection to the Branscombe household, and he has now thrown that into question, whether he's acting the part of spy or not.'

'I haven't been pushed out,' Sergei said defensively, but that was indeed his main complaint. He'd thought it would be a simple matter of courting Tessa, wooing the list out of her if she knew where it was, or finding it and stealing it out from under her. Peyton Ramsden's presence had changed all that and quickly, too.

Ramsden was cleverly keeping Tessa too busy to see him. These last days, she'd been swamped with shopping, fittings, even a few visits to friends of Ramsden's aunt. There was suddenly no time for him, when just a few days ago she'd been so grateful for his escort to the market.

'I respectfully beg to differ,' Vasilov continued. 'You have indeed been pushed out. In the past three days, our watchers report Ramsden has been there three times. The other day, he came early to wait for Miss Branscombe and his aunt to come home from shopping. He was alone in the house. How many days have you been there since Ramsden showed up? Even when he's not there, his personally appointed servants are, while all we can do is hire men to watch from across the street.'

'I will tell Tessa our suspicions about Ramsden. I will do it tonight at the Broughtons' ball. She'll be furious and she'll evict him from their lives. You know what a shrew she can be,' Sergei said idly, unimpressed with the worries of old men.

They were alarmed with such a plan. 'No! You cannot tell her. She might tell Ramsden. It would be just like her to confront the scoundrel with her information. We can't have her raising a fuss and alerting all kinds of people. Besides, how can we explain to her why Ramsden would have been assigned to them without telling her about the list?' Gromsky argued.

'No, our original plan of action is still our best plan,' the third one, Ilanovich, said in reasonable tones. 'You must continue to court her as you did in St Petersburg. Win her trust.'

Vasilov gave Sergei a sly look. 'Perhaps it will be easier to court her here where she is far from the only home she's known. Perhaps nostalgia for St Petersburg will make your case stronger.' His tone suggested he had his doubts.

Sergei's eyes narrowed. He did not care for the man's insinuations that he'd failed to secure a marriage to Tessa before she left St Petersburg. Marriage would have made it much easier to keep her close and under surveillance until they found the list.

'I have no wish to be married to such an outspoken woman.' He twirled his ivory-handled knife again.

Vasilov's eyes gleamed. 'It wouldn't last long, only until death do you part and the Czar would not forget all that you sacrificed for your country. In the meanwhile, you could enjoy a beautiful woman in your bed.'

Tessa sat mannequin-still in front of the mirror, trying not to fuss while Lily's maid put the final pins into her coiffure. She was used to such attentions, of course. She'd dressed for several elaborate occasions in St Petersburg. But in the interim of her father's death and their travels, she'd conveniently forgotten how tedious an evening *toilette* could be. She had not realised just how much she'd come to enjoy the simple wardrobe of the past months.

This discomfort was all Peyton's fault. Naturally. Everything that had gone wrong could be laid at his door. Most recently, he could be blamed for the upheaval that had occurred that afternoon, trying to move her and her sisters to Lily's town house. Peyton had insisted she prepare for the ball at Lily's and that her sisters come along and spend the night.

She and Peyton had spent a large part of the morning arguing about it. Ostensibly, he'd argued that he wanted Lily on hand to help her dress and that he hadn't wanted to make the longer drive to Bloomsbury to pick her up. But Tessa was suspicious none the less. If they were gone, it would be all that much easier to search the house for whatever he thought was there. She'd countered that she'd been dressing for formal occasions for most of her adult life and had yet to appear naked at any of them. She'd also been quick to point out that the distance to Bloomsbury had not been great enough to keep him from darkening their doorstep the last three days.

The maid slid a final pin in and stepped back, letting Tessa take in the hairstyle with an uninterrupted view. 'There, miss. You will steal all the gentlemen's hearts tonight!'

'Oh, Tess, you look lovely, like something from a fairy tale,' Eva breathed from the bed where all of her sisters were gathered, watching the spectacle of her getting ready.

Tessa turned her head in the mirror to study the pile of curls expertly arranged on top of her head. Some of the blame she'd laid at Peyton's door dissipated. The woman had done an excellent job. While the coiffure was securely pinned, her hair was by no means scraped up and back from her face. Instead, the pile of curls gave the appearance of being loosely done up, leaving a few trailing wisps to strategically frame her face. Tessa knew Eva and Petra could not have contrived to do better back at the house.

There was a scratch at the door. The maid went to answer it. She hurried back, followed by Lily. 'Dursley's coach has arrived, my dear.' Lily passed a narrow box to the maid. 'Stand up, Tessa, I am eager to see the gown.'

Tessa stood up and shook out her skirts for Lily's inspection, feeling self-conscious. Surely Lily would notice that the neckline was too low? Tessa couldn't resist a quick tug at the bodice. The gown was gorgeous, but indecent, no matter how much Eva raved it was the height of fashion.

'Stop fiddling,' Lily scolded, catching Tessa's tug. 'We're going to a ball, not a nunnery.' Lily stepped forward and tugged the bodice back into place. She stepped back to study the results. 'You look stunning. There will be a line of suitors coming to call tomorrow and the Season is not even in full swing.' Lily gestured towards the maid. 'The pearls will be just the thing.'

Before Tessa could resist, the maid clasped a strand of pearls about her neck and handed her ear-rings with matching pearl teardrops to fasten on her lobes.

'I can't possibly accept these,' Tessa began, but it was hard to protest in earnest when they completed her *toilette* so perfectly. Lily urged her over to the long standing-mirror and the sight of the woman in it conjured up a multitude of emotions in Tessa.

The woman in the mirror was positively lovely. The gown of eggshell on eggshell lace lent an ethereal aura to the ensemble. The pale yellow-ivory colouring of the gown was set off simply, but effectively, with narrow sky-blue ribbon at the bodice, hem and

at the small puffed sleeves. Instead of ruining the fall
of the lightweight fabric with fussy frills and bows,
the modiste had used Tessa's height and a slightly
fuller but unadorned skirt to show off the exquisite
flow of the material.

Yes, the woman in the mirror was not only
lovely, but proud. In spite of her complaints about
the task of dressing for the evening, Tessa had to
admit to herself that she had missed this. The
woman in the mirror reminded her of what her life
had consisted of in St Petersburg. She'd loved
moving in the diplomatic circles, talking to people
from all over Europe, sharing thoughts with intelligent individuals and doing so fluently in three languages. Her father's death had changed all that. She
was no longer needed in those circles, but now
Peyton Ramsden had given her a chance to make
new connections.

'We must go. Dursley will be impatient,' Lily said,
handing her a wrap of embroidered summer silk.

'I'll be just a moment. I want to say goodnight to
my sisters.'

Tessa faced her sisters after Lily left the room. Even
though she'd been to countless balls, the occasion felt
momentous. In some ways it was. This was her first
night among English society in London. She was doing
this for all their futures, hers as well as theirs.

'Eva's right. You look beautiful, Tessa.' Petra took
her gloved hand. 'We'll be all right here. This house

is huge. We'll be so busy exploring we won't even know you're gone.'

'Make sure Annie is in bed soon and don't wait up. I don't know how long I'll be.' Tessa gave last-minute orders. She hugged them all, careful not to crush the gown.

'Oh, no, you're not getting rid of us that easily,' Eva said. 'We're walking you to the stairs. We want to see the Earl all tricked out.'

'Don't use slang, Eva,' Tessa chided automatically but she couldn't deny them their wish. At the top of the stairs she left them peering through the newel posts. She could hear Eva whisper in awe, 'He's so handsome.'

Privately, Tessa had to agree. The man waiting at the bottom of the steps, chatting with his aunt, was absolutely riveting in his masculine appeal. He wore the standard black evening apparel of a gentleman better than any man she'd yet encountered, and she'd encountered many in all shapes, sizes and ages.

The dark coat was well cut across his shoulders, showing off their breadth without giving the impression of being glued on. And the trousers... Well, recent experience had taught her she'd better not think about his trousers. Still, she stole a glance just to be sure that his legs were as long, his hips as lean, as she remembered them.

She was halfway down when he caught sight of her and looked up from his conversation. She was acutely aware of his gaze following her every step. There was no doubt that she had captured his full attention.

He was there to meet her at the bottom of the stairs. He took her hand and lifted it to his lips. 'Miss Branscombe, you certainly know how to light up a room.'

The Broughtons' ball was one of the first of the Season. The Royal Academy art exhibition in May, which was one of the highlights of the social whirl, wasn't for another week. But the Broughtons were close with the Home and Foreign Offices and wanted to be the first to entertain the Russian delegation. It was the perfect social occasion for Tessa to experience *ton*nish life in London.

The dancing was already underway by the time they gained the ballroom. The receiving line had been surprisingly long for an early Season ball and Peyton had had to stop several times and greet acquaintances. Lily had smiled and suggested slyly that Tessa had increased Peyton's popularity immensely.

There were countless introductions to be made in the ballroom as well since there were both Lily's and Peyton's circles of friends to greet. They slowly worked their way around the perimeter of the ballroom. They were deep in conversation with an acquaintance of Peyton's when Lady Broughton approached, the Russian delegation in tow.

Tessa stiffened involuntarily, her light grip on

Peyton's arm tightening. She recognised the men with Sergei: Gromsky, Vasilov and Ilanovich. She knew them from her father's work. They were considered dangerous men at court. It was widely known among the right circle of people that these men were by turn diplomats, spies and assassins when all else failed to render the anticipated results. That they had been sent to England lent credence to her fears—she was the cause of their arrival.

'Dursley, I want to introduce you and Miss Branscombe to our guests of honour tonight. I thought Miss Branscombe might enjoy seeing someone from her former home.' The hostess gestured to the three men behind her. 'Ambassadors Gromsky, Vasilov, Ilanovich and Count Androvich, this is the Earl of Dursley and Miss Tessa Branscombe, recently of St Petersburg.'

'Miss Branscombe and I are old friends. I spent much time at her father's house during his tenure at the Czar's court.' Sergei stepped forward and bowed low over her hand. 'It is a pleasure to see you again.' He shot a look at Peyton. 'It's a pleasure to see you again as well, Dursley.' Sergei's icy gaze met Peyton's searing stare. The tension in the little coterie escalated.

Lady Broughton looked overtly uncomfortable. 'I did not know you were already acquainted.' Her eyes moved noticeably between Peyton and Sergei.

Tessa moved in to alleviate the awkward moment, focusing her attention on the other ambassadors. She couldn't let them see her fear. If there was a chance they were here for other purposes, her nervousness would alert them to something more. 'How do you find London?' she asked smoothly in French, the language of the St Petersburg court.

After an appropriate interlude of small talk, during which Peyton and Sergei continued to glare at each other, the orchestra struck up a waltz.

'Miss Branscombe, may I have this dance?' Sergei asked.

Tessa accepted, although she could feel Peyton bristle beside her. In truth, she was oddly disappointed that it was Sergei leading her on to the floor and not Peyton. But she'd dance with anyone to get away from the other ambassadors, and Sergei was an old friend.

Sergei and she swung effortlessly into the pattern of dancers. They'd danced together often enough.

'Like old times?' Sergei asked with a smile.

Tessa gave a little laugh. 'A little. It seems surreal that you and I are dancing together a thousand miles from the dance floors we're used to.'

'Are you missing St Petersburg?' Sergei navigated them through the turn.

'Of course I miss it. Practically my whole life was spent there. But I don't miss the way it was at the last.' She didn't need to say more. Sergei knew to what she referred. There was comfort in knowing at least one person in London understood her worries.

'It could be that way again, Tessa,' Sergei whispered in her ear, drawing her close as they danced. 'I was wrong to let you leave St Petersburg without declaring my intentions. It was such a confusing time—your father's death, the break-in—I hardly knew what to do. Then you left early without saying goodbye. You must forgive me for letting you go.'

At one time, Sergei's proposal would have met with joyous acceptance from her. For over a year there had been an unspoken courtship of sorts between them in St Petersburg. During that time, she'd never been quite sure if his regular escort to social functions had indicated something more than friendship. She'd spent nights hoping that it did. She'd fancied herself in love with the dashing count. But tonight, that original attraction seemed diminished. That was probably Peyton's fault, too.

'It was a trying time for all of us. No one was thinking clearly,' Tessa responded evasively. The dance was coming to a close.

'Would you come outside with me? I'm in need of some fresh air.' Sergei directed them towards a door out on to the wide terrace.

'Ah, this is better.' Sergei took a deep breath. 'I find myself missing the sharp cold of Russia at times.' Sergei leaned back against the railing and gestured towards the ballroom. 'How is your guardian? Not too high-handed, I hope? Although that hope seems misplaced.'

Tessa chuckled. 'He's all right. He's very confident.'

'I don't see you tolerating such shenanigans,' Sergei offered shrewdly. 'I am surprised to see that you've accepted him at all and yet he's the one who has escorted you here. I would have, you know.'

She heard the hurt in Sergei's tone and felt guilty. It wasn't right to throw over her friendship with Sergei for the demands of a man she'd only known a short week.

'I checked all the paperwork. It seems legitimate. He and his Aunt Lily have decided I must have a Season. Lily hopes I'll catch a husband, but I am doing this for the girls. Petra will be out next year.'

Sergei gave a gentle smile, his voice intimate. 'You have no need to catch a husband. I would willingly marry you and take you back to St Petersburg where you belong. I should have done so long ago.' He reached for her gloved hand, making small circular movements on the back of her hand with his thumb. 'Just think, Tessa, we could marry here by special licence and spend the summer in London. Then, in the autumn, you could come home with me as my countess. The universe would be restored to its rightful order.'

Tessa studied Sergei closely. The offer held its degree of temptation. No more strange city, no more starting over and making new friends, no more uncertainty. Being with Sergei would solve a lot of problems. She would lead the life she knew, a life she was good at. Her sisters would have opportunities to marry well, thanks to Sergei's title and position. Never had he spoken of his feelings or intentions so plainly. Yet his gallant words seemed to lack a certain ring of truth. What reason did he have to play act, and with her of all people, his friend?

She was so wrapped up in her own internal thoughts she hadn't realised what Sergei was up to until it was too late to prevent it. He had her in his arms, his mouth on hers in a deep kiss, his tongue wet where it ran across her lips. The kiss was not entirely unpleasant, but certainly far too intimate for their surroundings. He was kissing her as if no one else could see. This was a kiss between lovers and it was disappointingly empty of all sensation. After her encounter with Peyton on the stairs, she rather thought there would be. But she felt nothing.

Tessa drew back, struggling to do so when Sergei seemed reluctant to let her establish a decent distance between them. 'Sergei…' she began.

He put a finger to her lips. 'Shh. Say nothing. Promise me you'll think about it.'

The bastard was kissing her as if no one else could walk out and see them, and she was doing a fair imitation of liking it. Peyton's fists curled at his side. Tessa's prolonged absence had prompted his hasty search. He'd been worried and here she was, playing kiss the count!

He'd not been oblivious to Tessa's well-concealed anxiety regarding the Russian delegation. He'd felt her grip tighten on his arm. She'd done admirably, making general conversation, but she'd been all too glad to escape to the dance floor with Sergei, a man she thought she could trust. Well, Peyton wasn't so sure about that. What kind of gentleman would take such liberties in a public place?

In hindsight, he should have anticipated such a manoeuvre. A woman far from home would be susceptible to the wiles of a fellow compatriot. It begged the question of what the Count was here for—was Brimley right and Sergei merely here to win his bride or was he part of something more sinister involving Ralph Branscombe's list?

Tessa suddenly gave a brief struggle, pushing at Sergei's chest. That was all the invitation Peyton needed to make his presence known. The cur thought to kiss her secrets out of her. Well, not when he was around. He was Tessa Branscombe's escort. If anyone was doing any kissing, it would be him.

Chapter Seven

Peyton strode towards Tessa and the Count, crossing the terrace in three strides. 'Miss Branscombe, I have been looking for you,' he said without preamble, situating himself between the two. 'Your absence from the ballroom has been duly noted.' He was gratified to see Tessa blush slightly.

'You may return inside at your leisure, Count Androvich. Miss Branscombe will return with me. It's almost time for the supper waltz, which is mine, I believe.' The Count's dislike for him was palpable as Peyton dismissed him. Peyton discreetly looped Tessa's arm through his and began retracing their steps, taking a certain amount of satisfaction in routing the Count. But his victory was short lived.

Beside him, Tessa bristled. 'How dare you treat Sergei with such disregard!'

Peyton stopped and turned to face her, careful to

keep his features and tone even. 'How dare *I*? How dare *he* treat you with such flagrant disregard for propriety! Can you imagine what would have happened if someone else had seen you? You would have been compromised beyond redemption and well on your way to marriage, whether you wanted it or not,' Peyton scolded in cold tones.

It would not serve to have her suspect the real motives behind his behaviour when he did not fully understand them himself. Jealousy was not a familiar emotion to him. It was too petty and beneath his notice, yet it was remarkably akin to the primal urge that had surged through him at the sight of her in Androvich's embrace.

Tessa was spoiling for a fight. 'Sergei has been my friend far longer than you've been my guardian. He has seen me through difficult times and stood by me. He deserves better.'

Her defence of the questionable Russian sat poorly with Peyton. '*You* deserve better, Miss Branscombe—no friend would play so carelessly with your virtue. I find that, of the three of us on the terrace, I was the only one watching out for your reputation. Come, our waltz is beginning.'

They resumed the short walk back into the ballroom. But the stiffness of Tessa's posture hinted she was not through with their conversation. Peyton guided her towards an open spot on the floor and set aside his own irritation in order to cajole her into good spirits. 'The interlude is behind us, Miss Branscombe. The waltz is my favourite dance. I wouldn't want to spoil it with a sour mood.'

'This discussion is not over,' she said resolutely as he placed a hand at the small of her back and took her other hand.

Peyton smiled tightly. 'The discussion *is* over. I am right and you arc merely arguing because you're irritated that I am right.'

Tessa's blue-violet eyes sparked at that. Whatever rejoinder she had in mind was cut off by the opening strains of the waltz. She might have even left him on the dance floor if he hadn't had such a grip on her waist. As it was, she had no choice but to let him lead them into the patterns.

But Tessa was in no way defeated. Her eyes sparkled dangerously and her temper sizzled between them, a sharp contrast to the civilised steps of the dance. It soon became clear to Peyton that there was to be nothing civilised between them. The dance became a silent competition. The harder he tried to maintain the proper conventions, the harder Tessa pushed him to break them, using his gentleman's code against him. The distance between them shrank until he was forced to hold her tightly. The rapid pace of her steps forced him to greater speeds.

Peyton only fought back because he didn't like losing in any form and he avoided scandal like the plague. In truth, the temptation to hand her the victory was nearly overwhelming. He liked the feel of her body against his. The press of her breasts to his chest, as they whirled through a turn, was positively erotic. Then a miraculous transformation occurred. The speed of their dancing flushed her cheeks and the anger in her eyes faded to be replaced by something else that resembled pleasure.

The Fury had become an angel again. The combination of her pleasure and beauty was a stunning mixture. In spite of his vaunted self-control, Peyton felt his member stir at the sight and feel of her in his arms. Never had he wanted a dance to go on indefinitely. But he could have danced all night with Tessa Branscombe.

She was flushed and breathless when the music ended. Others swarmed passed them on the way into the supper room. Peyton was reluctant to give up the magic of the dance floor and quietly led her aside to an alcove where she could catch her breath and have a quiet moment apart from the crowd. Goodness knew he could use a moment, too, in order to let his growing arousal subside.

'What is this?' Tessa looked around their surroundings. 'We're alone.'

'Not entirely.' Peyton gestured to the throng just beyond them. The crowd was near, but, in their excitement to get to dinner, they were oblivious to anyone who had stepped out of the flow of foot traffic.

He was dismayed to see the exuberance fade from her face. The angel was gone.

'I see,' she said in a cool tone Peyton was coming to recognise all too well. 'You want the playing field levelled.' She gave a dramatic sigh. 'Very well, if you insist.'

Although Tessa was tall, she rose up on her toes to bridge their differences in height and kissed him full on the mouth.

The movement surprised him. Now he understood. She thought he was jealous of Sergei. His first reaction was protection. With a searching hand, Peyton groped successfully for the curtain that would shut off the alcove. His second reaction was to show her a thing or two about proper kissing.

She might have been bold enough to start it, but the kiss was no longer hers. Peyton took over, his tongue gently exploring the surface of her lips, testing her level of willingness. Her lips parted, and he deepened the kiss. With seductive skill, he caressed her tongue with his in slow circular strokes, allowing her to participate in this languid duel. He knew empirically this was the way women liked to be kissed. To prove his point, a small moan escaped her.

Her pleasure was potent. At the sound of her moan everything changed. The kiss was no longer an instructive lesson in technique. It was now a prelude to something much stronger. He had not meant to take things further. But possessing her mouth was no longer enough. He had one hand at the back of her neck and the other just below the underside of her breast. It was a mere adjustment of inches to cup the fullness of her breast in his palm, his thumbs reaching up to stroke her nipples through the cloth. She gasped in wanton delight and Peyton felt her knees buckle. He bore her backwards to the window seat and followed her down.

Her eyes were rich amethysts, dark with her desire, encouraging him onwards.

She wriggled beneath him, her untutored moves teasing his arousal where it lay heavy and obvious against her leg. Her movements indicated he was not in this alone. She was as aroused as he.

He *knew* what he wanted in that moment and it shocked the hell out of him. He'd never given in to such a burst of spontaneous passion before. Yet here he was, wanting to and even willing to ravish the beauty beneath him. This had to stop. Immediately. For a thousand reasons. Not the least being his honour as well as hers.

Peyton drew back with a hard breath. 'This is not the time or place. I must apologise.' He tugged at his waistcoat and extended a hand to help her rise. 'Are you all right, Miss Branscombe?'

'Yes,' Tessa replied curtly. 'And I think after *that*—' her eyes flicked towards the window seat '—you can call me Tessa.'

Her aplomb was laudable, Peyton thought, but his angel was unsteady on her feet, unsteady and beautiful, her golden hair loose about her face, her lips noticeably well kissed. Under no circumstance could she return to the ballroom looking like that. 'Wait here, I'll send Lily to you. You can tell her you're feeling out of sorts,' Peyton offered. It was the least he could do. His behaviour had been beyond the pale. He'd nearly seduced an innocent in an alcove as if he was a veritable rake. He needed time to sort things through, to make sense of his own feelings.

Peyton found Lily and discreetly sent her after Tessa. Lily would take Tessa home and send the carriage back for him. Peyton couldn't imagine riding home with Tessa just now, sitting across from her well-kissed lips and slightly tousled hair, knowing that he could do nothing for his aches or hers with Aunt Lily next to her. Right now he didn't need that form of exquisite torture. He needed distance. Secure in the knowledge that Tessa was taken care of, Peyton took himself off to a deserted library to await the return of his carriage.

The library was dark with the exception of a dim lamp on the fireplace mantel. Peyton found a long sofa and took the luxury of stretching out. Since dancing had resumed in the ballroom, no one was likely to come along.

Tessa Branscombe had turned his ordered world topsy turvy in a short time. He'd be more careful with what he wished for in the future. It seemed ages ago that he was bemoaning the fact that his life felt empty. Now, it practically burgeoned with activity.

Instead of smooth days, there was conflict. Tessa attempted to thwart his authority at every turn. Instead of predictability, there was now mystery everywhere he looked. He'd forgotten what that was like. Since he'd met Tessa, he'd been argued with, defied, held at gunpoint, soundly kissed and thoroughly aroused. It was no wonder his emotions were out of joint.

Peyton sighed in the near darkness. Riotous emotions were not what Brimley had hired him for. He'd been entrusted with uncovering a dangerous list for his government. He was getting nowhere with that. He suspected that wouldn't change until he'd acquired Tessa's full trust. Until then, he had no idea how much Tessa knew. Did she know there was a list? Did she fear the presence of the Russian delegation in town? What would she do if she had the list or found the list? Would she turn it over to the Russians?

A large part of Peyton hoped Tessa knew about the list. He very much feared a scenario in which Tessa accidentally uncovered the list among some family possessions and, unaware of its value, showed it to Count Androvich. Such a scenario was not so farfetched. The Count was a family friend. It would be natural to go to him, to see him as a trusted confidant.

Tessa did know something, though. There had been the one reference she'd made the first day he'd called about her concern over safety. Tonight, the Russian delegation had unnerved her. There was the gun in her reticule and her perception that a disturbance in her home must be due to the presence of an intruder. The last had been most telling. Many women he knew would have concluded anything amiss was due to new items laid out by the servants or the general upheaval of the unpacking process. It would have been beyond the imaginings of these pampered women to conclude someone had been sneaking around. Yet Tessa had not bothered to think otherwise.

Not for the first time, Peyton wished he knew more about what had happened in St Petersburg. His best chance of finding out was to get close to Tessa and win her trust. Tonight's events indicated that might not be as hard to do as he'd originally thought. In spite of their stubborn quarrels, their passion boded surprisingly well. But Peyton was reluctant to use such techniques, especially when it was clear they both had something more than politics at stake. Lydia would laugh at the irony of it. Just when he needed his emotional detachment, it was being sorely tested.

The door to the library opened. Peyton thought to call out and make his presence known. When he realised who it was, he decided against it. Count Androvich and the two Russian ambassadors entered the dark room. Due to the gloom and the position of the sofa, they couldn't see him. They took seats in a cluster of chairs at the long library table running down the centre of the room. Peyton couldn't see them from there, but he could hear them, even with their lowered voices.

It was obvious they wanted their meeting to be private. Such a realisation increased the level of peril Peyton was in. They would not want to discover he'd lain there for the entire conversation. Peyton thought about the sharp, slender knife he carried under his trouser leg. He would not be unarmed if it came to a fight.

'We must make plans,' one of them said. Peyton thought it was Vasilov.

'Speak in French,' Gromsky insisted.

'Speak in English,' came a sharp retort. That was Androvich. 'If anyone overhears a foreign tongue, they'll know it was us. How many Russians speaking accented French would all be meeting together? If we speak in English, it will be less likely to pinpoint us. Even with accents, we could always blame other foreign nationals in town,' he reasoned.

The conversation went forward in English. Peyton was relieved. While he had a decent command of French, Peyton had yet to grasp the intricacies of the language in fast-paced conversations. It had been an eye-opener tonight to hear Tessa manage the tongue so effortlessly.

'I am making progress with Tessa Branscombe,' Androvich bragged. 'Tonight, I reminded her that I would gladly take her home with me in the autumn, that I would marry her and restore her to her rightful place in St Petersburg.'

'Is she amenable to that?' Gromsky asked.

Androvich snorted. 'Amenable? When has Tessa Branscombe been amenable to anything?'

'So you're saying she refused you?' Vasilov put in, a sneer evident in his voice.

Androvich's retort was quick and crisp. 'No, she has not refused. She is tempted, I think. But she is a woman and she wants to be wooed. Where is the romance in accepting right away? I know women. I will woo her and convince her this is the right course. She was infatuated with me once.'

'That was when we should have struck!' Vasilov said in hushed frustration. 'You let her get away when she was most vulnerable to us.'

'She left St Petersburg earlier than expected,' Androvich protested quickly.

'Now we have the Earl sniffing after her,' Vasilov continued his rant.

'He's not after her. He's after the list,' Androvich countered, his male pride hurt.

'It's starting to look that way,' Gromsky said, taking Androvich's side. 'New intelligence from a few embassies suggest he's highly accomplished and respected in diplomatic circles and not just for his overt negotiations. Rumour has it he once was a trusted member of the Filiki Eteria. Secret societies don't let outsiders in as a rule, and yet he was accepted.'

'I've told you, he's a fraud,' Androvich all but snarled.

Peyton was gratified to know that the Russian

team wasn't in the best of standing with each other. Those kinds of dynamics could be used against them if needed. Unfortunately, Peyton would have preferred to keep his identity a secret from the Russians a while longer.

'We need to treat him as if he's more than an ill-timed suitor.' Ilanovich spoke up for the first time. 'As I think we've suspected all along, he's been injected into this wild treasure hunt for the purpose of finding the list. You've got to get back into Miss Branscombe's good graces quickly.'

Vasilov began to plan. 'The best way to do that is to contain the Earl. We must act quickly. We cannot afford the Earl turning her head. Anyone looking at them on the dance floor tonight can't doubt their mutual attraction. More than a passionate flirtation, we cannot allow the Earl to fill her head with suspicions about you, Androvich. You must woo her and make it believable. If the Earl is nothing more than a love-struck guardian, he'll do the honourable thing and step aside once you make your intentions known. If not, then we'll know what his agenda is.'

'I doubt it. Stepping aside isn't in his vocabulary,' Androvich said derisively. 'If there's any stepping to be done, it will be me stepping over his dead body.'

'That can be arranged,' Gromsky said with more relish than Peyton would have liked.

'Yes...' Vasilov's tones entered the conversation,

contemplative. 'A dead earl would certainly make access to Miss Branscombe easier as long as it's done right. We don't want to cause an international incident.'

'If anyone does in the Earl, it will be me,' Androvich put in. 'He's insulted me one too many times.'

The conversation ended shortly after that. Peyton lay on the sofa, unmoving for what seemed like hours, making sure they were truly gone, that they'd had time to clear the hallway. There would be no explaining how he materialised in the hall if he walked out and they were still there.

Listening to one's own death being plotted was definitely high on the list of unpleasant experiences. There was no doubt that these ambassadors were hardened killers. The calm matter-of-fact discussion of who would live and who would die, who would be manipulated and who would be shoved aside, was quite unnerving. None the less, the conversation had been instructive. Peyton had confirmation both that Tessa was in the dark about the list and that Androvich was clearly the villain here, using their friendship to trap her. 'Not that you're much better,' Peyton's conscience reminded him. 'Ah, but I'm not going to kill anyone to do it,' he rejoined easily, although it didn't make him feel any better. He'd rather not have his motives listed in the same category as Androvich's.

Plans began to form in Peyton's mind. He would

talk to Brimley in the morning. Then he'd call for re-inforcements. He was going to need someone to watch his back on this and that's what brothers were for.

Chapter Eight

The particular brother in question, Crispin Ramsden, let the letter dangle from his long fingers as he sat back in his chair and studied the other two occupants of Dursley Park's private family sitting room. His younger brother, Paine, and his wife, Julia, stared at him expectantly. Julia gently rocked the infant in her arms. At least one of the room's occupants wasn't going to like the news.

'Well?' Paine said at long last. 'What has Peyton got to say for himself?'

'I am going up to London for a spell,' Crispin declared, trying to avoid the difficulty by not mentioning it at all.

Paine looked at him suspiciously and Crispin knew his ploy was about to fail. 'Is Peyton in trouble?'

'Can't a brother go up to town without there being trouble?'

'Yes, but it seems unlikely that you would go to the bother of facing London during the Season just to pay a social call on Peyton, who should be returning any day now,' Paine argued.

Crispin sighed and rose from his chair, taking up a position at the window overlooking the gardens. 'Julia, may I speak with my brother alone?' He knew he sounded harsh. Julia was hardly ever excluded from family issues. He adored his brother's wife. She was everything a man like Paine needed for balance in his life. But right now, he wanted the liberty of speaking freely, man to man. No matter how endearing a woman was, women had a way of squelching that ability.

'All right, tell me what's going on,' Paine said, staking out his own position at the fireplace mantel, arms crossed and slightly irritated over Crispin's manner.

Crispin passed the letter to Paine. 'It's all there.'

Paine took the missive and scanned it, a quizzical look crossing his brow. 'What's there? There's news of the city, a friend named Brimley, a mention at the end that he's lonely and thought you might like to come up to town since he's got to stay longer than anticipated. I am afraid I don't see the cause for alarm.'

'He's *lonely*. Have you ever known Peyton admit to being lonely?' Crispin pressed. 'He's in trouble and he's worried enough not to disclose it directly in his letter.'

'You got all that from a single line?' Paine's disbelief was evident.

'I know Peyton better than you do.' Crispin hadn't meant for it to come out so bluntly. Paine would be offended, but it was the truth. Paine had been away from the family for twelve years of exile over a duel in his wilder, younger days. He'd only recently returned. While the rift imposed by distance and time apart had been overcome by healthy doses of love, forgiveness and Julia's presence in their lives, there was still a significant amount of time unaccounted for in each other's lives. Crispin willingly admitted he didn't fully understand what Paine had been doing in India all those years, just as Crispin knew Paine had no concept of what Peyton had been up to.

'Is that why you banned Julia from the room? To insult me? To doubt my filial affections?' Paine was bristly. Crispin reminded himself to tread carefully. Paine was a new father who had been kept up all night with a colicky infant.

'Paine, I banned Julia from the room because I didn't want her to worry.'

'What's there to worry about? This nebulous "trouble" you think Peyton is in?'

'Exactly. Look, Paine, you don't know Brimley.'

'The man mentioned in the letter?'

'Yes. Brimley isn't just another politico haunting Whitehall and Parliament. He's an important player in the Home and Foreign Offices. If Brimley is mentioned in the letter along with being lonely, there's no questioning that something's up.'

'What does this Brimley have to do with Peyton?'

Crispin drew a deep breath. 'Once upon a time, not so long ago, Peyton worked for British interests in Vienna while I was in the military.' He let the information settle with Paine, letting him grasp its full import.

'My brother was a diplomat?' There was incredulity in Paine's tone.

Crispin nodded. Peyton had been a diplomat, sometimes acting in a grey area between diplomat and spy. 'I'll go up to London and see what's going on.' Perhaps the news would be enough to distract Paine from the rest of the news. He wasn't that fortunate.

Paine took a moment to consider the situation. 'I'll come with you.'

Crispin shook his head. 'No. You have Julia and the baby to think about. You can't leave her and you certainly can't bring her and the baby to the city.'

'I could just come for a while, a few days, to make sure everything's all right,' Paine argued.

'No, Peyton asked specifically that I come alone.' There. He'd said the worst of it. He knew Paine wouldn't like hearing it, but Peyton's instructions had been clear.

'Exactly where does he say I am not to come?' Paine said, scanning the letter again.

'He only names me in the letter,' Crispin said shortly.

Paine read the line Crispin referred to out loud. '"I

am lonely in the city. Crispin, you should come up for a visit and lend me your good company." I suppose in the special language you and Peyton have devised what that really means is "please leave Paine at home and let him worry from afar".'

Crispin smiled at his brother's acerbic tone. 'You're learning.'

'Well, you can't really expect me to wait here. I am a grown man. I can handle myself in a fight.'

Crispin's demeanour softened. He understood Paine's reluctance to be left out, but he could not capitulate to it. 'Peyton does not want to risk you.' He gave a dry chuckle. 'I'm expendable if there's a real danger. You're not. He would not risk widowing Julia and leaving your son fatherless. If his reluctance to have you come to town is not enough to prove the perilous nature of his circumstances, I don't know what is.' Crispin strode to the door of the room, clapping Paine on the shoulder as he passed by him. 'Hold the fort here in case we need to make a hasty retreat. I'll leave this afternoon. I can make a fair distance on horseback before dark.'

Up in his room, it only took Crispin a half-hour to pack. He liked to pretend that it was his military training and ability to live an unencumbered life that made packing so easy. He also pretended that he liked the freedom such a situation provided him. The reality was that his existence wasn't so much unencumbered as it was rootless and pointless. Watching

Paine and Julia with their son had driven that aspect home relentlessly over the past months.

Although Crispin deliberately eschewed London and all the mamas who thought snagging Dursley's brother a worthy prize, it would be a nice change from the stifling domesticity of Dursley Park and all the reminders of what he didn't have. Crispin threw a pair of fighting knives on to the bed, followed by a brace of pistols. In London he'd be useful.

'You say Crispin is coming?' Brimley asked confidentially over brandies at White's. 'Crispin will be useful. He's a good man in a fight.'

Peyton nodded, all too aware that meeting Brimley at White's was becoming a commonplace habit, a sure sign that the situation was nearing its zenith. He'd shared the Russians' conversation with Brimley. Brimley had concurred that bringing Crispin to town would offer the Branscombes and Peyton some extra protection. With luck, the Russians wouldn't see Crispin as an assistant, but merely as a brother who had come to town to enjoy the Season.

Crispin would be a good addition. He could act as a buffer between him and Lily, who had been furious over the events at the Broughtons' ball. One look at Tessa and she'd guessed exactly what had transpired. She'd given him a severe tongue-lashing the next day that had included a scolding for stealing kisses as well as a scolding for poor behaviour on the dance floor. What had he been thinking to pull her so close? Miss Branscombe had enough disadvantages—no fortune, no social connections—to overcome, without a dubious relationship with him. He was her guardian, for heaven's sake. He was supposed to help her avoid scandal, not court it.

Yes, the scolding had gone something like that, followed by Lily's assurances that she'd effectively scotched the budding rumours about the beautiful Tessa Branscombe, who had appeared from nowhere on the Earl's arm, spoke French and Russian fluently and had prior acquaintance with the four Russian men who'd arrived in town, particularly the young, dashing Count.

'What are you going to do about Miss Branscombe?' Brimley inquired, breaking in. 'Has she told you anything useful?'

This was the part Peyton detested the most: reporting to Brimley about his relationship with Tessa, as if it were nothing more than a negotiation process. His gentleman's code warred with his duty to his country. A gentleman didn't kiss and tell. But duty often demanded hard choices. Still, to say anything felt like a betrayal.

'She needs more time to become accustomed to me. We can't expect her to spill her secrets immediately,' Peyton said firmly, knowing this to be the truth. 'She does suspect trouble, though.' There was no harm in telling Brimley about the incident with the gun on the staircase.

Brimley raised his bushy grey brows at this. 'She is on the lookout for an interloper. That means this is likely not the first time she's feared one. We have to make her feel safe, Dursley.'

'I want to move her to my aunt's. Bloomsbury isn't secure enough for my taste.' Peyton spoke his plan out loud. He'd been thinking about it since the Broughtons' ball. 'She won't like it.'

'Well, make her like it. Sell it to her with a kiss if you have to,' Brimley rejoined sharply. 'I am sure women find you attractive, Dursley, with all your good looks and manners. Put them to use before the Russian competition does. My wife was going on at dinner recently about how handsome that Count Androvich is. We can't have him kissing her and manipulating the advantage of his so-called friendship.' Brimley took out his pocket watch. 'It's seven o'clock—don't you have somewhere to be?'

Peyton smiled thinly at the older man. To Brimley this was just another chess game. Usually Peyton respected that about him. Tonight, that quality seemed to have lost its lustre. He rose. 'Actually, I am supposed to look in on the Branscombe girls.' Not that he was looking forward to it. The girls had corralled him into spending an evening playing parlour games with them, since there wasn't a social event demanding his presence. Parlour games and a growing irritation with Brimley were just two signs as to how far Tessa Branscombe was getting under his skin.

Lamps burned in the front windows of the town house in Bloomsbury, throwing a welcoming light into the night. Peyton stepped down from the coach and sent his coachman off with instructions to return in two hours. There was no sense having the man wait in the cold when he could wait at a respectable nearby inn and stay warm.

Peyton stood on the pavement, surveying the house, reluctant to go in. He knew Tessa would balk at his suggestion about removing to Lily's. It might go over better if the request came from Aunt Lily.

He could understand Tessa's unwillingness. The house was respectable enough for women of their circumstance. More importantly, it was *hers*. He felt the same way about his property and his people. They were his—his to take care of, his to protect. It would take a legion to move him by force. Oh, yes, he understood very deeply what motivated Tessa's stubbornness. He was coming to realise that what appealed to him most about Tessa Branscombe was that, beneath her beauty and her quick-flaring temper, she was very like him.

The girls were thrilled to see him. He could hear Eva and Petra vying to see who would open the door for him. Fortunately, Arthur beat them to it and actually got to perform his job.

'Good evening, milord,' Arthur said, automatically reaching to take Peyton's coat and hat. '*Everyone* is here in the drawing room.'

Peyton took note of that and stiffened. 'Everyone' could only mean Count Androvich. 'How long has the Count been here?' he asked Arthur in low tones.

'A half-hour—he's been regaling the girls with his outing to the Tower today.'

Peyton pasted on a cool smile and entered the drawing room. Tessa sat next to Androvich on the sofa with Annie at her knee. Petra and Eva had resumed casual poses in the chairs. The domestic scene twisted Peyton's gut. Anyone else might see familial tranquillity at its finest, but he saw danger. Based on what he'd learned last night, Androvich could have a knife in Tessa's ribs before anyone was the wiser. The girls wouldn't last much longer after that. A throwing knife and a gun would put paid to them in short order.

Peyton shoved the morbid thought aside. Tessa was safe for the moment. Androvich didn't want Tessa dead yet. She would live as long as he was convinced she still had information he needed regarding the list. It was he whom Androvich had deadly intentions for.

Tessa looked up, aware he'd entered the room. 'I'm so glad you could make it. The girls are looking forward to a night of games.' She stood up and crossed the room to greet him. Peyton thought she

seemed rather glad to have an excuse to leave Androvich's side.

'Can we start?' Eva asked impatiently. 'We have to
pair up for teams.' Peyton caught a glimpse of mischief
in Eva's eyes. She reminded him at times of Paine when
he was younger. It had been the bane of his existence
to keep Paine in line. He pitied the eligible bachelors
when Eva came out. She'd keep everyone on their toes.

'I will partner Sergei,' she began. 'Tessa, you can
be with Lord Dursley and Petra and Annie will be
together.' Eva plopped down next to Count Androvich, who appeared to take the edict in good form.
He was an excellent actor.

At least fate was on his side for the moment,
Peyton thought, taking a chair next to Tessa. If he had
to play parlour games, he might as well have Tessa
for a partner.

They played charades, with enigmatic word de-
scriptions, rather than acting out scenes. There was
much laughing among the teams and even Tessa
relaxed beside him, taking part in the game with zest.
This was a side of Tessa Branscombe Peyton hadn't
seen yet. It was intoxicating to watch Tessa among
her family, her temper leashed, whatever fears she
harboured momentarily restrained. The peace of the
setting added to her beauty.

Did she understand how much of an illusion the
evening was? Two representatives from two kings
sat in her drawing room, playing charades with her

sisters, acting as if they were her friends, people she could trust with her family, with her very life, all for the sake of a list. At least Peyton could say on his part that he wasn't acting. It made his conscience feel slightly better.

'Ah, this is just like those winter nights back in St Petersburg when we would sit by your father's fire and play games,' Androvich said after he and Eva won handily at charades. The girls looked at him enrapt, their faces dreamy with remembrances of better times, happier times. But Tessa looked down at her hands, refusing to meet Androvich's gaze. Peyton wondered about the awkwardness between Tessa and Androvich tonight.

As for himself, Peyton wanted to haul the Count outside and pummel some decency into him. No self-respecting gentleman would declare war on such un-suspecting girls. The girls thought he was their friend. Peyton had to stop right there. What did that make him? Meg entered with a tea tray, and saved him from too much speculation.

Peyton had been prepared to wait out the Count. He had no intentions of leaving the man alone in the house with Tessa. Fortunately, he didn't have to wait long. Perhaps the Count had sensed Tessa would not be receptive to whatever he wanted that night or perhaps the Count had another destination in mind to wind down the evening. After tea, Androvich took his very proper leave of the girls and Tessa.

'I would like to take all of you sightseeing tomorrow if your schedules are free,' Peyton offered to the room at large, but he looked at Tessa as he spoke. It had occurred to him during the course of the evening that the girls would want to see the sights of their new city. If he didn't take them, Androvich would. He could imagine all kinds of horrors that could befall young girls in the city with Androvich on watch.

His offer met with success. Even Annie seemed excited by the prospect. 'Please, Tessa?' Eva and Petra begged.

'Of course we can go,' Tessa acceded. 'Are you sure it's not too much trouble? We don't mean to interrupt your schedule. You must be very busy.'

'I would not have offered if I didn't mean it.' Peyton held her gaze over long until she was the one who looked away.

Quickly, Tessa said, 'If there's to be an outing, everyone needs to get to bed.' The order cleared the room efficiently and Peyton had what he'd wanted all night, a chance to be with Tessa alone.

He told himself it was for business purposes, but his body argued otherwise. The passion he'd tasted with her still lingered, coupled with an intensified desire to protect her from that snake Androvich. All night, his body had been teased by the mere proximity of her: the smell of lavender in her hair, the scent of soap, the clean smell of lemon and starch that hung about her clothes. The teasing didn't stop there.

The sound of her light laughter had been entrancing, the sight of her face lit with enjoyment had all combined into a potent elixir. Tessa Branscombe had definitely got to him. When he was with her, he could feel his objectivity slipping away, replaced by something subjective and primal.

'May I have a word with you before I go?' Peyton asked, all formal politeness, pleased that none of his inner longings flavoured his voice.

'Of course.' Tessa resumed her seat, habitually sweeping her skirts behind her as she sat.

'I couldn't help but notice that you seemed cool to the Count tonight. Is everything all right? He hasn't pressed you unduly since last night?'

Tessa gave a light chuckle. 'Playing the guardian, are you?'

'The gentleman,' Peyton corrected.

'Sergei is an old friend.' Tessa looked down at her hands. 'That's all last night was,' she added softly.

'You do not return his feelings?' Peyton probed.

'Not any longer. I do not see Sergei as more than a family friend. I fear his *tendre* for me has only developed out of loyalty to my father.'

'Is that all you fear?'

Tessa looked at him sharply. 'Whatever do you mean by such a question?'

'Well, I'm not the one carrying a gun in my reticule.'

Tessa stood up. 'Do not mistake one kiss in an alcove for more than it was. It does not grant you permission to snoop through my life. My business is mine alone. I am capable of taking care of myself and my sisters.'

Peyton rose to meet her, his own temper rising with hers. Lord, the woman was stubborn beyond all good sense. He knew instinctively that she would argue *ad nauseam*. He could think of nothing else to do except to take Brimley's advice and kiss her.

'One kiss might not qualify, but perhaps two will.' Tension sparked between them. Thank providence the Ramsden brothers counted kissing among their many accomplishments.

Chapter Nine

The girls were nearly giddy in their excitement over sightseeing the next morning as they gathered in the front room, fighting over a spot to look out the window and be the first to spy the Earl of Dursley. Tessa tried to share their enthusiasm. The sun was out and the prospect of seeing London under blue skies was quite tempting. But she'd rather see the sights without the pompous Earl of Dursley by her side.

The irritating man had had the audacity to kiss her not once, but twice. Once, she could countenance. The spirit of their dance had transmuted into energy that had needed an outlet, as unconventional as it was. There were multiple ways to explain what had passed between them in the alcove. Curiosity on her part—were all kisses as empty as Sergei's? Envy, maybe, on his part. He clearly had not approved of Sergei kissing her and she didn't believe his chagrin was solely motivated out of a need to adhere to the codes of propriety. But to kiss her twice? The earlier reasons simply hadn't applied to their kiss last night.

His kiss last night had been commanding, challenging, even, as if there was a hidden dare behind it. To her credit, or maybe not, she'd met that challenge, answering his kiss with a kiss of her own. Before she knew it, her back was against the wall, her hands were in his hair and they were both fully engaged.

How embarrassing! No one had ever kissed her in the manner Peyton had. Never had a kiss evoked such a flood of feelings. Simultaneously, she wanted to both give in, see where such abandon led, and to slap the arrogant Earl across the planes of his handsome face. How dare he make such presumptions! Possibly he wouldn't presume so much if she didn't give him leave.

Oblivious to the turmoil plaguing their older sister, the girls gave a squeal of delight as Peyton's carriage drew up to the kerb, the top pulled down in acquiescence to the good weather. He jumped down and headed towards their steps, looking well turned out in buff Inexpressibles and a blue morning coat for the outing.

With surprising little chaos, everyone was settled in the landau. Tessa sat facing forward with Eva and Annie, while Petra took the seat next to Peyton, who sat with his back to the driver. Tessa had originally thought the arrangement would be much more to her satisfaction. Sitting across from Peyton would somehow be less intimate to her way of thinking. There would be no chance for the natural contours of the road to jostle them into one another. There'd be no knees knocking, no shoulders brushing. But now there would be eye contact. She had not reckoned on how disconcerting it was to be the focus of his gaze.

'I thought we'd stop at the Tower of London first,' Peyton said as the carriage pulled into the street. Tessa hated how collected he sounded, as if their kiss hadn't happened, or, if it had, didn't matter. He had the unnerving ability to carry on as if nothing out of the ordinary had occurred. The nasty side of her posited a theory: maybe that kiss was not out of the ordinary. Maybe he kissed every woman he met. But that was hard to believe. The immaculately dressed, mannerly Earl did not strike her as one to engage in light dalliance.

Tessa spent the trip making small talk with Dursley, trying to pretend that he hadn't given her quite a thorough kissing on the last two occasions they had met. The trip to the Tower seemed endless, although, in reality, she supposed it hadn't taken all that long. Traffic was not that bad in the streets.

The coachman found a place at the kerb for them to get down, and Tessa was pleased to see that the girls remembered their manners, letting Peyton exit the carriage first in order to help them down.

When it was her turn, Peyton lingered over her

hand. 'Miss Branscombe, you look especially lovely today. Yellow becomes you.'

A wicked retort came to mind, but Tessa fought it off. Surely the daughter of a diplomat could do better? She opted for a more mundane but safer comment about the sun and the weather.

The Tower was an intimidating spectacle. Tessa had been eight when the family had left London, far too young to be out sightseeing. She was as new to the sights as her younger sisters. They were all suitably impressed and Peyton was a natural tour guide.

'The Tower has long been used in a variety of roles from a prison, a mint for the treasury, a home for jewels, and a garrison for soldiers. Up until last year, the Tower was even the home of a great menagerie of animals, including lions,' Peyton said.

'What happened to the animals?' Petra asked, concern evident in her voice. 'Surely they weren't killed?'

'No, not at all. The menagerie has been moved over to the zoo in Regent's Park,' Peyton allayed her concerns.

'Can we go there some time?' Annie asked shyly, surprising Tessa. Annie hadn't spoken directly to Peyton since his appearance in their lives.

To his credit, Peyton favoured the little girl with a rare smile. 'I will arrange it. Regent's Park is a lovely spot. There's boating and the gardens will be in full bloom. We can picnic and make a day of it.'

Annie beamed and Tessa was inexplicably moved by his kindness. She cocked her head beneath the brim of her hat and gave him a long, considering look. Peyton Ramsden was fast becoming the most complex man she'd ever met. His outward demeanour of urbane politeness gave him an aura of constant coolness, as if the world could not reach him with all of its busy, noisy messiness. However, that was not the sum of him. Beneath that well-cultivated surface lay a man with intense passions and mysterious depths, a man who intrigued her against her will. If their circumstances and stations in life were different, she might feel compelled to attract his attentions.

As it was, this was not the time to engage in a little romance. Nor would there ever be a right time. She had Sergei's feelings to consider. If she turned her attentions to the Earl so soon after she'd refused his proposal, Sergei would think Peyton was the reason for her rejection.

Then there were her concerns about potential danger to consider. True, there had been no other incidents to raise her suspicions since the day she'd mistaken Peyton for an intruder. Regardless, she couldn't help but feel that all was not as it should be. If there was anything amiss, she didn't want to drag Peyton into it. He'd gamely taken up his duties as a guardian and that was enough. Anything further would be an imposition.

Besides, nothing could come of such a flirtation than what had already occurred. Part of her thought this was the real reason. For all that her mind called him 'Peyton' and thought of him as a man, this man was a peer of the realm. The Earl of Dursley could not be expected to seriously consider courting a diplomat's daughter without any substantial monetary or social consequence to her name.

There would never be anything more than the kisses they'd already shared. And those, while quite stirring, had not been prompted by courtship or growing affection. They'd been brought on by the heat of conflict and the passions of the moment. She would be mistaken to construe them as anything else.

'Miss Branscombe, I do believe you've missed my fine dissertation on the armoury,' Peyton said drily at her side, a hand cupping her elbow to guide her through the crowd towards the exit.

'My apologies, I am sure it was riveting.'

'Apparently not as riveting as your wool-gathering. I will expect your full attention at the Jewel House.'

At the Jewel House, they gathered with other visitors on wooden benches to watch one of the daily ritual unveilings of the Crown Jewels. It was not terribly crowded, as it would be later in the day, but some jostling behind them drew Peyton's attention. Tessa could feel him tense beside her as he discreetly looked around for the source of the commotion.

'What is it?' Her own senses were on alert now.

'Do you recognise that man in the tan coat?' Peyton asked in a low voice. 'I seem to recall having seen him before, but I can't place him.'

Tessa studied the man covertly from beneath her hat. He was of middle years, a bit portly around the middle and dressed respectably in the clothing of a merchant. He didn't look menacing, but rather like a friendly father-figure, someone who might be a likeable neighbour. Tessa stiffened. It was probably nothing but a mere coincidence.

'He resembles a man who reads the news sheets on the bench by the garden near our home,' Tessa said softly. 'I can't say for sure if it's the same man. I've never approached him. I assumed he lived in the square with us. We haven't met many of our neighbours. Perhaps that's where you've seen him.' She added the last bit lightly, trying to hide her growing concern. It had only been the noise that had drawn Peyton's attention. Peyton had no reason to share her suspicions. She had to remain calm, lest she arouse his suspicions. He was already curious as to why she'd had a gun with her.

The girls gasped in appreciation, drawing her attention to the curtain, which was being pulled back to reveal the jewels of the monarchs. The group of people gave a collective gasp of awe at the opulence on display. An old woman came forward and stood next to the collection. She held her head high and began her recitation on the treasures. 'Ladies and gentlemen, behold the treasures of the ages,' she began in a pompous manner that made Tessa stifle a laugh. Peyton gently elbowed her and shot her a sideways glance that suggested he saw the humour in it, too.

Afterwards, Tessa looked around for the man in the tan coat. She caught sight of him exiting. He did not appear to be interested in the whereabouts of her group. Later, as they toured the rest of the exhibits, she saw him near them in some cases, but he did not attach himself to the group of people they moved with, nor did he seem to notice them at all. Her initial fears began to subside, but it was privately quite telling to her just how deep-seated her fears ran these days when she was alarmed by such an encounter. It wasn't a good sign that she was seeing danger everywhere.

The day progressed without incident. Peyton took them to Gunther's for ices and had them deposited at his Aunt Lily's town house promptly at four o'clock, so that Tessa had time to rest before the Ashmore rout that evening. Meg was already waiting at Aunt Lily's with Tessa's gown and the girls' things for spending the night.

The move had been accomplished so effortlessly that Tessa could hardly complain. Peyton's efficiency made it easy to let him handle the details and, for a change, it was nice to let someone else take care of things. 'Your management skills amaze me,' Tessa said as he handed her down from the landau. 'This could easily become habit forming.'

Peyton held her gaze for a long moment. 'I sincerely hope it does, Miss Branscombe.'

Tessa dressed carefully for the rout in an evening gown of a becoming shade of lavender that brought out the colour of her eyes. She was looking forward to the rout for far different reasons than she'd looked forward to the Broughtons' diplomats' ball. At the Broughtons', she had been excited about the idea of participating in a milieu she knew well and missed during the long months since her father's death. Tonight, the excitement that fluttered through her had very little to do with the venue and everything to do with a man.

Tonight, she'd be on Peyton's arm. He would dance with her. Perhaps they'd waltz again. She was almost certain they would. The thought of his hand at her waist sent a delightful shiver through her.

He might kiss her again if they could manage to be alone. When they were alone together, he behaved like an entirely different man than when they were surrounded by others. The neutral ambience of the sophisticated Earl would vanish in private, to be replaced by a man of an entirely different nature.

Meg popped her head into the room and announced the arrival of the carriage. Lily was already downstairs. Tessa said a quick goodnight to her sisters and sailed down to meet Peyton.

Peyton waited at the bottom of the stairs in the foyer, but he was not alone. Along with him and Aunt Lily was another man, equal in height to Peyton and with hair just as dark, although far longer. Her first thought was that Lily, still intent on seeing her engaged before the Season was out, was playing matchmaker.

A wave of disappointment rolled through Tessa. She'd thought to have Peyton all to herself. It was silly, really. At a ball one was never in great risk of being alone with their escort. The rules wouldn't allow her to dance with Peyton more than twice and they'd be surrounded by a crush of people all night long.

'Ah, Miss Branscombe,' Peyton said as she approached, firmly entrenched in his public role of the urbane Earl. 'Lovely as always, I see. Allow me to introduce you to my brother, Lord Crispin Ramsden.'

'It is a pleasure to finally meet you,' Crispin Ramsden said. 'I can see why my brother has found his time in the city extended beyond his original intentions.'

Up close there was no mistaking the resemblance. Crispin Ramsden physically aped his brother: dark hair, blue eyes, a commanding height and presence. But only a fool would miss the stark differences between them, Tessa thought. Crispin might be able to deliver a polite line, but he lacked Peyton's inherent ease in social situations.

There was a rough, wild quality to him that set

him apart from his elegant brother and from others, which became quickly apparent once they arrived at the Ashmores' rout. People gave Crispin a wide berth and might have avoided him altogether if it hadn't been for his brother's presence. Those mamas who did dare come forward for an introduction, daughters in tow, were sent scuttling back to their *chaise longues* with a sharp comment and dark look.

'Play nice, Cris,' Peyton warned in low tones after a fourth mama was routed. 'I'm going to waltz with Tessa now. Don't bite anyone until I get back.'

Tessa had waited all night for this. She'd been out on the dance floor with partners Lily had arranged and with several others who had voluntarily signed her card. None of them had equalled Peyton's grace.

'You're becoming quite the sensation, despite not having been on the town long,' Peyton commented as the music started.

'I don't mean to be,' Tessa said honestly.

'Why ever not? You're a beautiful woman, Tessa.'

She should have revelled in the compliment, but she hardly noticed it. He'd called her 'Tessa'. It was the first time. Of course, she'd given him sardonic liberty to do so after their kissing bout at the Broughtons', but it had been correctly 'Miss Branscombe' all day today.

'I like it when you use my name,' she said boldly. 'Since circumstances have required we spend so much time together, it seems ridiculous to do otherwise.' In truth, she was having difficulty recalling that Peyton had not always been a part of her life, which was a ludicrous sentiment given how little time she'd known him. If she thought about it too much, it was alarming how easily he'd woven himself into the pattern of their days.

'Perhaps you should call me Peyton, at least when we're alone, then,' he replied, swinging them expertly through a turn. 'It shall be our rule. We are indeed in an awkward position, are we not? Social protocol demands you call me "Dursley". But since we're practically living in each other's pockets, it seems far too formal.'

His eyes darkened and, for a moment, Tessa felt his gaze on her lips. With a slight pressure at her waist, he drew her infinitesimally closer to him. Her breath caught in expectation.

'I find that sometimes formalities can be used to build barriers between people and I don't want any barriers with us, Tessa.' His voice was deliciously low in her ear. 'You can come to me with anything, trust me with anything. I will be your bulwark, always.'

In spite of her warnings to herself not to get swept away in an entanglement with Peyton Ramsden, Tessa was losing the fight and gladly. It wasn't simply because he was a handsome man, although that could hardly be overlooked. She'd met handsome men before who were no more than their fair visages. Peyton was far deeper. Watching him with her sisters at the Tower, she'd begun to feel she could trust him. The time might come when he was the only one she could turn to, trust or not. Sergei was a foreign diplomat and a diplomat associated with the origin of the trouble. If there was difficulty, Sergei would be of little use to her. She'd need an Englishman. It felt good to know there was somewhere she could turn.

The invisible burden she'd been carrying for months lifted from her shoulders. She felt physically free in Peyton's arms as he waltzed her about the ballroom. She never guessed she'd have to test his resolve to stand as her bulwark so soon.

It took two carriages to transport them all back to the house in Bloomsbury the next day. Peyton and Crispin had decided to come along with Aunt Lily to see them home. Tessa had argued that it wasn't necessary. She was becoming acutely aware of the amount of trips Peyton and his family members were making between their rarefied homes in Mayfair and her neighbourhood. But Peyton had insisted, saying he wanted to show Crispin the area.

They pulled up to the kerb, more than a few heads peeking around lace curtains to peer out at the group. Tessa noticed immediately that the man from the Tower was reading his news sheets on the bench. She nodded discreetly to Peyton.

'I'll have a word with him for my own peace of

mind,' Peyton said. 'It can't hurt. If it's nothing, we're just being neighbourly.'

Tessa laughed at the thought of the Earl of Dursley being 'neighbourly'. Peyton shot her a teasing look. 'Can't I be neighbourly? He doesn't know I am an earl.'

Crispin laughed, too, unable to resist a chance to rib his brother. 'No, he'll think you're a duke instead. You might do better to tell him you're an earl.'

'Your faith in me is touching,' Peyton responded drily, but Tessa could tell he'd taken the teasing in good stride. She liked this Peyton quite a lot, the laughing, human, approachable Peyton.

Everyone clambered out of the carriages. Peyton and Crispin went across the street and she went up the steps to the house, her key in hand, Petra right behind her. Tessa unlocked the door and stepped across the threshold. Tessa took two steps and came to a shocked halt. She wavered, collapsing against the door jamb for support, mentally digesting the sight inside. The house was destroyed.

'What is it, Tess? Are you ill?' Petra made to move around her. Tessa flung out an arm in a protective reaction, barring Petra from the sight. 'No, don't come in. Get Peyton, quickly—we've been burgled.'

Chapter Ten

The conversation with the news sheet-reading neighbour was not going well. Instead of being happy to engage in friendly conversation, the man was proving to be taciturn, giving short, single-syllable answers. He was even quite defensive at one point, declaring, 'I can read my bloody news wherever I want. This is a free country.' After that rhetorical turning point in the conversation, Crispin had been ready to plant the man a facer and Peyton's own concerns about the man were heightened.

He hadn't wanted to say anything alarming to Tessa yesterday at the Tower. The damnable game he was playing for Brimley didn't allow him to. Tessa didn't know he knew something of her situation. To suddenly have misgivings about a stranger would be out of place. He couldn't have suspicions unless Tessa shared her suspicions with him first. She hadn't done so, although he could see that she was unnerved by the 'coincidence' of her supposed neighbour showing up at the Tower.

He had to win the stubborn woman's trust, not just for the sake of Brimley's game, but for his own male pride. He wanted to take on Tessa's burdens as his own, regardless of Brimley's dictates. She was in danger and the sooner he could openly convince her of that, the safer all of them would be. His mind ran ahead of itself. Once Tessa was acquitted of this deadly game with the Russians, he could devote himself to a different kind of game with her, a courtly one. But romance had no place between them right now while a more perilous game was afoot. He needed all his sharp-witted faculties to protect her.

A burst of activity on the steps across the street caught his attention. Peyton saw Petra run down the steps and stop briefly to say something to Lily, whose reaction was to gather Annie to her and clasp Eva's hand. He exchanged a quick glance with Crispin and was up and running.

'Lord Dursley! We've been robbed,' Petra gasped as soon as he was in earshot. Panic was never discreet and he could hardly blame the girl. But he wished she hadn't announced it so openly for anyone to hear.

Peyton bolted across the street, but not before he heard Crispin say in falsely polite tones to the would-be neighbour, 'It seems we have something else to talk about.'

Peyton bounded up the town-house steps, his protective instincts on full alert. Tessa was still inside. Did the woman have no sense? The intruder could still be there. At the threshold, Peyton bent swiftly and pulled the knife from his boot, a long, slender, lethal-looking blade. He found Tessa in the drawing room, her gun out. Apparently her thoughts had run along the same lines as his.

'It's just me, Tessa,' Peyton said in even tones before she was inclined to whirl around and point her gun at him. 'You should be outside until I can determine if the prowler has left the premises.'

'Peyton, my house has been destroyed.' Tessa turned to face him and he could see the struggle she waged not to fall apart.

He did not miss her use of his Christian name; while a part of him thrilled to the sound of it on her lips, he knew he'd trade that accomplishment to spare her this moment. He wanted to take her in his arms and conceal her from the sight of the carnage, but propriety would not allow such a liberty. All around them the drawing room lay in shambles. Furniture had been overturned, stuffing ripped from chair cushions, the fireplace mantel pulled loose, leaving the wall scarred where it had been mounted.

Those were the big items Peyton noticed immediately. There were smaller signs of devastation, too: a shattered vase, an overturned table, a shredded book. He imagined the rest of the house would look the same.

'Who would do such a thing?' Tessa sighed, kicking aside a ruined chair cushion.

Peyton had some very good ideas. The break-in told him two things—first, the intruder had been looking for something. That explained the wanton destruction of things like the mantel and the cushions. The intruder was seeking out a hiding place. The second was that the intruder also wanted to send a threatening message with his destruction. That explained the errant acts of violence, like the overturned table and the shattered items that clearly weren't likely hiding places.

He wasn't ready to voice his thoughts to Tessa yet. He wanted to wait until he'd searched the whole house and seen the entire pattern of the prowler's destruction.

'Tessa, fetch your sisters. We need to get them off the pavement. Explain the situation to them. I am going upstairs to look around. We'll meet in the drawing room,' Peyton directed, starting up the stairs before Tessa could counter-plan.

Upstairs, the devastation was as complete as downstairs. Peyton drew a deep breath. In some ways what had been done upstairs was even worse because it involved the desecration of highly personal items. Clothing had been flung from wardrobes, beds had been torn apart. In Tessa's private office, papers had been thrown out of drawers. There was no choice now but to move Tessa and the girls to Aunt Lily's.

Downstairs in the drawing room, Peyton broke the

news to the Branscombe sisters. 'You cannot stay here. The mess alone is reason enough, even if there weren't concerns about the safety of this location. There's plenty of room at Aunt Lily's.' He studied their pale faces. The girls were trying hard not be overwhelmed by the situation, but they were clearly quite shaken and rightly so.

If he could give them something to do in order to stay busy and not dwell on the crisis, they would fare better. 'Aunt, if you could take the girls upstairs and have them gather up anything they want to bring, anything salvageable, we'll get packed up and get them settled at your place.'

Aunt Lily ushered the girls upstairs, but Tessa remained behind. 'We don't need to burden your aunt,' she protested. 'Once the mess is cleaned up, we can make do here. Within a few hours, the worst of this can be cleaned up,' she said bravely.

Peyton shook his head. He placed his hands on her shoulders. 'Supposing that were true, what would you do if the intruder came back? I have my doubts that the burglar found what he was looking for. If he did find it, he didn't find it right away. This prowler is dangerous, Tessa.'

'You're acting like this prowler isn't a common thief intent on a bit of jewellery.' Tessa tried to dismiss his concerns, but Peyton could hear the lie beneath her words. She didn't believe the statement any more than he did.

'You're exactly right. I don't believe for a minute that this break-in was conducted by an amateur looking for valuables to fence. Amateur thieves don't stick around to wreak havoc on furniture. The fewer signs there are that testify to a thief's presence, the better in most cases. But this thief wanted you to know that he'd been here. I don't believe this is the work of a regular burglar and neither do you.'

Peyton motioned with his eyes to the reticule hanging from her wrist. 'You carry a gun. You were expecting something like this and have been for quite some time.'

Crispin chose that moment to enter the room, preventing Tessa from responding to his charges. It was rather poor timing on his brother's part, Peyton thought. He needed Tessa to tell him what she knew, what she feared, and he'd given her a perfect opportunity.

'Your neighbour isn't very neighbourly,' Crispin said to Tessa sourly, flexing his fingers. 'I got him to warm up a bit, though. If he comes sneaking around again, we'll recognise him right away. He's missing a tooth and he'll be sporting a facer for a while.'

Tessa gasped. 'I am sure such violence was uncalled for.' She shot Crispin a scolding glance. 'My sisters and I have to live here among these people. I can't have you beating people up.'

'You won't be living here for a while,' Peyton

reminded her. 'Until this is settled, you'll be with Aunt Lily.'

Tessa shot him a withering look. 'I will decide what is best for me and my sisters.'

'I'm the guardian.' Peyton scowled. He could see Crispin's mouth working to suppress a smile. How dare she challenge him in front of his brother? On the other hand, he could understand how she felt. Her home had been violated and circumstances were now out of her control. It was natural to want to try to exert some influence on the direction of things.

Crispin intervened swiftly, his inappropriate inclination to laugh successfully suppressed. 'Has anything been taken?'

'Not that we can tell. But we haven't looked all that closely yet,' Tessa said, diverted from her brewing argument with Peyton.

'If you have an office of sorts, it would be a good idea to check there to see if family papers have been taken,' Crispin suggested.

Tessa nodded and took herself off up the stairs.

'Nice diversion,' Peyton said, watching Tessa sail off.

'I wasn't sure you wanted me to share my news in front of an audience.' Crispin shrugged.

'Tell me before anyone comes down.' Peyton shot a quick look at the staircase.

'The man isn't a neighbour. He claimed to live at

Number 4, but when I questioned a maid in the park afterwards, she said he couldn't possibly live at Number 4 since that house employed her to watch their two children.'

'What else did you learn?'

'After I roughed him up a bit, he said some foreign men with accents asked him to keep an eye on this place, wanting to know where the girls went, when they weren't home, when the servants were out, as they were today. Paid him in gold.'

Peyton nodded. It affirmed what he'd suspected. He wished he'd been more alert to the man earlier, and he would have been if Tessa had called it to his attention. It was becoming painfully obvious that he was limited in his capacity to protect her without full knowledge of the danger she was in. He would remedy that tonight. He could wait no longer. Tessa and he would have a long overdue discussion. The Russians were on the move.

Tessa kissed Annie and turned down the light in the spacious guest room at Aunt Lily's. Although there were several rooms and the girls could have had their own chambers, they'd elected to sleep together, at least for a few nights, until they could trust their security again.

Eva and Petra were snuggled together in the big four-poster bed. Annie was lodged on a wide couch at the foot of the bed.

'You all did so very well today,' Tessa told them, and they had. They'd gathered up their things and stoically driven over to Aunt Lily's, leaving the servants, who had arrived back before they left, to follow them, after securing the house. Even now, a few pieces of salvage from the house were strewn about the chamber. Among the items retrieved was the portrait of their father from Tessa's office. It was one of the few items left completely intact, even though it had been removed from the wall.

'It was good to have Dursley with us today,' Petra murmured from her blankets. 'I don't know what we would have done without him. And Lord Crispin, too,' she added sleepily.

'We would have managed just as we always have,' Tessa responded, hiding her hurt at the comment. Before Peyton had come along, her sisters had looked to her for guidance. How quickly their allegiance had shifted.

Eva propped herself up on one arm. 'I like Dursley immensely. Perhaps he could be your husband, Tess, if you'd stop quarrelling with him over every little thing. He thinks you're pretty. I could tell by the way he looked at you today.'

'You called him "Peyton",' Petra said. 'You like him, too, no matter how much the two of you fight.'

'Oh, yes,' Annie piped up. 'We could go on fabulous outings all the time. Do you think he'll still take us to the zoo?'

'I am sure he will. Now, go to sleep,' Tessa chided, glad the darkness hid the rising heat in her cheeks. She shut the door behind her. Perhaps it was a good sign that her sisters were focused on such silly things like a romance with Peyton Ramsden after the trying events of the day.

Tessa wished her mind was as easily diverted. But it had been awash with controversy. She was not looking forward to going downstairs and the impending interview. She had to speak to Peyton to thank him for his assistance and to remind him that she was capable of taking care of things. That was not all she needed to discuss with him. She should not delay in telling Peyton all she knew. It was time he understood the danger he'd inherited when he'd taken on their guardianship.

Maybe he'd already left and she could put the discussion off until morning. But, no, that was the coward's way out. Although him being gone was a distinct possibility, it was one she did not prefer. Better to be done with this tonight.

She found Peyton in Aunt Lily's study, a decidedly male domain done in dark woods and burgundy. The room had clearly belonged to her late husband. A fire burned in the fireplace, giving the imposing interior a more comforting feel.

'I wanted to thank you for today,' Tessa began. 'I hope I am not interrupting?' Peyton was behind the desk, writing and looking entirely at home in the masculine room.

'Not at all. I am glad you're here. We must talk.' Peyton rose and gestured to the sofa near the fireplace. 'Are the girls settled comfortably?' He kept up a gentle stream of small talk until they were seated. Tessa was immediately alert to the informality of their proximity. The edges of his roles were blurry tonight. Was he the polished Earl managing the business of his guardians, or the man who promised in seductive tones on the ballroom floor to be her bulwark?

'I meant it last night, Tessa, you can trust me. But I cannot help if there are things you are not telling me. Do you know why someone would want to break in to your home? Is there anything they could be looking for?'

'I don't know,' Tessa said, hesitating only slightly. It was the truth. She'd been grappling with the same thoughts all afternoon and with another dilemma: how much to tell Peyton? Tonight, here in the intimacy of the firelight, she wanted to follow her instincts and tell Peyton everything. The horrors of the day had illustrated poignantly that she could not face this alone, whatever it was.

But she'd never been good at relying on others. If she told Peyton, he would feel obliged to assist her, even if it meant putting himself at risk. That was unacceptable to her. Others shouldn't shoulder one's own responsibilities. Yet the temptation was overwhelming.

Peyton seemed to sense her dilemma. One of his hands curled over hers where it lay on her lap. He pressed it lightly. 'I've been in your situation before, Tessa,' he said quietly. 'You don't do well when circumstances don't bend to your will. I don't, either. When my father died unexpectedly, I was suddenly the Earl. I was young, not much older than you are now, and my brothers were about Eva's and Petra's ages. I wasn't ready to be the Earl, let alone be a father–brother figure to two rambunctious boys.

'People tried to make decisions for me. Aunt Lily's husband offered to take Crispin and Paine under his wing. Another distant cousin offered copious amounts of advice regarding how to invest the family fortune. They might all have been well meaning, but I would have none of it. Perhaps I feared that if I showed weakness, they'd for ever be assuming they could run roughshod over me, that I'd be Dursley in name only as opposed to deed.

'I can't say I was the easiest person to be around in those early days.' Peyton gave a chuckle. 'There's probably still quite a few people who think that. But I got the job done and successfully, too, even though there are some days I wonder if I might have gone about it a little bit better, more graciously. My autonomy was bought with the sacrifice of a few friendships.'

He'd voiced her sentiments precisely and Tessa was nearly undone by it. Maybe at last here was one person who *did* understand. And if he understood, he'd know how important it was that she not surrender all of her control to his will. Maybe, at last, she could trust someone enough to lay down her burden.

Tessa's eyes filled with tears. Perhaps it was the intimacy of the fire, the honesty of Peyton's disclosure, or the events of the day. It might have been all three of those combined. 'Peyton, would you do something for me?'

'Anything.'

She shouldn't have asked, but her emotions were running high. 'Make me feel safe, at least for a little while, like you did on the stairs.'

Chapter Eleven

Tessa moved in to his arms in one fluid motion or was it the other way around? Had he been the one to take Tessa in to his arms? The moment happened so rapidly, it was impossible to tell who did the moving. Regardless, the outcome was the same. Tessa was warm and invitingly soft against him. His arm was about her and she leaned against his chest as if she fit there, her golden head resting in the hollow of his shoulder.

He ran his hand up and down the length of her arm in a gentle, soothing gesture, but his body was well aware that he was not comforting a child. He was acutely aware of the breast that rose and fell against his side as she breathed. He was conscious of her hand where it lay on his thigh, more out of a need to simply be somewhere in their current posture than out of any seductive intention. But it did occur to him that her hand only had to move a few inches in order to come into extremely intimate contact with him. Certain parts of his body were becoming excited about that.

Peyton shifted slightly to manage his member's growing arousal. Did the vixen have any idea what she was asking? Did she have any idea how difficult it would be to offer her the comfort she was seeking without taking things too far?

It was not unreasonable for her to want the physical reassurance of strong arms after what had happened. Emotions ran high in circumstances like the ones they'd encountered today. It was greatly satisfying to know that she wanted him to be her comforter, that she hadn't sent off a note to Androvich seeking the reassurances of the Count's arms. Oh, yes, her need was understandable. That wasn't what made the situation difficult.

What made the situation difficult was that he knew better than to accede to her wishes. No gentleman ruined a lady, and certainly not a lady under his care. Taking advantage of his position in her life and the emotional duress she was under was most unfair. Only a cad of the lowest order would misuse his position in such a manner.

But logic compelled him just so far. All the arguments in the world about honour could not overcome one single fact that outweighed all other rationales. He wanted her with a single-minded possession that swept traditional considerations out of its wake.

Her emotions weren't the only ones to consider. His own feelings were quite piqued over the events of the afternoon. Well, 'feelings' might be a bit strong. Peyton didn't make a habit of having his feelings engaged in most situations. It would be more accurate to say his temper was fully engaged over the break-in. Yes, he felt more comfortable with that assessment. His temper had risen to the fore upon seeing the wreckage of Tessa's home and the subtle messages that had been left behind by the malicious intruder. None the less, the afternoon had stirred a primal urge in him that would not take kindly to being denied.

Next to him, Tessa sighed. 'This is nice. We're not quarrelling.' She gave a little laugh. 'Eva says you and I argue all the time.'

'Only because you disagree with me.' Peyton hazarded a little teasing, enjoying the peace of the moment.

'I do not,' Tessa said and then laughed again, catching her error. She pushed up from her position against him. He immediately missed the warmth of her body. 'You did that on purpose,' she scolded, mischief flirting in her eyes.

'No, I didn't,' Peyton answered before he could stop himself. He grinned. 'You've caught me at my own game.'

'So I have.' Tessa smiled back, utterly enchanting in the firelight. Her hair had come loose, curls randomly framing her face. She sat cross-legged facing him, her yellow skirts tucked about her. She looked entirely girlish. Her blue-violet eyes held his as they shared their little joke. The personal quality of the moment was heady.

Desire for her physically shook Peyton. He wanted this beautiful, brave angel right here, right now. Peyton could not recall a moment in his life when he'd felt so desperate to *be* with another human being. Peyton leaned towards her, a hand moving to cup the nape of her neck and guide her into his kiss. She came willingly.

She melted into his body, compliant and eager. There was no hesitation on her part and Peyton claimed her with his lips and his hands. The sofa could no longer hold them and they moved in one accord to the rug spread before the fireplace, a memento of one of his uncle's many exotic hunting expeditions. Peyton didn't much care at the moment except that it was soft and accommodated their needs.

He pushed the shoulders of Tessa's yellow gown down. His mouth found her breasts and sucked gently. Tessa arched against him in her newfound pleasure. She felt her hands reach up to tackle the fastenings of his shirt. They found success and Peyton shuddered at the contact of her palms against his own nipples, his own stimulation heightened by the idea that his own pleasure at her hands mirrored the pleasure he was giving her.

Tessa's hips pressed against his trousers, a moan of frustration escaping her at the limits allowed by the fabric between them. Peyton answered her with a kiss that claimed her mouth entirely, moving a hand to push up her skirts, searching out the core of her womanhood, determined to give her what satisfaction he could. Unerringly, his fingers found her sheltered pearl. She shuddered in her delight.

Intuitively, her hands grabbed at the front of his trousers, wanting to rectify the incompletion of the ecstasy that welled between them. He let her take him in her hand, her fingers exploring the hard, living length of his member.

Her eyes, wide and shining, stared into his face, reflecting her awe. 'Peyton, please. I want you to finish this, to find your own pleasure,' she whispered.

It was his undoing. The last thoughts of offering her pleasure while taking no further release for himself evaporated at the sound of his name on her lips as she made the most intimate of requests.

'Tessa?' His voice was hoarse. He was incapable of further speech. He hoped the questioning quality of his single word conveyed all that he meant it to. Was she certain of this next step? Did she understand he was willing to do this, wanted to, even needed to do this? That doing this placed her under his protection more firmly than she already legally was? All arguing aside, he was glad for it—he welcomed this addition to his life.

Her eyes were bright with the passion that drove her. 'Come into me, Peyton. Do not cheat us.'

Peyton. Us. The words were an aphrodisiac. Peyton took her lips in another searing kiss and brought himself into her, calling on all the skill he'd acquired in the beds of his mistresses, until she was as physically ready for him as she was mentally.

Beneath him, Tessa gasped at the sensation of his presence inside her. He felt her move, tentatively at first, looking for ways to meet him, to share this with him. He revelled in her need to participate. He should have known his Tessa would be no wilting, merely tolerant bedfellow. Peyton placed his hands on her hips and helped her find the rhythm.

Tessa's hips against his, the intimate joining of their bodies, her soft moans of delight, comprised a joy beyond imagining. Peyton hoped he would last long enough to show her the possible pleasures that existed between a man and a woman. Tessa writhed against him and he knew they were both close. He increased his pace, felt her own pleasure near. She cried out her achievement and Peyton's world exploded into a magnificent release.

He was drained, paradoxically sated and filled all at once. Peyton drew deep breaths, trying to reconcile the riot in his mind with the physical bliss that lulled him into drowsy placation in front of his aunt's fire. Against his shoulder, Tessa dozed, her golden hair sweeping his chest.

His body was completely at peace with what they'd done. Never had the act of sex been so fulfilling for both himself and his partner. What had transpired on his aunt's carpet was the physical pinnacle of human existence. Their bodies were designed to bring each other such pleasure. There was a tranquillity that came in being able to overcome the social constraints of their stations and situations and achieve such bliss.

Peyton wished his mind could accept such a natural rationalisation. But all his mind could comprehend was: sex in the study and not even his own study at that! He'd behaved scandalously. This was behaviour he had expected from his brothers in their wilder days. Paine and Crispin were perfectly capable of such shenanigans. Scandalised as his mind was, his brain couldn't decide on exactly what the scandal was. His gentleman's mind argued the scandal was that he'd taken a virginal young woman on the floor in front of a fire, not even bothering to do more than unbutton his trousers and push up her skirts—such actions were trademarks of how men took the whores against the walls in Covent Garden alleys.

A young woman of Tessa's background deserved a bed and fine sheets. Of course, the irony of such a conclusion was that a young woman of Tessa's background should not be inducted into love making at all without the benefit of a wedding ring.

She's twenty-two, for heaven's sake! the other

portion of his mind contended. She is capable of knowing her own mind and there was no doubt she was a consensual participant. You did nothing more than use the tools the situation put at your disposal.

Brimley would certainly applaud his actions. He'd done no more than what duty demanded. But something deep inside Peyton knew that he could not camouflage what had transpired with Tessa as merely 'duty'. Something in him would not let him paint their love making with such a superficial brush.

Tessa stirred, reminding Peyton they couldn't stay this way indefinitely. What they'd done in his aunt's study was risky. Crispin was out for the evening and Lily was gone as well, but there were still others in the house that could accidentally walk in on them: servants come to douse the fire or a sister who couldn't sleep.

Peyton gently dislodged Tessa and rose, taking time to adjust his clothing. His hands went to his trousers and his member roused a bit in remembrance of other hands that had recently passed that way.

He knelt down and took a moment to arrange Tessa's skirts and bodice decently before scooping her up in his arms. She made a mild protest that made him laugh. Of course his Tessa would protest, even though she was in no condition to walk to her chambers.

Peyton made the walk up the stairs to her bedroom and deposited her on the bed, taking time to remove her shoes and stockings. He pulled back the bedspread, debating whether or not he should try and get her into a nightgown. He didn't trust the reaction of his body and opted against it. He'd made the long walk with her in his arms—no easy feat—she could do her part and think what to tell the maid in the morning.

Peyton tucked the blanket about her. She reached for him in her sleep. 'No, Tessa,' Peyton said a quiet whisper. 'If I am going to get caught in your bed, I might as well have left us on the study floor and saved myself the effort. Sleep well.'

There was a chance she might rest well, if her current state was any indicator. There was no chance he would, Peyton reasoned. He had too much to think about and the night air on the way home would be bracing on the short walk back to Dursley House. He'd known what he was doing with Tessa. No matter how consensual their passion had been, there were still certain facts that had to be faced. He'd taken her innocence. His gentlemanly behaviour might have lapsed on the floor of the study, but he knew his responsibilities. When a gentleman took a young lady's innocence, there was only one acceptable reaction. Tomorrow would be a very busy day, starting with a visit to Lambeth Palace for a special licence and ending with a proposal.

The prospect actually filled him with satisfaction in spite of its precipitous nature. He'd not originally planned to marry Tessa Branscombe. He'd not planned to make love to her in his aunt's house, but he did not find the idea of marriage to her an un-palatable consequence. Peyton began to make lists in his head. He would propose over a quiet supper on the terrace of Dursley House before the dratted Academy Ball. He'd need roses, the ring from the vault, candles, the good champagne...

Tessa woke the next morning to brilliant rays of sunlight streaming through the windows of her room, the maid humming happily while she laid out clothes.

Tessa stretched, realising she was still in her dress. Then she remembered why. She had a vague recollection of Peyton carrying her to bed. But there was nothing vague about why he'd done so. That was very clear. Tessa wondered how quickly she could get rid of the maid. She devised a short errand and breathed a sigh of relief when the maid left the room to carry it out.

Oh, lord, what had she done? She was glad no one was there to see her embarrassment. She and Peyton had made love on the study floor. Strangely enough, that wasn't the embarrassing part. She'd not been ashamed of anything they'd done last night and that was still unswervingly true this morning. No, it wasn't the nakedness or the physical intimacy which caused her to blush. It was the motivations for it.

What must Peyton think of her? Did he think she'd seduced him? Tessa recalled her words—'make me feel safe'. Did he think that had been a ploy? A flirtation? This morning, she regretted the words. She had not meant them as any kind of coy game. She'd not suspected such words would lead them to the situation they found themselves in. But perhaps Peyton had taken them as such.

It was embarrassing to think Peyton might have taken pity on her. Surely that wasn't the case? Surely Peyton, with all his stiff-necked notions about propriety, didn't make a practice out of bedding young women on study floors because he pitied them?

No, that notion didn't fit at all. Tessa would have been relieved if it hadn't led to another notion. Peyton *was* a stickler for propriety. He was a gentleman of the highest order in both title and behaviour. She rather hoped such attitudes wouldn't lead to an embarrassing proposal. Peyton might feel compelled to make some kind of outlandish offer, all for the sake of her lost virginity.

She needed to make sure he didn't have a chance to do that. Today would be difficult to navigate. She would be with Peyton all day. The Royal Academy had its annual exhibit today and there was a ball afterwards to mark the opening. He would be by her side all day and all night. Fortunately, they'd be in very public venues and surrounded by people. With luck, there would be very little opportunity to hold a private conversation.

Tessa threw back the covers and began to strip out of her dress before her maid came back. Today would be a very demanding day.

* * *

'We can do it today,' Sergei Androvich said coldly from his seat at the table in the private with-drawing room of the Russian embassy. 'We could have done it last night if you'd allowed it.' He took a moment to fix Vasilov with a sneer, giving the man a taste of his own medicine. 'The Earl *walked* home alone in the late hours from his aunt's. It could have looked like footpads had simply stabbed him for his purse. We could have made it look like things turned rough when he tried to fight back and was outnumbered.'

'And I told you it would look too coincidental to have that happen on the same day the Branscombe house was burgled,' Vasilov retorted hotly. They'd been arguing about how best to eliminate the Earl for the last two days.

'Why is today any different?' Sergei said testily.

Gromsky intervened. 'Because, today it will be in public. Everyone will see. The man we've hired is supposed to look like a political radical. Everyone will think it is about his opposition to a bill in Parliament. No one will connect it to the Branscombe house. Best of all, we'll be there, all of us. Even those who might be aware of the reasons behind the Earl's involvement with the Branscombes won't be able to connect us to it. We'll be there, clearly talking with others and enjoying the occasion when the deed happens.'

Ilanovich turned to Sergei. 'After the Earl's

demise, Tessa will be ready to turn to you. She'll need comforting after the loss of the Earl.'

Sergei bristled at the implication. 'She does not love him.'

Vasilov chuckled. 'We'll see. I think you're losing your touch. But that's for another day. Today, we have an Earl to assassinate. It's all been arranged.' He looked at his pocket watch. 'Three hours until the curtain rises.'

Chapter Twelve

The courtyard of Somerset House, where the Royal Academy of Arts was located, was filled to near-capacity with people anticipating a grand social event of the Season. Up until now, the routs and balls had been modest events, growing ever more crowded, but today, the Season was on display in all its well-tailored finery.

Eva and Petra had argued without success to be allowed to come with them. They'd only accepted their fate once Peyton promised to bring them later in the Season on a quiet afternoon. In part, Tessa was glad to know they were at home, safe at Aunt Lily's. She had enough on her mind without trying to keep an eye on her two sisters. Most of her concentration was absorbed with the task of walking beside Peyton with her hand on his arm and pretending nothing had transpired between them. She took a small sense of pleasure from recognising that this was proving difficult for Peyton as well.

Certainly he did nothing that outwardly gave away the change between them. But privately, she knew he was behaving differently. She noticed the firmer grip he kept on her arm, the constancy of the light pressure of his hand at her back; little things that were not out of place to the outsider but were remarkable to her because she'd known him *before*. Tessa wondered if the rest of her life would be divided up that way—all the things that happened before Peyton and all the things that would happen after.

'Here we are. We've arrived at last,' Peyton said, leaning close to her ear in order to be heard over the crowd's conversations. 'The Great Room of Somerset House.' Peyton gestured to the enormous hall they'd entered. 'This is the most prestigious room in the exhibition. All the artists strive to have their work on display in this room.'

Tessa looked about her, taking in the overwhelming display of art. Not an inch of the high walls was left uncovered. Paintings of all sizes hung everywhere. 'It's nearly impossible to focus on just one!' Tessa exclaimed.

'There are other exhibition rooms, of course, that we can reach off this main room. Perhaps you'd like to start there?' Peyton offered. 'They might be less crowded.'

That would not do. Less crowded might provide an opportunity for a conversation she didn't want to have. 'No, this will be all right. I will accustom myself to the abundant display.' Tessa laughed, dissuading Peyton.

Lily and Crispin trailed behind them and the foursome made slow but steady progress about the room, taking time to admire the canvases and occasionally chat with friends.

Peyton turned out to be a well-informed escort on the subject of art, pointing out certain aspects to the artists' work. At John Constable's *Opening of Waterloo Bridge*, Peyton stopped for a while in front of the colourful painting, silently comparing it to a nearby Joseph Turner canvas depicting a seascape. He gave a short chuckle.

'What's so funny?' Tessa asked, following his gaze from one painting to the other.

'Joseph Turner has got the last word in on this, I think.' Tessa gave him a perplexed look and he hurried on to explain. 'Last year, there was some controversy between Constable and Turner. It seems that Constable took Turner's exhibition spot and hung his own painting in it, ousting Turner from the Great Room. This year, my friends associated with the Royal Academy told me that during the time period the artists can come in and touch up their paintings, Turner knew he'd hang his work next to Constable's, so at the last minute, he painted this yellow buoy into the canvas to steal attention away from Constable's colours.'

Behind them, Crispin snorted. 'What sissified nonsense, squabbling over where to hang a picture.'

Peyton shot him a quelling look. 'Cris, do try to appreciate the finer things.'

'I like that one over there, the one with the half-dressed, drunk lady in it.' Crispin tossed his head towards a picture entitled *The Swoon*. Peyton grimaced.

They moved through the room into another series of smaller chambers featuring other exhibits. They were examining a collection of Chinese art when Sergei Androvich found them.

'Tessa, I thought I might find you here today.'

Tessa fought the urge to cringe at Sergei's easy use of her name. True, he was a good family friend, but things were different here in England, her life was different and it struck her that his use of her first name was no longer appropriate. In all likelihood their friendship would end soon. She would not be marrying Sergei. She knew that now after her night with Peyton. Regardless of what that night meant, she knew that something magical was possible with the right man—whether or not Peyton was the right man, Sergei definitely wasn't. His kisses were empty of fire and Peyton had proved it didn't have to be that way. She looked about for any signs of the other ambassadors, relaxing slightly when she didn't see them in the vicinity.

As he stood beside her, Peyton's grip tightened. 'Count, how do you find our Academy?' He was all cool politeness.

'I suppose it is passable,' Sergei said with equal steel. 'It's not the Winter Palace. Tessa and I had a chance to survey the Imperial art collection on several occasions.'

'Perhaps your monarchs should spend more time and money on taking care of their people instead of scouring Europe for fine art. It's hard to eat paint, but I hear it burns well,' Crispin snarled, bluntly referring to the growing unrest between the Czar and the Russian populace. Tessa was all too aware of the volatile situation she'd left behind in St Petersburg. Building palaces and collecting art seemed like poor priorities when people were starving and the very social fabric of the country was on the brink of unravelling.

'Muzzle your dog, Dursley,' Sergei spat. 'I would willingly face you at twenty paces for the honour of Mother Russia.'

'Muzzle me yourself,' Crispin shot back, not willing to be ignored.

'Gentlemen, this will not do,' Lily swiftly put in, to Tessa's relief. 'Crispin, I want to look at that lovely Chinese statue over there. Come with me.'

'Tessa, my apologies,' Sergei said with a short bow as Lily led Crispin away.

Tessa smiled wanly.

'How are your sisters? I have not seen them since we played charades. That was a lovely evening,' Sergei said, taking a smoother conversational avenue.

'They are well. We've had a few—' Tessa began, but to her surprise Peyton cut her off.

'We've had a few outings,' he said swiftly. 'I've been showing the girls around town. We had a wonderful day at the Tower not long ago,' he added.

He was being pompous again, acting as if she couldn't speak for herself. Why didn't he want Sergei to know the truth? Why not tell Sergei about the house? When Sergei asked if he could show her some of the items on display in the next room, Tessa accepted, just to give Peyton a taste of her independence. He did *not* own her.

Peyton's gaze narrowed and she knew he saw the reason for her acceptance. She'd hoped she wouldn't be that transparent. 'I've been eager to see that display myself. I'll come, too,' he said evenly. He shifted his gaze to the Count, studying Sergei with an intensity that unnerved Tessa. She suddenly felt like a complete outsider. Under the veneer of this petty squabbling they were conducting over her, something else was going on between them.

The three of them made their way towards the other room. It was slightly more populated and there was not room to walk three abreast in many cases. Tessa felt Peyton slip behind them and her anxiety escalated. Something felt unnatural. Sergei was trying too hard to keep her with him. His grip on her arm was firm beyond politeness. When she tried to manoeuvre closer to Peyton, Sergei manoeuvred the situation otherwise. Something was dreadfully wrong, but what was it?

Tessa saw it all at once only because she'd turned her head behind her to say something to Peyton. A man dressed in a gentleman's clothes was moving swiftly through the crowd towards them—too swiftly, Tessa thought, for it to be natural movement in these close confines. Metal flashed in his hand, partly concealed by the cuff of his shirt.

Instinctively, she knew the man had set on her group as his target. Was the man after her? Her fear rose, but not for herself. If the man was after her, he'd have to get through Peyton first. Peyton was all that stood between her and the man advancing towards them. She cried out a warning. 'Peyton!'

The man charged, forced to hurry now that his attentions had been noticed. But her warning was enough to save Peyton from the brunt of it. He sidestepped, taking the slice of the knife in the side instead of in his vital organs. He crouched in reaction to the initial pain and came up with a knife of his own from some secret place on his person, the knife he'd had yesterday at the house.

Around her, women screamed. She heard her own voice call out for Crispin. She struggled against Sergei's iron grip as he forcibly restrained her and hauled her to safety. 'Let me go! Don't bother about me, help him!' she railed at Sergei. 'Please, go help him.' But Sergei did nothing.

'The bloody Englishman looks like he can take care of himself, Tessa.' He gave a low whistle at the sight of Peyton's blade slicing into the arm of the would-be attacker.

Out of reflex, Tessa turned her head into Sergei's shoulder at the sight of blood. She felt Sergei's arms about her, but she couldn't feel safe. These weren't Peyton's arms and they conveyed none of the strength of Peyton's embrace.

'You can look now,' Sergei said after long moments, disappointment peppering his tone. 'The guards have come to manage the situation. Quite the dangerous guardian you've acquired, Tessa. He carries a knife and apparently for good reason. Don't you think that's a little odd for a gentleman?'

Tessa lifted her head to see Crispin and three soldiers hired for the exhibition enter the fight. The soldiers inserted themselves between Peyton and the stranger so that Peyton could disengage and step back. After that, the man was easily subdued and led off, Crispin following close behind to mop up the details.

Tessa broke from Sergei's side and went straight to Peyton, pushing through the crowd of people gathered around him. She didn't care that people stared at her or that some murmured the beginnings of rumours: *That's the Branscombe girl, the one who danced so close to him, the one who speaks Russian. Did you hear her call him by his Christian name?* 'Excuse me, let me get him out of here,' she said in her most authoritative voice. It worked. Before long, she had Peyton outside and had summoned the carriage.

The carriage took an eternity to make its way to them in the courtyard. They seemed to be the centre of everyone's attention, but Tessa staunchly ignored the stares that came their way. Instead, she devoted herself to a quiet inspection of Peyton, who stood silent and stoic at her side. He didn't appear hurt, but that could be deceiving. This was not a man who would admit to injury, although she knew he had taken at least one cut.

The carriage pulled up and they climbed in. 'Are you badly hurt?' Tessa asked now that the crowds were behind them. She pushed aside his coat, searching for damage. She'd seen the knife slice his side and his coat was ripped.

Peyton snatched at her hands, trying to fend off her ministrations. 'Tessa, don't. I'll be all right.' But it was too late. She'd already discovered what Peyton wanted to hide. Her hands were wet when Peyton pulled them away, covered in his blood. In the dim carriage light it had been hard to see the blood against the dark blue pattern of his waistcoat. But on her hands, there was no mistaking it.

'Oh, God, Peyton.' Tessa felt herself tremble. She had to be strong at least until they got home.

'It's all right,' Peyton said, but he gritted his teeth as he said it and Tessa knew he was in pain now that the initial adrenalin rush from the fight was gone.

Tessa suffered a terrible pang of guilt. This was her fault. She was certain now that the attacker was meant for her. Why would anyone try to kill an earl? Yet, he'd almost been fatally wounded on her behalf. She shuddered to think what would have happened if she hadn't turned when she did, if she had called out her warning a second later. Peyton would be dead in her place. She had waited too long to tell her secrets and the man who'd made love to her had almost paid the ultimate price for her choice.

'I am so sorry, Peyton,' she whispered.

'Why?' Peyton studied her. 'It's not your fault.'

'But it is.' Tessa shook her head. 'That knife was meant for me. You were simply in the way. I am sure of it.'

There was no stopping Tessa Branscombe when she was determined. And she was determined to tell him everything. Peyton sighed, leaning back against the pillows of his big bed at Dursley House. At least she'd had the decency to wait until the doctor had cleaned his wound and bound it. But he could tell her impatience was getting the better of her. She paced the length of his room, oblivious to the fact that she was alone with a man in his private chambers.

But nothing mattered to her right now except her guilt.

Now that the moment of truth was here, and he was minutes away from having all the answers

Brimley wanted, he wanted to tell Tessa to stop. He wanted those answers, not just for Brimley and the British troops facing potential war, but for Tessa's own safety. Yet he knew there would come a time when Tessa would hate him for this. She would feel betrayed, and rightly so.

He should blurt out right now that he knew the knife attack was for him. He'd been accidentally privy to the Russians' scheme. Count Androvich didn't want her dead, Androvich wanted *him* dead. He had to be out of the way first in order to clear a more direct path to Tessa. Peyton had worried about just such an attempt once Androvich had shown up and started provoking Crispin. He'd thought the man might be angling for a duel. Then, when the Count had made the attempt to separate Tessa from him, Peyton's other suspicions had risen. The Count didn't want to take the chance that Tessa would be in the line of fire and become an accidental casualty.

There was no doubt in Peyton's mind that the attack had been meant for him alone. Tessa's warning had saved his life. But Tessa did not know that. She saw the situation only through the lens of what she did know. She knew only one thing: someone was after her, and so she blamed herself for his injury. Brimley would be overjoyed.

'Do you need water?' Tessa asked. 'Are you comfortable?'

'You would make a terrible nurse,' Peyton tried to tease. 'I have a slight knife wound, not a fever.'

'All right.' Tessa relented and came to sit on the side of the bed, her face earnest. 'You have to listen to me. You have to stay away from me. This is all my fault. Someone is after me and you could be killed if you stand in the way.'

Peyton raised a hand to her lips. 'Shh, Tess. Slow down, start at the beginning and let me be the judge of all that.'

And for once in her life, Tessa Branscombe did as she was told.

Chapter Thirteen

'After my father's funeral, our house was broken into, not unlike what has happened here, only with less damage,' Tessa began, trying to marshal her thoughts into some cohesive order. It had been so long since she'd shared any of this aloud. 'We lived in a prestigious neighbourhood in St Petersburg, one not troubled by common crime or criminals. I thought at the time how odd such an act was. It was so out of place for our surroundings. Such things did not happen.' Tessa pleated the coverlet between her fingers.

'Was anything taken?' Peyton asked.

Tessa shook her head. 'No. Just like the break-in here, nothing was missing, although, in both instances, the thief was obviously looking for something in earnest and there were items of value that could have been taken, but weren't.' Tessa thought of the few silver pieces in the kitchen cabinet that Arthur had so lovingly arranged and the brightly coloured Russian samovar. Those items would have fetched a good price, but the thief had left them behind.

Tessa continued with her story. 'Over the next few days I felt as if I were being watched every time I ventured from the house, which was quite often. There was a lot of business to wrap up at the embassy regarding my father. In some instances, I am quite sure I was followed, but I can't prove any of that.' She studied Peyton closely, watching for his reaction. 'You're the only person I've discussed this with since coming to London. Of course, I told Sergei about it in St Petersburg and he escorted me everywhere. After that, the feeling that I was being followed disappeared.'

Tessa regretted mentioned the last bit about Sergei. She could see Peyton's dislike for the man rise in his eyes. 'I know you don't care for him, but he acted as a good friend to us in a difficult time,' she scolded lightly.

'He was no friend to me today,' Peyton said coldly. 'The coward was more than happy to let me face the knife alone.'

Tessa bit her tongue. There were defences she could make for Sergei's choice: he was busy protecting her, it all happened too quickly. But she'd thought the same thing. Indeed, she'd urged Sergei to assist Peyton and Sergei had foregone the opportunity outright in a very blunt manner.

Tessa continued with her story. 'I felt it was best

we leave St Petersburg right away. We left quietly before the deadline I had put about in our social circles. I'm not sure Sergei has forgiven me for that small deception, but I think it was successful. There were no incidents on the road, nothing until here.'

'And the arrival of the Russian delegation,' Peyton added.

Tessa looked at him sharply. 'What are you implying? Those men were my father's colleagues. They'd worked together for years.'

Peyton struggled to sit up straighter against his pillows. 'That is exactly my implication. Who would know better if your father had secrets, diplomatic secrets, than the people he worked with most often? Besides, I've noticed they make you nervous.'

'Secrets?' Tessa questioned. 'I doubt that very much. My father was a most unassuming man. He was quiet and straightforward in his dealings. It was what made him so popular. People knew they could trust him, that he was there to do a job. He was not a man who had hidden agendas like so many of the others.' She was growing irate at Peyton's suggestion that her father might have been hiding something.

'It only takes one secret, Tessa,' Peyton said.

Tessa got up from the bed, no longer able to contain her agitation. She paced the length of the floor. 'All right, then, you tell me what you think is going on, since it's clear to me you see this in an entirely different light.'

Peyton recognised he was on very tenuous ground. Tessa was telling him all she knew, or at least all she thought she knew. But there were details he wanted. He had to ask his questions in a way that would help her expose those details without him appearing to be overly informed on a subject that he'd supposedly just heard about moments ago.

'Did your father ever talk with you about his work?'

'Always. He felt it helped me be a better hostess,' Tessa answered.

'What about anything unusual towards the end? Any new developments or people who had entered his circle?' Peyton probed carefully. He watched a certain amount of understanding dawn on Tessa.

'You think the people following me thought I knew something or had something in my possession that wasn't in the house when they broke in,' Tessa guessed, fitting the ideas together.

Peyton nodded. 'It makes sense. The item wasn't in the house, so they may have reasoned it was small enough to easily keep on one's person. Maybe they didn't know for sure that the item was a physical thing. Perhaps it was and still is some information they believe you remember. Perhaps, even, they followed you in the hope that you were going to retrieve it from somewhere. I am assuming most people were aware that your father kept you well educated.' He studied her, watching her mind work as her pacing slowed.

'So whoever is looking for this nebulous something believes I still have it?'

'Yes.' That was all Peyton could afford to say. It was positively killing him not to shout out that 'it' was a list of Russian revolutionaries willing to overthrow the Czar with the help of English pounds and arms.

'I wish I knew what it was.' Tessa sighed heavily. 'I don't think I have anything of use. All their terror is for nothing. No matter how much they frighten me, there's nothing I can do. If I knew what it was, I'd have some negotiating power.'

That truly frightened him. 'No!' Peyton sat up too far and winced. 'No,' he said in a softer, firmer voice, easing back on his pillows. 'Tessa, these men do not negotiate. They have ruined your home in two cities and have put you in personal danger. Promise me under no circumstance you will try to manage them.'

Tessa tossed her gold hair. 'That's an easy promise to give. I don't have any inkling as to who they might be.'

Peyton snorted. 'You're too intelligent to be that naïve, Tessa. You should look very closely at the Russian delegation and at Sergei Androvich before declaring them innocent. Whatever it is that you have, they are pursuing it actively and covertly.' He dared not go any further with what he shared, but he could not in good conscience keep Tessa unaware of the danger she put herself in every time she had contact with Androvich. He could at least put the idea into her mind.

'I have known Sergei for years!' Tessa protested. The rest of her tirade faded. Peyton didn't like the look on her face. 'That is precisely what Sergei said about you today.'

Peyton cocked a cool brow her direction. 'What did Count Androvich have to say that merits repeating?'

'He said I should not be so quick to trust you. Actually, what he said was "Quite the dangerous guardian you've acquired…carries a knife and apparently for good reason".'

Peyton tamped down his temper. There was no sense in letting his anger get the better of him, but that didn't change the fact that he wanted to show Androvich just how dangerous he could be. The fool was twisting the truth, creating doubt about him in Tessa's mind when the one Tessa ought to fear was Androvich himself.

'What is going on?' Tessa demanded from the window, hands on her hips as she faced him. 'I feel as if there is a game within a game being played out around me and I don't know all the rules. I will not stand for it.'

The door opened without warning and Crispin entered, picking up the conversation. 'Haven't you ever had two suitors fighting over you before? I would think a beautiful woman like you would know exactly what's going on.'

Peyton groaned, knowing the words Tessa would fling at him before she even spoke them.

Her blue-violet eyes flashed. She speared him with a stormy look. 'Is that what last night was? Some kind of gentleman's competition to get there first?' It was as bad as Peyton had expected. Really not the tone he wanted to set for his proposal. But what she said next chilled him entirely. 'Sergei was right. You are not to be trusted.' She pushed past Crispin and left the room, slamming the door behind her for good measure.

'What did I say?' Crispin said, pulling up a chair beside the bed.

'When are you going to think before you open your mouth?'

'What happened last night?'

'Nothing to comment on,' Peyton said, trying to push the issue aside, but Crispin noticed the briskness in his tone for what it was.

Crispin slapped his leg and hooted. 'You seduced her. At Aunt Lily's? In the study where I left you? This is grand. Is the rug as soft as it looks?'

Peyton tried to look more annoyed than embarrassed. His brother was the only one who could cut him down to size by painting his adventures for what they were. 'Really, Cris, a gentleman doesn't kiss and tell.' And, apparently, he wasn't going to propose either. He had the special licence, but it appeared that it would have to wait.

'You did more than kiss the delectable Miss Branscombe. This is so unlike you, Peyton. Wait until

I tell Paine. You've lectured us for years about a gentleman's responsibility.' Crispin gave a haughty pose and pointed a strict finger. 'Young ladies of good breeding are off limits. They're only for marrying. Taking the innocence of a young woman of good standing is tantamount to a marriage proposal.'

'I haven't broken any of my rules,' Peyton said, finally drawn into the argument. 'I do intend to marry her, if she'll have me.'

Crispin chuckled. 'I'd be more worried about the last part of that than the first. She was angry enough about you and Sergei competing over her. Can you imagine how she'll cut up if she finds out you've known about the list all along and that you're not really her guardian?' Crispin let out a low whistle.

Yes, he could imagine. It was a scene he preferred not to think about for many reasons. He hoped when the time came there would be a way to avoid the discussion altogether. 'We'll deal with that later. Now, help me up. I want to put my shirt on. We're going to see Brimley and you can tell me what you found out from the man with the knife,' Peyton said firmly. He refused to think of the aftermath this little episode would cause. Tessa would be beyond furious at his deception, but if they both lived through it, maybe there was a chance she'd forgive him.

She would *not* forgive Peyton for what he'd done! Tessa jabbed the needle mercilessly through the fabric of a small tapestry depicting the Nevsky Prospekt in St Petersburg. It wasn't going well. The river was crooked and the buildings looked wobbly. She had Aunt Lily's second-floor sitting room all to herself. Her sisters were gathered in the music room with a tutor Aunt Lily had hired.

It was just as well. She couldn't talk to anyone about the things on her mind. She couldn't tell Petra or Aunt Lily what had happened with Peyton. Unmarried women didn't go around making love to men who couldn't possibly wed them. It was a poor example to set for Petra, and Tessa feared Aunt Lily would think it a low attempt to take advantage of her nephew. Everyone knew the Earl of Dursley was fated to marry someone of high standing and enormous wealth. Like married like.

Even if there had been a chance, the ensuing scandal that had erupted from the attack at the Academy had scotched what hope there was. The *ton* had marked her as trouble. Their sympathies were with the Earl of Dursley, the poor man saddled with the Branscombe girls. How much could a man, even of Dursley's impeccable background, be able to reform what had taken years to instil? She'd heard those rumours, too.

At twenty-two she was nearly on the shelf. Such flagrant behaviour as dancing too close to a man and calling him by his Christian name assured her a place on that shelf. No man would want to marry a woman with those low tendencies. But what could be expected from her eccentric upbringing in foreign places and no mother to guide her? Tessa didn't mistake the last for genuine pity. Her circumstances were merely more grist for the gossip mill.

Most assuredly, Peyton would not consider aligning himself with a woman who fomented scandal on a grand scale. She could appreciate that reticence. He had his family to think of, an obligation he took seriously. His alliances affected all of them. He would not risk them by embracing more than guardianship with the Branscombes, and it was all Tessa's fault.

Knowing all that, Tessa still couldn't believe Peyton had done what he did just for the sake of competing with Sergei. He hadn't struck her as a man who felt anyone was worth competing with. Yet, Crispin's words made sense. The alternative was too horrific. If Sergei and Peyton weren't competing over her, then what was really going on? Was one of them right about the other? Was one of them capable of committing treachery of a magnitude she could not contemplate? Peyton and Sergei had both intimated as much about each other. If so, which one was it? Tessa made the cases in her mind.

Sergei was a long-time friend. He'd courted her and proposed to her, motivated, if not by love, then by honour. She was convinced Sergei felt he owed it to her father to take care of them the only way he knew how: through the security of marriage. Sergei had warned her about Peyton because he cared for her. To be fair, however, she needed to remember that her troubles in London hadn't started until the Russian delegation had arrived and she knew the dark reputations of the three men travelling with Sergei.

On the other hand, she could also say that her troubles had not started until Peyton appeared, coincidentally the first day Sergei had come to visit. That did not leave Peyton in a strong position. Peyton had blown into their lives like a thunderstorm, carving out a place in their family with his codicil and arrogance. Within days, he'd displaced Sergei as the main male in their little world. He'd put his servants in her home, he'd been making free of the upstairs rooms in her absence. He knew their schedules. He knew when they'd be out with Aunt Lily.

She had not thought of that before. Peyton would know the best times for a burglar to gain entrance to the house without any surprise residents being home. Her stomach twisted at the thought. Had Peyton planned the break-in? Her mind rallied in his defence. To what purpose? Peyton had known nothing about her circumstances until today. He had no motive. She immediately discarded the thought. But she couldn't discard the niggling notion that something about Peyton didn't ring true. Even if he couldn't be involved with her problems, he was dangerous.

Sergei's comment was strongly etched in her mind: 'He carries a knife and apparently for good reason.'

It wasn't the first time she'd seen the knife. He'd pulled it out at her house. It wasn't the first time either that he'd acted with such reflexes, if she counted that day on the stairs. Peyton Ramsden was not a soft earl accustomed to the easy life. He was a man with highly trained, potentially lethal skills. But to do what? Tessa shivered at the thought. She had been impetuous last night. It was unnerving to think she'd quite possibly slept with the enemy. Worse, she had liked it.

Chapter Fourteen

Sergei eyed the newly arrived folder on the embassy's conference table with ill-contained glee. Inside that folder lay the answers which would guide the next steps of their mission. More importantly, if those answers were what Sergei expected, he would be able to take a more aggressive approach where the quarrelsome Earl of Dursley was concerned.

It was all he could do to refrain from sneaking a peek inside while he waited for his comrades to arrive. Finally, there'd be some forward movement in their assignment to retrieve the list that had the Czar so concerned. He had not so much followed Tessa Branscombe to England as he had followed that list. It was here, somewhere, accidentally transported by Tessa Branscombe, whom he was increasingly sure had no idea what she'd done. While Sergei was certain Tessa had no idea the list existed, his comrades were not as convinced. But they hadn't seen first-hand what he'd seen. In the days he'd escorted her about St Petersburg, wrapping up her father's work, she'd not retrieved anything from a secret place, had not met clandestinely with anyone. Yet, the Czar had believed so strongly that she'd taken the list with her that he'd sent this coterie of ambassadors to ferret it out before it could be turned over to British officials.

The three others trickled in one by one, Vasilov being the last to arrive. 'This had better be informative considering the amount of money we paid to acquire it,' he groused, reaching for the dossier.

He reached inside. 'One sheet?' He pulled out the one piece of paper inside the leather folder and waved it. 'This is almost laughable.'

Sergei's hopes sank as Vasilov passed the sheet on to Gromsky. 'Not so laughable, it would seem,' Gromsky said.

'Our friend the Earl was not a close acquaintance of Ralph Branscombe. But he is a close acquaintance with a Whitehall conspiracy expert, Moreton Brimley.'

This got everyone's attention. They all knew who Brimley was. They'd met him at a few social occasions since their arrival. If there were plans afoot, Brimley would know.

Gromsky went on to read out from the page. 'While it cannot be empirically substantiated, it seems likely Peyton Ramsden is involved with

Brimley's latest project. Private sources informed me Ramsden had not expected to be in town very long. He certainly had not planned to join the Season. Socially being seen with a diplomat's daughter seems too much of a coincidence given that he's worked with Brimley extensively in the past and his original timetable for staying in town.'

'Aha!' Sergei said triumphantly. 'Our earlier suppositions were correct. He is indeed after the list, too. He's now a proven threat to Russian national security. We must move more quickly to eliminate him. No more relying on a third party to do our work. The attacker at the Academy was a poor excuse of an assassin.'

The three men exchanged glances. Gromsky coughed. 'Androvich is right. We've been less aggressive with the Earl because we haven't been sure of his role. That's weakened us.'

'I say we use a slow-acting poison like the one we used on Branscombe,' Ilanovich put in. 'Something we can slip in a glass of champagne at a ball and will take six or seven hours to work.'

Sergei humphed. 'I want to quietly run him through and dump him in the bushes somewhere.'

'Too much scandal,' Vasilov said. 'Ilanovich is right. Slow-acting poison would be very discreet. There'd be no scandal, no disrupting of an event. No hostess would be beside herself at thinking the Earl died in her ballroom or her rose bushes.' He shot

Sergei a withering look. 'We need to do it soon, before the invitations run out.'

There was no real fear of the invitations running out. There were plenty of circles they were welcome in, plenty of people in government who would gladly entertain foreign ambassadors and Sergei knew his own good looks had ensured a large level of interest, too. All the same, he knew what Vasilov meant. The Earl ran in lofty circles. Once the novelty of being the new Russian Count around town wore off, the invitations to events Dursley attended at the higher reaches of society would taper off. The chance to encounter Dursley would shrink, especially if Dursley put it about that there was a certain level of animosity between him and the Russians. Society would become a shield around Dursley.

So far, Dursley had thwarted him at every turn, subtly taking away access to Tessa and thus to the list. First, the man had insinuated himself into Tessa's life and taken time away from him. No longer could Sergei simply drop by and find Tessa able to receive him. Next, Dursley had physically removed her, putting her in his aunt's house. Even if there had been time to see her, now there was no place he could see her without being watched. Not that it mattered. She didn't know about the list, but she was the gateway to the Branscombe possessions.

Worst of all, it appeared Vasilov was right. Dursley was succeeding where Sergei himself had fallen short—the Earl was wooing Tessa with some success. She'd certainly been frightened for Dursley at the Academy. That moment in his arms, when Tessa had turned her head into his shoulder, he knew her fear for Dursley was far more than the sum of her friendly affections for him had ever been. To a man of Sergei's charms, such a realisation was quite lowering. He didn't love Tessa Branscombe, far from it, but it was a matter of male pride.

'Where are they today?' Ilanovich broke into Sergei's thoughts.

'The zoo in Regent's Park and then the Berrybourne rout tonight, to which we are invited. We'll need to be early. They'll probably move on to the Viscount St Just's private gala.'

'To which we're not invited,' Vasilov hastily put in.

'To which most of London is not invited,' Sergei corrected. 'It's a quiet supper for thirty to show off the Viscount's new rose breeds.'

'Gentlemen, please,' Gromsky put in. 'This bickering will not help. We'll be at the Berrybournes' early and see what can be arranged. Are they being followed today at the zoo?'

Sergei shook his head. 'No, there seems no point in it now that we know who all the players are. Tessa doesn't know about the list, so she's not manoeuvring to meet anyone about it, and she has nothing dangerous to tell Ramsden that he doesn't already know.'

'That's probably for the best,' Vasilov said slyly,

unable to resist one more jabbing remark. 'We're running out of people to enlist since Crispin Ramsden has decided the quickest route between questions and answers can be travelled with his fist. I had no idea how long it took a black eye to heal.'

'This is wonderful!' Eva flung her arms wide and spun a circle in the wide grass lawn of Regent's Park. 'The sun is out and the weather is perfect.'

Tessa smiled from her place on the large picnic blanket they'd spread out. She shared most of her sister's sentiment. This was a gorgeous day. She'd loved watching her sisters enjoy the sights of the zoo, especially Annie. Best of all, there had been no mishaps. They hadn't been followed. She could feel it. That knowledge alone had given her an enormous sense of freedom and well being. The only blight on that freedom was that she and Peyton had not talked since their stormy encounter.

More than ever, she felt she and Peyton were living two lives: the polite life they played out in front of society and her sisters, and the explosive, private life where nothing was quite clear beyond their intense physical attraction.

Even now, watching him play tag with Annie and Eva on the park lawn, Tessa was hard pressed to summon up her sinister thoughts about him with any validity. How could a man who was so good with children have such a dark side as the one her mind tried to accuse him of? He looked magnificent out there. He'd taken his coat off for tag and Tessa found the sight of him in only shirt and waistcoat physically compelling. Peyton Ramsden was a well-made man, a fact she'd had chances to verify on more than one occasion. He'd caught Annie and was swinging her around until the little girl couldn't stop laughing. An amazing feat considering he must have still been sore from the encounter with the knife at the Academy.

'He'll make a wonderful father,' Lily said, accurately interpreting the source of Tessa's wide smile.

Tessa quickly wiped the smile off her face, embarrassed to be caught so openly ogling the Earl. 'I am sure he will. It is good to hear Annie laugh and enjoy herself.'

The deflection wasn't good enough for Lily. Tessa was conscious of Lily's studious gaze. 'My nephew is a man of honour. He will always put family first. There are few things a person can bet on with any regular success, but that is one of them. In that, the two of you have much in common.'

'What a kind thing to say, thank you,' Tessa said as evasively as possible. 'I must remind you that I have no intentions of marrying.'

Lily only laughed. 'It seems you and Peyton have another item in common. That's what my nephew says, too, especially now that his brother has a new baby boy to ensure the estate is inherited by a close family member.'

Peyton returned to the blanket, carrying Annie on his back. 'I've found a rare, wild species that laughs when she's tickled.' Peyton dumped her on the blanket beside Tessa and Tessa picked up her cue. It was far easier tickling Annie than it was deciphering Lily's messages. Was the woman playing matchmaker, or testing the waters in terms of what Tessa's agenda was where her nephew was concerned? Surely Peyton had not told his aunt what had transpired between them? It was likely Lily wanted to be certain Peyton wasn't tainted by the rumours surrounding her. If Lily thought she held any ambitions where Peyton was concerned, the older woman would not hesitate to warn her off.

'There are ducks on the pond, Aunt Lily. I thought the girls might enjoy seeing them while Tessa and I talk a bit,' Peyton suggested.

Within moments, Lily had the three girls organised and headed towards the pond.

'There's a place that rents boats, too. I should have liked to have taken you out for a row, Tessa. It's a pretty venue for two. But sometimes such privacy is not possible with a family to look after.' Peyton waved an idle hand after the girls. 'Having the girls around reminds me of the days when Crispin and Paine were younger. Sometimes I thought I'd never have a quiet moment to myself.' Peyton shrugged, sobering a bit. 'Then there was a time when I had all the silence and privacy I wanted and I discovered I didn't like it as much as I thought.'

'It must have been hard to be the brother, the father and the Earl to them,' Tessa said.

Peyton reached for her hand. 'Yes, just as hard as it is to be guardian and lover to you, Tess. We have some unspecified roles between us. We would do best to settle them and clarify our positions. I had meant to speak to you the day of the Royal Academy show.'

Oh, oh. Tessa saw where this was headed. 'Peyton, if this is about what happened at your aunt's, you needn't worry.'

'Needn't worry?' Peyton looked appalled at her response. 'We may have made a child. We may have decided to launch a new being into this world. That cannot be dismissed.'

She had to handle this better. Lily had just told her how important family was to Peyton and she'd blithely ignored that in her opening argument to dissuade him out of a marriage proposal. Well, Peyton might be stubbornly loyal, but he was also practical. 'Let's not be hasty in our assumptions,' Tessa said. 'The odds are definitely against us.' This answer did not please him entirely, but he did seem somewhat flummoxed. Tessa plunged ahead.

'Peyton, I did not engage in what we did the other night out of any attempt to coerce a proposal from you. Marriage to you was the furthest thing from my mind.' *Oh, lord, that sounded even worse.* She should stop now. But Tessa found she couldn't. 'What I mean to say is that there are no obligations to be met on your part because there are no expectations on my part.' There, that sounded much more pleasing, much more as if they were equals in this.

Peyton's features were hard, unreadable as he studied her. 'Did you like what we did?' he asked quietly.

Tessa blushed, although she knew no one else had overheard. 'Yes, of course I liked it.'

'I did, too, and I find myself wanting to be with you again and again. Certainly, such a situation is tolerable only in marriage.' A glimmer of a smile played on Peyton's lips, giving him a look that bespoke sin and seduction. He was positively irresistible—not that she really wanted to resist at all. But her world was too complex to introduce another element into it at the moment. Beyond the physical satisfaction they'd found together, she wasn't entirely sure it was safe to link herself in such a way to Peyton for him or for her.

She shook her head. 'Peyton, my world is a dangerous place right now. You're wearing the evidence of that beneath your shirt. Someone is hunting me for reasons I can only speculate on. Until that situation is resolved, I cannot contemplate marriage.'

'What if the first situation is resolved? Would you consider marriage then?' Peyton asked casually.

'If it was for more than lustful reasons, Peyton,' she said. 'Lust is not a good standard for a marriage. We can have that without a wedding.'

The girls were coming back from the pond. 'I'll take that as a "yes", then, since I would not seek to demean you in any way,' Peyton said politely, 'and it seems that is the best answer I'm going to get from you today.'

'I wish it could be different,' Tessa offered tentatively. 'I'm not good for your reputation and I know it.'

'Let me be the judge of that, Tessa.'

'No, *listen*, Peyton. I regret the rumours that are circulating, but I can only be myself. That won't change, it can't change.' She would like to have explained more, but the girls would be within earshot shortly.

Peyton saw them, too, and spoke quickly. 'I need to apologise for Crispin's comment the other day. He was out of line and I wanted you to know that I had said nothing to him about us. You need never fear for your reputation with me.'

'I accept your apology. It was a difficult day for all of us.' She did accept it, what there was of it and what it covered. But it wasn't near enough to cover the entirety of their recent feud. It was interesting to note that he'd apologise for his brother's errant comments, but said nothing at all about his own comments, which had fanned the fire to start with—the implication that her father had been involved in something clandestine and unsavoury, that Sergei was no true friend.

It would have made her life much easier if he'd apologised for those remarks, too. Then she could have chalked them up as nothing more than male jealousy or emotions over the moment, over being stabbed on behalf of a woman who had not been entirely forthcoming about her situation in St Petersburg. Without an apology, those comments could not be discounted and swept aside. She had to consider them and with them the dark thoughts she'd had about Peyton himself.

The girls began picking up the picnic things, signalling the end of the outing, and the little group began the short walk to Peyton's carriage. Tessa slid a careful glance at Peyton. He was busy talking to Annie about the ducks. They were back in their other world now—their public world where they were Miss Branscombe and Lord Dursley, where their interaction and behaviour were limited by the circumspection of society. He would drop her off at his aunt's house in a half-hour and pick her up a few hours later for the Berrybourne ball where they would dance, drink champagne and pretend that everything was all right.

The word 'crush' seemed highly inadequate to describe the Berrybourne affair. Peyton thought 'squash', 'squeeze' or perhaps 'cram' would do more justice to the situation. The massive amount of attendees at the ball gave it an inelegant quality and Peyton was glad he had a legitimate engagement to move on to as he surveyed the ballroom, taking stock of the event.

Beside him, Tessa was beautiful and coolly accepting of her surroundings, no more pleased than he about the quality of the Berrybourne entertainment. The gown she wore tonight upstaged the other gorgeous gowns she'd worn on previous occasions. The gown was the iciest of blues, so pale that it appeared to be white until she moved and the gown picked up a hue of blue or on occasion even lavender. Every movement changed the viewer's understanding of the gown. To Peyton's eye, it was a most appreciative work of illusion, no doubt done to keep the wearer of the gown the centre of someone's attention.

Peyton thought the gown was succeeding admirably and he might have attributed Tessa's outward coolness to the qualities of the gown with its pale, ice tones except that he knew better. Tessa *was* playing it cool with him. She had refused his marriage offer because of what she felt was her complicated life and her refusal to drag him into it. Tonight, in the carriage, between the Berrybournes and the St Just supper, he would remove her concerns. The rumours would pass eventually, replaced by someone else's scandal.

After dropping Tessa and her sisters off from their outing, Peyton had gone straight to Brimley and demanded the right to tell Tessa at least some of what was going on around her. He'd argued on grounds of her own personal safety, her own ability to protect herself. At the very least, she had to know about Sergei Androvich. It was no longer enough for him to make suggestions about Androvich's character. Doing so simply made him look like a jealous man and Tessa did not take a jealous man's claims seriously, as she'd so aptly demonstrated.

Brimley had thought for a moment and agreed, within reason. She could know about the list and about Sergei. Those were the limits of Brimley's 'reason'. She could not know about Peyton's own involvement. Brimley feared it would drive her away.

The orchestra was playing a waltz. Peyton shot Tessa a dubious look. 'Do you think we dare?'

'I think we must or our hostess will be offended. Do you think it's safe?' Tessa said, looking around apprehensively at the hordes of people migrating to and from the dance floor.

Peyton immediately understood her concerns. Tessa was very courageous, braving a crowd of this magnitude after the incident at the Academy. It was hard to stop wondering who would come charging out of the crowd next with a knife or a gun. Suddenly everyone was a potential enemy. Peyton thought of the ever-present knife in his boot, which was under his trouser leg even now. For a professional, it would be easy for a knife to do damaging work here, courtesy of an accidental jostle in a crowd this size. Getting away wouldn't be as simple, which was why he felt fairly safe. But Tessa was still intimidated by the sea of people.

With as much protection as propriety would

allow, Peyton steered Tessa on to the dance floor and into a slow, careful waltz, all that the room allowed in its current overpopulated condition and just the right pace for a man who'd taken a knife wound in his side recently.

'There, see nothing untoward happened,' Peyton said as their dance came to a close. A footman walked past and offered them the last two glasses of champagne on his tray.

'That was fortuitous.' Peyton clinked his glass against hers. 'Who would've thought we'd get so lucky?'

'We're due for a little bit of luck.' Tessa gave a small laugh, her eyes sliding towards a movement in the crowd. 'Sergei's here with the other ambassadors,' she said quietly. 'They're standing by the French doors.'

'Hopefully the dolt won't have the bad manners to come over here after he failed to assist me.' Peyton's tone was light, but he knew what Tessa did not, at least not yet. The attempt at the Academy had been about an effort to kill him specifically. It would have been counter-productive for Sergei to fight against his own hired assassin. Peyton knew perfectly well why Sergei had acted as he had.

Peyton let his gaze wander to where Sergei stood. The other man raised his glass in a silent salute and drank, the gesture designed to encourage Peyton and

Tessa to do the same. Peyton gave a cool, assessing nod to the Russian and raised his own glass. The liquid slid towards his mouth, the fruity scent of it tangy in his nostrils, and the elusive presence of something sweet he couldn't place. At the last moment, Peyton brought the flute down, instincts on high alert.

His movements had arrested Tessa's own. She'd paused, the glass halfway to her lips, distracted by his gesture. Peyton rapidly reached for Tessa's hand, roughly jerking the glass away from her mouth. Some of the liquid splattered on her skirt. 'Stop, Tessa. Don't drink it,' Peyton warned in low tones.

Chapter Fifteen

'The champagne is poisoned,' Peyton said, leaning close to her ear. He did not care to be overheard. He didn't want a scene. He wanted only to get Tessa away from here and explain to her what danger they were in from Sergei, to convince her once and for all that Sergei Androvich was no friend of hers. Sergei was no friend of his. That had always been clear. But Peyton had expected their fight to be fought with covert blades. He had not anticipated Sergei would come after him with poison. That was traditionally a woman's weapon. Because he had not anticipated such a move, he couldn't be sure both glasses were tainted. His certainly was.

Beside him, Tessa trembled involuntarily, realising she still held a poisoned glass in her hand. Peyton moved to take it from her, but not soon enough. The fragile glass slipped from her shaking hand and shattered on the floor. Now, he'd never know if Sergei had tainted her glass, too. People around them turned in the direction of the noise.

It was definitely time to go. Peyton muttered a few excuses and took Tessa's arm, leading them through the crowd. He was careful to hang on to his remaining glass of champagne and to steer clear of Sergei. The longer it took the Russians to realise he'd left, the better. He wasn't sure what kind of poison Sergei had slipped him, so it was hard to gauge the reaction Sergei would be looking for—something immediate or perhaps a more latent effect that would take place hours from now.

In the hall, Peyton called for their things and sent for the carriage, trying to make their departure look ordinary. Peyton set his glass down and slipped Tessa's evening cloak around her shoulders, taking a moment to let his hands linger on her shoulders. 'Are you all right, my dear?' She was still shaking.

'Who would do such a thing?' Tessa breathed. 'What could I have that would cause someone to take such desperate measures?'

'I will tell you in the carriage,' Peyton said, close to her ear. He wanted to take her in his arms and reassure her all would be well. But words were all he could give her in this crowded venue. Such an embrace would not go unnoticed, especially with the *ton* on high alert to see what Tessa Branscombe would do next. Other actions would be less conspicuous, however. With his free hand, Peyton found Tessa's gloved fingers and gripped them tightly in the folds of her skirts, hidden from casual view.

She turned her head to the side. 'What do you know, Peyton?'

'Wait. Just wait,' he cautioned.

Waiting was not her strong suit. It seemed ages before they were settled to Peyton's satisfaction in the carriage. After he'd seen her situated, he'd taken time to tie a handkerchief over the top of his champagne glass before he'd let the coachman drive. But the delay had given Tessa time to transmute her horror over the episode into something sharp and useful.

Now that the initial shock had passed, she would not allow herself to wallow in the powerless sensation of being a victim. In the dim light of the carriage, she fingered her reticule and the familiar comfort of the gun inside. Tonight proved what an irrational type of comfort her little weapon actually was. Firepower was no protection against the silent threat of poison. All of the guns in the world would have failed her tonight if it had not been for Peyton's quick thinking.

I guess that makes him innocent, a little voice challenged in her head. Indeed, her mental accusations the other day seemed hugely misguided in light of what had happened. Villains didn't poison themselves. Neither did they attempt to protect the very people they were trying to betray.

Across from her, Peyton leaned back against his seat and fixed her with all his attention. At last, he was ready to talk, ready to give her the answers she craved. His presence filled the carriage and she was entirely aware of him. It was heady to think that she held the complete sum of such a man's attentions.

'Tessa, there are two things I shall tell you tonight. I'll tell you who is after you and why. I do not think you will like the answer, but you must believe me and you must keep this information in the strictest of confidences. If you cannot do these things, then I cannot tell you what I know.'

Tessa nodded slowly. 'That is a hard bargain to ask me to make when I don't know the merit of what I am trading for.'

Peyton chuckled. 'Spoken like a true diplomat's daughter. I would expect no less from you, Tessa. But I will ask for your pledge anyway. You know I hold you in the highest of regard. I would not trifle with you. Your pledge is well worth it.'

'Then it seems I have no choice.' Tessa held steady. Such a claim was bluff only. She'd never had a choice. Her curiosity would not allow such an opportunity to go by.

'There is a list that is said to have been in your father's possession. The list is of great value to the Czar. It contains the names of revolutionaries who are plotting to seize the throne.'

'Someone is after a list?' Tessa repeated. She tried

to search her mind for a reference her father might have made to something of the sort. Nothing. She shook her head. 'Are you sure? That doesn't sound like my father's usual line of work. Why would he be compiling a list for the Czar? He wasn't a Russian citizen.'

'He wasn't acting for the Czar. It is believed that he was acting on behalf of some British businessmen who were looking to fund a revolution in exchange for trade benefits and water rights when a new government came to power,' Peyton said quietly.

'That would be quite a dangerous proposition. Going against the Czar could mean the literal signing of your own death warrant—' Tessa broke off with a choked cry. 'You think that's what happened. Someone found out what my father was up to.'

'Not just "someone", Tessa. Sergei Androvich.' There it was, the second piece of information he'd promised to deliver. She didn't like it any more than she liked the first. The idea that her father used his position to sell information to private British citizens looking to further their own interests smacked of unethical behaviour at the highest level. Not once to her knowledge had her father ever engaged in anything of a questionable nature—no expensive gifts, no grandiose bribes, nothing. Now this threatened to taint his legacy.

If the list became known, his reputation would be tarnished. Her sisters would be devastated. Tessa could barely get her mind around the implications of

Peyton's first bit of information, let alone the second. Sergei had betrayed them.

In some ways, that was worse than the first piece of information, because she knew in her heart and her mind that this last bit was indisputably true. Too much made sense. There'd been no disturbing followers in St Petersburg once Sergei began accompanying her, because there'd been no need for that. The culprit was right there, legitimately attending her meetings as her escort. There'd been no problems in London until the Russian delegation had arrived. There had been Sergei's insistence that they marry.

Sergei had played the suitor very convincingly. He'd played the friend convincingly, too. She'd been all too glad to accept his friendship and let him into their lives. She'd had real affection for him, albeit a lukewarm one. How could she have been so foolish? Why hadn't she seen it? Was Peyton telling the truth? She wanted to dismiss the notion as ludicrous. Of course he was. What motives did he have for lying about Sergei? Yet, there were still things that were unclear to her.

'Peyton, how is it that you've come by this information?' Tessa asked with steely quietness. 'It seems odd that you would know so much that has been obscured from me.'

'You know I've done some diplomatic work in the past, Tessa. I mentioned to you that first day that I'd worked in Vienna. I have kept my connections. It was not hard to discover.' He leaned forward and grasped her hand. 'Tessa, I asked you to believe me. We are at a point where there can be no distrust between us. I need to know that you are fully with me. I can't have you running to Sergei. I need to know you'll support the decisions that need to be made.'

Tessa felt the intensity coursing through him in the simple power of his grip. 'What decisions?' she asked carefully.

'I want to send your sisters to Dursley Park with Crispin as escort. You and I need to find that list. We can't risk one of your sisters finding it accidentally or Sergei deciding to make one of them a target. I do not want to be in the position of bartering that list for Annie, Eva or Petra.'

Tessa nodded, seeing the wisdom of the choice. 'We'll do that.'

'Then you are in agreement? I have your trust, Tessa?'

Tessa bit her lip, feeling the magnitude of the commitment he asked from her. But, in truth, this last step was not as monumental as other decisions she'd already made with regard to Peyton. She'd given him her body, her passion and told him her secrets. In many ways, she'd already pledged what he asked now. 'Yes, Peyton. You have my trust.'

The carriage came to a halt and the coachman set down the steps. Peyton handed her out and Tessa was surprised to see they were nowhere near the St

Just address. Instead, the structure of Whitehall loomed in front of them. She looked quizzically at Peyton, who reached back inside the carriage for his carefully preserved glass of champagne.

'I want someone to look at this,' he said shortly. 'I have a hunch this might be the same poison that killed your father.'

Tessa blanched. Her world had taken a dark cast these days with poisons and assassins. 'My father died in his sleep.'

'With help,' Peyton commented. He took her hand and guided her faultlessly through the winding dark halls of Whitehall until they came to a door with a light shining beneath it.

Peyton opened it without ceremony. 'Brimley, I've brought you something,' he said without preamble, drawing her into the room with him.

The man in question lifted his gaze from the paperwork in front of him. 'You've brought me a girl?' he said drily.

'Brimley, this is Miss Tessa Branscombe. Surely you recognise her? What I've brought you is this glass of champagne. It smells off and I strongly believe it contains poison. You would be best placed to know if it's related to the substance that killed Ralph Branscombe.'

Brimley took the glass and sniffed. 'It's definitely not right, but I can't tell exactly what it is. I'll have some of our experts get back to you. Courtesy of our friends?'

Peyton nodded. 'Yes.'

'They must feel they have some growing influence if they can ensure you receive a tainted glass at a large affair without mishap,' Brimley commented, shooting a tight look at Tessa. 'You are completely with us, aren't you, Miss Branscombe? Not selling secrets to the enemy?'

Tessa bristled at the bald-faced comment. She edged closer to Peyton, her hand tightly wrapped in his. 'What are you suggesting, sir?' Tessa challenged.

A knowing smile creased Brimley's lips. 'Nothing at all, my dear. I can see that you're entirely with Peyton here and that's good enough for me.'

'Goodnight, Brimley,' Peyton offered tersely, cutting off further conversation.

'Were you protecting me back there?' Tessa asked, trying to keep up with Peyton's long-legged stride. She didn't dare fall behind. She'd never find her way out.

'Brimley doesn't go about among polite society much. His manners are a bit blunt for many,' Peyton said. He made a shushing motion with his hand and pulled them both against the wall.

Tessa stiffened, straining her ears to hear what he'd heard. She caught the sound of footsteps clicking in a nearby empty corridor.

In a quick motion, Peyton swept her behind him, pressing her to the wall. With his height and dark clothing, she was entirely obscured. A fact, she realised belatedly, she could not have claimed for herself. Her light-coloured evening gown would have stood out like a beacon. The footsteps neared and Tessa held her breath. Then they veered in a different direction and faded. She relaxed, feeling the warmth and strength of Peyton's back. Not for the first time, she was amazed at this man's willingness to place himself between her and danger. This incredible man was hers if she'd trust herself to claim him.

Tessa snaked her arms about his waist. 'Is he gone?'

'Yes. It was probably nothing more than a night watchman on his rounds. But it pays to be safe. The fewer people who know I paid a nocturnal visit here, the better.'

Tessa slid under his arm and came around front. 'There, this is much better.'

'Much better for what,' Peyton queried, not resisting when she put her arms around his neck.

'Much better for this,' Tessa said, stretching up on her toes and kissing him full on the mouth.

His arms were around her waist, he deepened the kiss. 'We have to go to St Just's,' he murmured.

'Do we? I'd rather go to your town house,' Tessa answered. From the feel of him through his trousers, she rather thought he'd prefer her option, too. This argument shouldn't be too hard to win.

'You are courting scandal, Tessa Branscombe,' Peyton whispered a warning, but she would have none of it.

She ran a hand down the length of him, exalting

in the power of his erection. 'The scandal is already a *fait accompli*. I might as well live up to it. Perhaps the carriage will do. I don't know if I can wait until we get home,' Tessa said breathlessly.

'The carriage is vastly overrated as a place to copulate,' Peyton ground out, his voice hoarse as his desire rose to dangerous levels under her attentions.

'As are the corridors of Whitehall, I am sure,' Tessa argued.

'Vixen.' But in the end, it was Peyton who led them to the carriage and gave the coachman orders to drive until he told him to stop.

Chapter Sixteen

Whatever the carriage lacked in convenience, it made up for in the exotic nature of the encounter. Peyton knelt on the carriage floor between her parted legs and pushed up her skirts. Tessa shivered deliciously as cold air met the moist warmth of her private juncture. This was positively forbidden territory and her body was awash with curiosity and sensation.

Peyton's hands massaged lightly at her thighs, fingers carefully brushing her curls, delighting in the little tremors they raised when they skimmed her woman's pearl. 'I love your passion, Tessa. Never hide it from me,' Peyton whispered, moving forward to take her lips with his. Peyton forged a trail of hot kisses down the bodice of her gown, to her waist and bared thighs below.

Tessa divined his intentions and gasped. But Peyton was gentle in his insistence. 'You'll like this,

Tess. Trust me.' Then he lowered his mouth to her, taking her most privately in the manner he'd earlier claimed her mouth and her breasts.

Whether it was the wicked decadence of their situation or the sheer magic of their intimacy, Tessa's senses were in utter thrall. She felt her hips lift, and pressed herself against Peyton's mouth, urging him to take her onwards to the place she knew waited just beyond this moment. She bucked once more and exploded, a completed cry escaping her.

Peyton fell back from her, his hair dishevelled, his evening clothes slightly wrinkled as he sat on the carriage floor, staring up at her. Tessa thought he'd never looked as handsome as he did now, his pleasure open in his eyes, his attentions entirely focused on her and not on his many responsibilities. Then she realised he had not had his pleasure.

'Is it possible for me to do that for you?' she asked.

'It is, but I'd prefer to wait and love you properly in my bed. We'll be at Dursley House shortly.'

On cue, the carriage lurched to a halt. Peyton lost his balance and laughed as he rolled against the seat.

'Oh, hurry and get up!' Tessa said, unable to restrain her laughter. 'What do you want your coachman to think?'

'I'm pretty sure he worked it out, Tessa.'

Tessa blushed. 'Is this a common occurrence, then?'

'Not for me, but I'm certain others have contrived similar proceedings.' Peyton was amused.

Tessa fluffed her skirts. 'We can at least pretend nothing happened.'

'I am sure that's what most people do,' Peyton said with mock severity as the carriage door opened.

They walked in stately propriety up the steps to Dursley House, although there was no one to see them at that time of night. They slipped inside and Tessa stifled a giggle. 'I don't think he suspected a thing. We're very good at pretending.'

Peyton laughed. 'Maybe he's very good at pretending, too.'

She liked this Peyton: playful, witty, so at ease. 'I like you this way,' Tessa said abruptly as they climbed the stairs.

'What way is that?' Peyton asked carefully.

'At ease,' Tessa said. 'Tonight, you're just a man.'

Peyton turned to look at her, his hand softly touching her cheek. 'Your man, Tess. Tonight, I'm just your man. I've waited a long time to just be someone's man.'

'Then I am honoured,' Tessa said, a bit choked by the honesty he put on display with his confession. Other men might make confessions of undying love and spout flowery praise, but such generic practices didn't suit this unique man.

Peyton drew her to him and cupped her cheek in his palm, his other hand at her waist, keeping her close against him. He gave her a sweet, deep kiss. 'I'll keep you safe, Tess, always.'

'We'll find the list, Peyton,' Tessa said fiercely.

'Shh. Don't mention such things tonight.' He reached a hand to her hair and pulled it loose. Tessa revelled in the feel of his strong hands in the loose tresses. His voice was low in her ear. 'Morning will come soon enough. Tonight, I want there to be nothing between us.'

She wanted that, too; understood better, perhaps, than he realized, just how much she wanted simply to be with him without the trappings of intrigue that had cast a pall over the potential of their relationship. She wanted to prove to herself that what she and Peyton had shared that night at Aunt Lily's was more than the product of adrenalin and crisis, that at its core there was something extraordinary and rare about what lay between them. Peyton took her hand and she let him lead her through the door to his bedchamber.

The chamber was dimly lit, the covers of the bed already turned down in anticipation of its occupant retiring. A robe lay on the bed, ready for Peyton. 'No valet?' Tessa asked lightly.

Peyton shook his head. 'I don't make a habit of having my servants wait up for me, especially when I don't know what time I'll be back. I am capable of undressing myself.'

'Makes it easier to sneak the ladies in, too, I'm sure,' Tessa joked. But Peyton didn't share her humour.

'You're the only one, Tessa. I am not in the practice of bringing my lovers home.' He grazed her cheek with his hand in a gentle, stroking motion. 'You're the only woman I want to have in this bed.'

Tessa swallowed. For a man like Peyton, who kept his emotions so heavily veiled, such a proclamation was quite possibly as close to the words 'I love you' as he would ever get. She wasn't sure how she felt about that. There was so much she couldn't promise him.

Peyton began working the fastenings at the back of her gown, his hands sure and competent at their duty. She revelled in the intimacy of his actions even as she rebelled against the sensations they aroused. What did she want from Peyton Ramsden? She wanted this night, she wanted this passion that surged between them. Did she dare want all that could follow? Could she allow herself to fall in love with all that Peyton Ramsden was and all that he was not? How could she ensure he wouldn't hate her for it in the end? The last thing she wanted was to ruin him.

Peyton pushed the gown and her chemise to the floor, the last of the fastenings undone. He placed a kiss on her bare shoulder, his hands moving to cup her breasts, thumbs gently tempting her nipples to pebble beneath their light strokes. It seemed her body knew the answer to that question already. It ached for Peyton and the pleasure it found with him. It knew instinctively that it could trust itself to him entirely. Her mind had only to follow.

She turned in his arms, reluctant to leave the pleasure of his hands on her breasts, but wanting to divest him of his clothes so they could move on in this passionate game of theirs. Peyton waylaid her efforts, scooping her up in his arms and carrying her to the bed. 'But...' she started to protest.

Peyton laid her down, his blue eyes glittering with desire. 'Shh, my dear. Tonight, you watch.'

Intuitively, Tessa found the idea strikingly titillating. Before, their passion had been confined by time and place, by layers of clothes subdued as best as circumstances allowed. Tessa unabashedly watched Peyton remove his jacket, his waistcoat, and finally his shirt, stud by careful stud laid aside deliberately in a small crystal dish on the bedside table. The anticipation of seeing Peyton's chest revealed heightened her desire. She'd seen his chest before, of course, the day he'd taken the knife wound, and she'd felt his bare skin beneath her hands the night they'd first made love, but this, seeing him deliberately disrobe for her, was entirely different. Tonight he was her lover, presenting himself to her in the most intimate of ways.

The shadowplay of darkness and light in the room displayed him superbly, limning the muscular perfection of his shoulders and chest, the sculpted form of his upper arms, and the tapered definition of his stomach. Peyton Ramsden sported not a single ounce of fat on his magnificent torso. Tessa wondered fleetingly if the women of the *ton* knew just how well made he was.

But Peyton was not done yet. His hands might have been concentrated on the task of disrobing, but his eyes were concentrated solely on her. His smouldering sapphire gaze did not leave her face as he bent briefly to remove his evening shoes. His hands skimmed the waist of his trousers and Tessa's breath caught. Within moments, Peyton had freed himself elegantly from his trousers and the small clothes he wore beneath. How he'd managed to do so with such grace, Tessa couldn't guess, but there was so much more to wonder at than the graceful mechanics of removing one's trousers.

Peyton was beautiful. There was no other word for it. Tessa had no idea how splendidly wrought a man could be. Without trousers, she could fully appreciate the length of his legs, the firm muscles in his thighs that spoke of long hours in the saddle, the leanness of his hips. And, of course, the great manly secret that lay at his core.

'Lay' wasn't precisely the word for it. Tessa could plainly see that it wasn't 'laying' about. Its length jutted out, begging to be recognised as its own unique entity.

'Peyton, you take my breath away,' Tessa whispered. 'I am entirely overwhelmed. I never imagined…'

He moved towards her. She could sense he was gratified by her words. 'I am glad it's only ever been imaginings. I want to be the first and only man you've seen naked.'

Tessa smiled in the darkness. Tonight such primal

claims carried a pleasing, erotic quality to them. Tonight, she wanted to be claimed, didn't want to fight for her position, didn't want to rail for acceptance as an equal.

'Come and claim me, Peyton.' She arched her back and reached for him, taking him in her arms and drawing him down to her, revelling in the feel of him as his weight covered her. She knew what to do. She parted her legs for him, taking pleasure at how easily he moved between them, how comfortable the intimacy of joining with him had become.

When he slid into her, it felt like the most natural of actions in the world. Her core was slick, enveloping his hot length as if welcoming a loved one home. She sighed her satisfaction and Peyton smiled knowingly above her. Then Peyton moved inside her and the pleasure began. All thoughts of comfort and rightness faded, replaced by intense feelings of primal delight. Tessa was not alone in her joy. Her cries of pleasure were matched by Peyton's own.

It was a heady discovery to realise that in wanting to surrender entirely to Peyton, she hadn't surrendered at all. What they'd achieved together in this bed hadn't been accomplished through the dominance of one person, but through mutual accommodation. They'd got their wish, Tessa thought sleepily. There'd been nothing between them tonight as they'd made love. There'd been only the shared desire to possess one another in the most complete way. And that had taken Tessa far beyond her wildest imaginings.

In her arms he was a god, immortal and strong. In her arms he could reach a place where he could set aside his burdens, where there was no longer a constant weighing of duty against pleasure, where he wasn't trading the lives of British soldiers for his personal desires, where there wasn't a list that would mark the end of the happiness he'd found with Tessa Branscombe.

In her arms he was the man he was supposed to be—her man. Peyton knew with a sharp clarity that one thing presupposed all else in the early dawn light. There would be no other woman who was Tessa's equal for him. *Ever.* She was the one woman who dared to challenge him, who dared to meet his passions, to unleash the real man he was. She was the one woman who loved him with all his conditions. She understood the duality of his existence, the Earl he needed to be, and the man he longed to be. She let him be both. Her very acceptance of his nature made him strong. She was the one woman who had not once tried to change him.

He recognised now how that had been Lydia's failing, the failing she had shared with all his other mistresses. He recognised how much he'd resented the attempt to mould him into a different man. No wonder he'd set a two-year limit on his arranged relationships. He wouldn't change, couldn't change. Then along came Tessa and it had not crossed her mind to change him because she couldn't fathom changing herself. She said as much at the park.

Too bad it couldn't last. The night had been amazing, fulfilling his wish to have nothing between them. But the morning, too, was fulfilling its promises of a less pleasing sort. Tomorrow had arrived and with it, the cares of the day. He needed to convince Tessa to send her sisters to safety. She'd agreed last night, but they'd not established a date of departure. He wanted them to leave immediately. He and Tessa needed to be free to search in earnest for the list.

It was something of a relief to have the list acknowledged between them. There was no more need for trying to pry information out of Tessa covertly, even though there hadn't been anything to pry. She'd known nothing about it. They could search openly and honestly for the list together.

But such an achievement had not been won lightly. Peyton knew it had cost Tessa greatly to accept that her father might not have been quite the man she'd believed him to be—a man with ethics above the norm—only to discover posthumously that those beliefs had been betrayed. Sometimes it was worse discovering it that way. He'd grown up thinking he'd understood his father, but he'd learned too late, when his father was no longer there to explain the truth to him, that his father had kept secrets, too, that life had not been precisely as it had appeared. Such realisations came with a price.

The other cost had been the rift between him and Tessa. She'd not taken his information well. He'd been lucky to get a second chance, but he was not fool enough to think she'd extend such courtesy again. Like him, Tessa valued honesty and straight-forwardness above all else. It seemed the height of irony that both of them should be drawn into a game that precluded direct disclosures.

He felt Tessa's warm hand slide to his groin, searching for him. She would find him hard and ready for one last bout of loving before they had to face the day's realities.

He was taking unrealistic chances there as well.

Every time he made love with Tessa, he was tempting fate. Not once in any of his relationships had he elected not to do his duty and complete a gentle-man's finish in the sheets or to use sheaths. It was not fair to risk getting her with child, no matter how much the idea thrilled him. Such an occurrence would bind her to him without giving her a choice. At least it would if she was a conventional woman. Peyton wasn't sure what he feared most: Tessa marrying him for the sake of a ill-conceived child or Tessa refusing to marry him and taking the child off into a new life without him. He knew legally she wouldn't stand a chance if he pursued her. But he knew, too, that he could not bring her such pain if that was her choice.

Still, when Tessa's hand closed about his member, her delight at her discovery coming in a little gasp, Peyton could not refuse the chance to give himself over to the peace he knew would come, if only for a little while.

Afterwards, Tessa lay content in his arms, her head in its usual place against his shoulder. They'd been silent for quite some time, neither of them wishing to speak of the day ahead. But Peyton knew they could not put it off indefinitely.

Carefully, he ventured the topic that mattered to him most. 'Tess, I want to ask you something,' he began, easing into the conversation. She murmured her assent.

'I would like to send your sisters with Crispin to Durlsey Park immediately.'

Peyton felt Tessa shift beside him, moving to raise herself up on one arm. 'It's become that dangerous, hasn't it?' It was worded as a question, but she knew the answer already, he could see it in her eyes.

'Yes, it has. Until we recover the list, they are fair targets for Androvich and he won't hesitate to use them. I understand how hard it is for you to be separated from them. I promise they'll be safe. Crispin and Paine will protect them with their lives. Julia will love the company.'

Tessa nodded. 'I agree. We'll tell them after breakfast.'

Peyton smiled and reached to take her back in his arms. 'It's a good decision, Tessa. You'll be with them again as soon as we find the list.' He wished he could say as much for himself. When he imagined the reunion Tessa would have with her sisters at Dursley Park, he wondered if he'd be part of that, or if Tessa would have shunned him completely by that point, disgusted by his duplicity. He was tempted to tell her everything right then, throwing himself on her mercy in the hopes that she'd understand the weight he carried, the depth of what his decision required of him. But Tessa chose that moment to fling back the covers and rise, determined to dress and meet the day head on.

Tensions were high in Aunt Lily's drawing room two hours later. Everyone was gathered. They were only waiting for Crispin's arrival in order to begin. Little conversations flowed awkwardly, a clear testament to the strained atmosphere. There'd been no way to disguise the obvious: Tessa had spent the night at his town house. While Peyton had no worries about his staff's discretion in such a situation, it was clear from the stern eye Aunt Lily fixed him with that she wholeheartedly disapproved of the developing circumstances.

Peyton shifted infinitesimally in his seat. It was hard to act like the family patriarch with one's aunt shooting reproachful looks across the room. Lily's baleful stare made him feel like a toddler in leading strings who'd got caught stealing biscuits from the kitchen. It wasn't as if he was unaware of his culpability. He was a gentleman. He should have taken the high road and fought his urges, although he couldn't imagine how he would have succeeded. And he had tried, was still trying in fact, to do the right thing by Tessa. She had been the one to refuse him, after all. Of course, Peyton could hardly imagine explaining *that* to Aunt Lily: *I have asked her to marry me, Aunt, but she only wants to have sex with me.*

The door to the drawing room opened and Crispin slipped in, flashing a quick glance in Petra's direction before taking an unoccupied chair. Peyton cleared his throat for attention. It was time to get started.

The decision to go to Dursley Park was met with mixed emotions. Eva and Annie were thrilled at the prospect of a trip to the Cotswolds. Peyton painted grand pictures of the idyllic fields populated with stone walls and sheep, fresh air and places to run. The beauty of an English summer in the countryside could not be underestimated and the girls were enthralled. He tried to persuade Petra, too, with the promise of his excellent stables. The girl loved horses and at Dursley Park there were horses aplenty for any level of rider. But she was loyal to Tessa and clearly had misgivings about leaving her sister. Those misgivings were no doubt fuelled by Tessa's absence last night.

Crispin shot Petra a sharp look that Peyton

couldn't ignore. The two of them had been quiet in the wake of his announcement that they were to go to Dursley Park.

Peyton had noticed they'd exchanged looks ever since the conversation began.

'Crispin, do you have something to say?' Peyton barked. Petra immediately looked down at her hands, blushing. Lord help him if Crispin was even contemplating trifling with Petra Branscombe. The girl wasn't even out yet. It would give Tessa one more reason to kill him and Tessa would have plenty of reasons in the days to come. Right now, Peyton was enjoying the unity of Tessa agreeing with him. She'd stood beside him literally and figuratively, supporting his decision.

It wasn't Crispin that spoke. It was Petra. 'I want to know why we're to go to Dursley Park. We haven't been given a reason. It was my understanding that we were to be allowed to remain with Tessa for the Season.' As always, she was quiet and forthright. While soft spoken, there was no mistaking the directness of her question.

Peyton glanced at Tessa. It should be her decision how much her sisters were told. Tessa drew a deep breath.

'It has come to our attention that Father may have been in possession of a list that the Russian government wants returned. It has become something of a sticking point and we are not sure just how explosive the situation might become,' Tessa said carefully.

Eva cocked her head thoughtfully. 'Then it's good that Sergei is here. He can take care of everything and tell the others Father didn't have a list.'

Petra's gaze shot between Eva and Tessa. Peyton could see her keen intelligence working quickly. 'Sergei *is* the Russian government, isn't he, Tessa? That's why he's here. It's his mission to retrieve the list.'

Tessa nodded slowly. 'I believe so.'

Eva looked incredulous. 'He's not here to win you back, Tess? I thought he was here to court you.'

'It's what he wanted us to believe,' Petra said, a hard look in her eyes that belied her seventeen years. She shot a look at her sister. 'Oh, Tess, I am so sorry. He's treated you poorly, making you believe he was in love with you.'

Tessa dismissed the concern with a wave of her hand. 'I didn't harbour any affections for him beyond friendship. Any betrayal I feel is that of a friend. It's of no account. What does matter is that you are all safe, so Peyton and I can look for the list. Crispin will go with you.'

'And I will go with you,' Aunt Lily put in with good humour. 'Crispin won't last a day on the road with three girls.'

Peyton nodded his thanks. 'Your offer is much appreciated.' He wondered if Lily had the same concerns he did. He'd been so wrapped up in his own troubles he hadn't noticed the developments between Petra and Crispin.

'When do you think everyone can be ready to leave?' Peyton asked Lily.

'Tomorrow, if we hurry. I'll assign a maid to each of the girls to help with packing. I'll have the groom start readying the travelling coach. My secretary can spend the day closing up my calendar. There's no need to close up the house since Tessa will still be here.' Lily speared Peyton with a sharp look.

He would take Tessa to Dursley House with him as soon as Aunt Lily's travelling coach was out of sight. He wouldn't leave Tessa alone in a big house, an easy target for Androvich. Her safety far outweighed any social concerns for scandal. But Peyton knew there were certain battles he wouldn't win with Aunt Lily outright, so he tactfully kept his argument to himself. Better to do what he planned and argue with Aunt Lily after the fact. If she knew what he intended, she might choose to stay and right now he needed her to watch over Petra.

'Tomorrow it is, then,' Peyton said, standing up as if to signal that the meeting was over. He watched Tessa move towards her sisters, ushering them from the room. She would be absorbed with them today, but she was already counting the hours until dark and he would be able to claim her again. He wasn't sure how, but he'd find a way. He motioned to Crispin for a private word, his gaze fixed on Tessa, watching her sail out of the door of the drawing room with her charges. He ached for her already. The countdown till night had begun.

Chapter Seventeen

Sergei Androvich sipped his morning tea in the breakfast room of the Russian embassy, impassively listening to the latest report from one of the men they employed to keep an eye on Dursley.

'The aunt's travelling carriage left at dawn,' the man said. 'Looked like a veritable convoy with a luggage carriage, servants and outriders and everything.' There was a touch of awe in the man's voice. Sergei snorted. The last thing he needed was his own informants starting to respect the damned Dursley clan.

He pondered the information. Leaving in great style didn't suggest an act of stealth. He remembered Tessa's quiet flight from St Petersburg. *That* had been an act of stealth—amateur stealth, of course; Tessa didn't have his training in covert activities. Dursley did have training, on the other hand. Sergei did not doubt the Earl could effect a stealthy removal if he wanted to. It appeared that he hadn't wanted to, that secrecy wasn't the aim of the early morning departure.

Such an action could only mean one of two things. It might mean the girls had tired of the city in the summer—and, really, who wouldn't? Sergei couldn't imagine being in London without the allure of invitations to grand balls. London was hot and crowded, much warmer than St Petersburg. Perhaps the removal was just that—an escape to the cooler countryside. If so, that meant Tessa and Peyton hadn't found the list. It might also mean that Tessa didn't know about the list yet, but Sergei doubted it. At this point in the game, Peyton would recognise he would be better off if Tessa knew what to look for, even if it meant encountering her wrath.

The other thing the removal of Tessa's sisters might mean was the scenario Sergei feared most. They had found the list and were getting ready to act with the understanding that it was going to get dangerous. Sergei could not let that list fall into the hands of the British government. If people had to die to prevent that from happening, then so be it. Peyton would understand that, even if Tessa hadn't grasped such consequences yet.

'Let the carriage go,' Sergei said. 'They're likely off to enjoy the countryside. The people who matter are still in town. We must double our efforts to see what Dursley and Miss Branscombe are up to. Follow them and report on everything they do.'

Sergei tossed a bag of coins to the man. 'Share this with the others. Keep your eyes sharp. We don't want Dursley to spot you.'

Sergei dismissed the man and rubbed a hand over his face. He was getting tired of this. All he'd been able to do was watch and wait: *watch* Dursley steal Tessa's affections, *wait* for the list to come to light, instead of being able to search for it himself. Dursley was calling all the shots these days. Something had to change quickly. He had no doubt that Vasilov would be happy to report his failings to the Czar. Sergei had a lot at stake personally in the success of this mission to bring back the list before it could be used to destabilise the Russian throne. A promotion and money were on the line, both of which he desperately needed.

It was frustrating to be reduced to such a minimal role, but Sergei would wait for his moment. Dursley couldn't be perfect for ever and Sergei knew how to use the slightest slip to his advantage.

Tessa had not been to the house in Bloomsbury since the day she'd discovered the break-in. Returning now with Peyton, she could hardly reconcile the vision against how it had looked that day. The devastation had been minimised. She stood in the doorway to the front room, taking in the details. It was clear Peyton's servants had been hard at work to clear the debris and restore order. There was still work to be done. The walls would need new paint and paper. New furniture would need to be purchased to replace the articles that had been ruined beyond redemption. The ruined furniture had been removed and Tessa could see that all the rooms were considerably emptier in their absence.

'You've worked wonders,' Tessa commented as they wandered through the rooms, Peyton giving her time to assimilate the state of the house.

'It's not enough. There is more to be done and it will be done, Tessa. Your house will be restored,' Peyton said in a surprisingly fierce tone.

Tessa shook her head. 'Not with your money, Peyton. This is my house, my responsibility.'

'You are my responsibility, thus your house is my responsibility,' Peyton retorted.

'I am not your mistress, Peyton. I've come to you out of my own free will. I have no intention of being a kept woman.' Tessa stopped walking and faced him over the scarred piano in the music room. 'You don't *owe* me anything.' They'd been intimate too often without setting ground rules. Tessa regretted that right now. At the time she'd known better. She'd known Peyton would see a responsibility in their intimacy and yet so great had been her desire for him that she'd put aside the discussion for more immediate pleasures. Now that pigeon was coming home to roost.

Peyton's jaw tightened. Tessa stood her ground. They might as well get things sorted out once for and all. 'Tessa, I have no intention of making you my mistress. I had not thought to bring this up in such a manner, but the timing seems to have forced it.' Peyton held her gaze. 'I mean to discuss marriage with you. I know this is not an opportune time. There are issues that need to be resolved, but would you consider it? Once the Russian issue is settled to our satisfaction, would you do me the honour of being my wife?'

Tessa recognised immediately that this was perhaps the worst marriage proposal in the history of proposals. There were no flowers, no words of love, and no flattering protestations of great passion. But there was a sincerity that Tessa appreciated, a sincerity that could only come from Peyton. The last proposal she had received had carried with it all the trimmings a proposal should have. Sergei had proposed with flattering sentiments, grand promises of a life together and burgeoning affection. But the proposal had been wrapped in deceit. Events had revealed the proposal to be a fraud. This proposal, Peyton's proposal, was practical and real. He understood now was not the time for commitments, the future was too uncertain for that.

'Peyton, you are chivalrous to a fault with your offer. But you and I know that even if the Russian issue were resolved, it's not in your best interest to marry me. You mustn't feel obliged,' Tessa said gently. 'I do believe we've discussed this before at the park.'

'I am very persistent,' Peyton said staunchly.

'Yes. And I am very stubborn, which is why my answer remains the same.' Tessa gave him a soft smile. 'There is enough to worry about without throwing that into the mix.'

Tessa made to move on to another room, but Peyton grabbed her arm. 'Tessa, I need to know, do you have feelings for me? Do you harbour any serious affection for me?'

The question took her aback. She had not thought to ever see the confident, arrogant Earl of Dursley in a vulnerable moment. But that's what she saw when she met his blue gaze. She had not meant for him to take her refusal as doubt of her affections.

'I am quite undone by you, Peyton. My feelings for you are complex and overwhelming. I scarcely know what to make of them beyond the fact that they are more powerful than anything I've known,' Tessa said honestly. 'It's the truth, although I fear admitting it will only serve to inflate your substantial male ego,' she jested.

'It seems we are in accord then, Tessa, for I am quite overcome by you.' His gaze was searing, his touch on her arm electrifying. She saw the early signs of a seduction.

'Then we'd better find that list,' Tessa said, finding it necessary to break the rising tension of the moment. If this went on much longer, Peyton could have her up against a wall and she'd be making promises she didn't want to keep.

They'd come to the Bloomsbury house with the intention of following the thief's lead. Whoever had broken in had been quite certain the list was in the house. They hadn't found it. If it was here, then it was *still* here.

'I'll start in my office,' Tessa volunteered. 'The family papers seem a logical place to start.'

Peyton nodded his approval. 'I'll start in the kitchen. There's a chance there's a false bottom or something in one of the silver pieces that's been overlooked.'

Tessa mounted the stairs to her little office. Unlike the other rooms that had been tidied, this room had been left just as it had been. The thief had been quite thorough in this room. Papers had been thrown out of her desk. Her father's papers, which had been stacked in crates, had been upended and strewn on the floor. But in all likelihood, the thief hadn't had the time needed to comb through the individual files and look closely at the content of each.

Tessa sat on the floor and began sorting papers, making stacks and restoring order, scanning the papers carefully for references that might be of use. Occasionally, she could hear Peyton in the kitchen and the clink of silver. The humour of imagining the proper Earl of Dursley pottering around a kitchen brought a smile to her lips.

After two hours of work, Tessa leaned back on her hands and stretched. Her back was starting to hurt and her shoulder was stiff. The room was beginning to look more orderly. Mentally, she took stock of what she'd organised. In one pile, she had her personal letters and correspondence. There was nothing of note there. In another pile, there were household accounts and bills. Again, there was nothing of import. In a stack of her father's things was a social calendar full of his appointments. This held some promise and Tessa reached for it, eagerly flipping through the pages. But there was nothing present in the calendar other than appointments she'd already known about with people she already knew. Well, she could hardly expect her father to keep a secret list in a public place. It was unlikely that he would have written down in plain view, 'Meet with Russian revolutionaries to discuss munitions shipments'.

He might not have written it down in an obvious place, but Tessa was sure he had written it down somewhere. He had been a meticulous records keeper and had admitted on more than one occasion that if he didn't write things down, he'd get the details messed up. The list was somewhere. Carefully, Tessa stood up and began re-boxing the papers into the crates. The room looked substantially better when she was through.

Tessa looked around the room. It seemed barren without the portrait of her father on the wall. As soon as the house was fit for inhabiting again, she'd hang the portrait back up where it belonged. That decided, she went downstairs to see how Peyton was doing with the silver.

Peyton had long given up on the silver and had made his way into the cellar. When Tessa found him, he'd discarded his coat and waistcoat, preferring to work in shirtsleeves.

'That suits you,' Tessa said appreciatively, from the top of the stairs.

Peyton pried a lid off a crate. 'Help me bring this upstairs. It's too dark to really examine anything down here.'

Tessa made her way down the stairs and helped Peyton haul the contents up to the kitchen. They spread the items out on the long kitchen work-table. The items were in good condition and smelled of the wood chips Tessa had packed them in months ago. She picked up a *matryoshka* doll. 'This was a birthday present from my father when I was eighteen.' Tessa began untwisting the doll's different layers. 'He had placed a piece of jewellery inside each of the dolls,' she said wistfully. 'It was a perfect gift for a young girl who was so desperate to grow up. He needed a hostess and I wanted so badly to fill that role for him.' Tessa set each progressively smaller doll down in front of her in a line.

Peyton was staring at her inquisitively. 'What?'

'You've never said anything personal about your life in St Petersburg before. I've only ever heard about the robbery and your father's death.'

Tessa moved on to pick up a lacquer box with a painted scene of the Winter Palace on it. 'This was my mother's. Father gave it to her as an anniversary gift. There was jewellery inside, of course. It was the year before Annie was born. The year before my mother died.' Tessa opened the lid of the box. 'I keep a picture of my mother in here.' She handed the little miniature to Peyton. 'Father says I look like her.'

'You're the only mother Annie has known?' Peyton probed gently, handing the miniature back to Tessa.

'Yes. It was winter and the birth was too hard on my mother. She was too old for another child. I was twelve, Petra was seven and Eva was five. Mother herself was in her late thirties. It was just too much. The midwife put Annie in my arms and I've done the best I could ever since then. She was so tiny and no one thought she'd live. But I would have none of it. I wasn't about to lose her, too.' Tessa snapped the lid of the box shut. 'There's nothing here but memories, Peyton. These are my personal things. I packed them myself. If anything was hidden here, I would have found it before we left Russia.'

'It's all right to talk about the past, Tessa,' Peyton said, reaching a hand out to her. 'You shouldn't hide these beautiful things away and pretend they don't exist.'

Tessa shot him a wry look. 'Would this be the pot calling the kettle black, Peyton Ramsden? You're not the most forthcoming man I've ever met.'

'Learn from my mistake, my dear.' Peyton chuckled. 'After all, I have attained the august age of my late thirties. I'm a veritable temple of ancient wisdom. Trust me, I am better with people now. It's only been recently, since Paine's returned, that I've recognised the value of memories, of expressing my feelings to those I care about.'

Tessa looked dubious.

'Don't look at me like that. I am better. I don't run around professing emotions every second I feel them, but I've learned to be more careful with those I love.' Peyton gave a self-deprecating snort. 'My last mistress won't agree with that, but then I didn't love her.' Peyton paused. 'I am sorry, that was tactless. I don't know what prompted me to say that.'

'It's all right. When you make mistakes, it reminds me that you're human like the rest of us.' Tessa smiled.

'Did you find anything upstairs?' Peyton changed the subject.

Tessa shook her head. 'No. I had hoped to find hints, clues, maybe, that would allow us to reconstruct the list from original sources. I thought there might be references in a variety of letters or in his social calendar. But I saw nothing to support that.'

'Let's go back to Aunt Lily's and have some lunch. Then afterwards we can go through the few things you brought from the house. There might be something we've overlooked,' Peyton suggested.

Outside at the carriage the coachman leaned down

to speak privately with Peyton. His mouth was grim when he turned to Tessa. 'Our watcher is back. He's not on the bench, but my coachman said a man kept walking by watching the house.'

'Sergei is hoping we'll lead him to the list,' Tessa said tensely, taking her seat in the carriage.

'Yes. He doesn't know where the list is or how to get to it now that he's lost access to you. But chin up, my dear, as long as he needs us, he won't be harming us.'

'That's not funny, Peyton,' Tessa scolded, all too aware of the danger that lurked around them. She was more than glad that her sisters were safely away from harm.

Lunch was a short affair, mostly because Peyton had found other exquisite uses for strawberries besides eating them out of the bowl. Tessa found herself in bed, thoroughly loved and smelling of strawberries in the middle of the afternoon with a drowsy Peyton beside her.

'This is what Aunt Lily feared would happen,' Tessa said coyly, reaching for the last strawberry in the bowl.

'She only feared it would happen if she closed up the house and let me take you to Dursley House,' Peyton corrected. 'Now we can tell her honestly that her fears were for naught.'

Tessa laughed. 'Someone is going to find out. Servants talk.'

'Mine don't,' Peyton said.

Tessa sat up in bed. Peyton made to drag her back down. 'Where are you going? The damage is already done. We might as well stay in bed and enjoy ourselves.'

'I'm going to turn the portrait of my father around. It's like he's staring at us.' Tessa swung her legs out of bed and padded naked to the portrait she'd leaned against the wall days ago.

Peyton laughed at her.

'Have you ever made love in front of your parent's portrait? Don't laugh until you've tried it.' Tessa gave him a mock scolding.

'No, because I keep all my relatives in the art gallery where they belong. There's a reason all the big houses have galleries, you know. That way we can have sex—'

'Peyton, come here,' Tessa interrupted, all seriousness. She knelt down in front of the portrait.

'What is it, Tessa?' Peyton was beside her instantly.

She gave him a steady look. 'I know where the list is.'

Chapter Eighteen

'Is it painted into the portrait?' Peyton asked, taking a moment to retrieve her robe from the bed and grabbing a bedsheet for himself.

'No, I don't think so,' Tessa said, squinting at the long scroll depicted in the painting. 'I think this scroll is merely a clue.' Tessa struggled to turn the portrait around.

'Here, let me.' Peyton reached around her and easily turned the awkward object. The back of the portrait was sealed up in brown wrapping-style paper.

'I bet if we rip the paper backing off, the list will be inside,' Tessa said.

Peyton nodded and they began to rip the paper. They'd only torn back a few strips when Peyton halted them. 'Wait. Ripping paper works if the list is separate from the backing. But if the backing is the list itself, then we're ripping the list up as we go. Let me get my knife and then we can remove the backing as a whole piece instead of tearing into it like a Christmas present.'

Peyton grabbed his knife from his boot and began the laborious process of detaching the backing as a single large sheet of paper. Halfway through, he pulled back the paper, searching for signs of the list. 'The backing is blank. We're safe. You can rip away if you like, Tess.' Peyton sat back on his heels.

Tessa grinned and tore the remaining paper away. Sure enough, at the bottom corner of the portrait was a narrow, folded piece of paper. It hardly looked big enough to be the source of so much commotion. Tessa reached for it, feeling like a treasure hunter who'd just unearthed a chest of jewels. She unfolded the paper and a second piece fluttered out. She looked at Peyton, who picked up the second piece. For a while, they sat in silence, surveying their lists. At some point, it crossed Tessa's mind how ludicrous this must appear—two half-naked people in bedclothes sitting in front of a portrait they'd torn apart and reading small slips of paper.

'There are two lists,' Peyton said eventually. 'My list contains the names of the British businessmen who were interested in backing a revolutionary group. I am guessing that your list contains the revolutionaries who were willing to consider outside assistance?'

Tessa nodded and they exchanged papers. 'Do you know any of the businessmen on the list?' she asked.

Peyton shook his head. 'No. My brother, Paine, might. Do you recognise any of the Russian names?'

'Not really. One or two of them sound familiar, perhaps because they might have been named in a news article. But they're supposed to be secret societies. Publicity can hardly be what they want.' Tessa shrugged. 'It's amazing this was overlooked during the break-in. The thief was so close. The picture had been taken off the wall. The thief held the list in his hands and did not even realise it.'

'He was probably looking for a hidden safe. It's fairly common to hide a family safe behind a portrait. He removed the picture to see if there was a hidey-hole behind it. When there wasn't, he moved on to other possibilities,' Peyton explained.

'What do we do next, Peyton?' The thrill of finding the list was starting to fade as realities and next steps started to set in.

'We get the list to Brimley at Whitehall,' Peyton said, matter-of-factly.

Tessa fiddled with the tassel on the robe's belt. 'What do you suppose he will do with it?'

'He has intimated to me that British diplomats in Russia will be able to use the list as a bargaining tool. Britain wants to convince the Czar to keep the Dardanelle Straits open to British shipping.'

Tessa didn't like the sound of that. She sat up straighter. 'Your Brimley is going to sell the list to the Czar for water rights?'

'He might,' Peyton answered.

'Does that bother you? It bothers me quite a lot.' Tessa rose and began pacing away her agitation. 'We've risked our lives for this list. You've been stabbed and nearly poisoned. And for what? So that the list can be used as a death sentence for Russian revolutionaries. Your government is going to use this list to betray men.'

'Calm down, Tessa.' Peyton stood up. 'It's your government, too. You're as British as I am. This is about what's right for Britain. Those revolutionaries have committed themselves to treason against their king and they know the risks they run.'

'That's no answer at all, Peyton,' Tessa stormed. 'You could do something about that. You don't have to be the one to send them to their deaths.' Tessa stopped pacing at the window and drew back the curtain a bit to see the garden below. Her voice softened an increment. 'We were in St Petersburg in 1825, you know. I was about fifteen at the time. Later, once the leaders had been sentenced, we were invited to watch the executions. I didn't go. I couldn't bring myself to do it. My father went, of course, out of a show of loyalty to Nicholas I, the necessities of diplomatic relations and all that. This was not a rebellion of unorganised peasants. This was an internal rebellion that reached as high as the Czar's own military—smart, educated men who believed in freedom.'

'They were soldiers willing to die for their

beliefs,' Peyton put in from his side of the room. 'You can't shout "Constantine and Constitution" and not expect the Czar to do something about it.'

'Peyton, men were hanged from the ramparts of the Peter and Paul fortress,' Tessa protested. 'They weren't shot down in battle. They were marched out and put to death. It will happen again if you turn that list in. I can't believe you'd deign to be part of that.'

'If we don't turn this list in, Tessa, there will be war,' Peyton argued, exasperation evident in his tone. 'There are already Russian troops amassing for an attack on Turkey. Turkey will not survive a Russian assault without British assistance. If Britain does not ensure a Turkish victory, then we'll lose critical water rights. War means British troops will die, perhaps by the thousands.'

Tessa stared thoughtfully out of the window. These were the situations her father had grappled with during his career. She had never been quite so close, quite so instrumental to one of those decisions as she was now. In her hands literally was the power to decide who lived and who died. Did she let Peyton turn the list in and risk sending those Russian freedom fighters to their deaths, or did she dissuade him from his course and send British troops into Turkey for a war with no certain outcome?

If she chose the former, Britain could use the list as leverage for maintaining water rights, a few freedom fighters in exchange for safe passage to

India should Russia conquer Turkey. British troops could stay out of the conflict and let Turkey and Russia fight it out, knowing that British water rights were secure regardless of the outcome. If she chose the latter, nothing was certain. The freedom fighters would not be betrayed by her, but British trade could very well be jeopardised and there would be war, a war which Britain might win or lose.

Tessa desperately wished there was a way between her options that would allow her to prevent a war and yet protect the revolutionaries. She wished her duty was as clearly defined to her as Peyton's was to him. It would make this decision easier, more obvious. Peyton had lived his entire life in Britain. He understood his role and obligations as a British peer. But while she was born British, she hadn't lived a British life. She'd seen first-hand the need for reform in Russia, the oppressive practices of serfdom and the consequences of the outmoded government practised by Russia's Czars. She didn't want to trade freedom for water rights. Maybe she didn't have to after all.

'What if we give Brimley only one list?' Tessa began to hypothesise out loud. 'Give him the list of British investors. It's still something to negotiate with. He can promise the Czar he won't let those businessmen fund a revolutionary cause if the Czar promises water rights should Russia seize Turkey. The right diplomat could build a persuasive case. Czar Nicholas is putting down revolts all over the country. He'll be paranoid enough to take the threat of sponsorship seriously.' Hope began to grow in her as she outlined her argument.

Peyton stared at her thoughtfully, weighing, considering what she proposed. She knew he was thinking of his ability to keep his word, to keep his countrymen safe. 'What about the other list?' he asked.

'We burn it. We tell no one that it existed. We can claim my father's work wasn't as far along as people had been led to believe. He'd not yet had time to make the connections,' Tessa said ardently.

Peyton nodded. 'Those men will have the chance to live and die on their own.'

'It is the best we can do for them. Are we agreed, Peyton?' Tessa pressed. 'I want you to do this because it's the right thing to do, not because of your affections for me.'

'Yes. I will take the list of investors to Brimley. He will be disappointed it isn't more telling, but he'll see its uses none the less.' Peyton reached for his clothes and began to dress.

'You're going now? I'll come with you,' Tessa offered, striding towards her pile of discarded clothing.

Peyton shook his head. 'No. I want you to stay here. You'll be safer. There are servants downstairs who would come to your assistance. You can lock the doors. I won't risk you at the last moment when we're so close to being free from this cloud.'

His words gave her pause. 'Do you think it's all

that dangerous? The Russians don't know we have found the list.'

Peyton looked at her, a frighteningly serious look on his face. 'I am not as worried about getting to Whitehall as I am about getting home. We know we were followed this morning. There is a great likelihood that I'll be followed when I leave the house. I'll try to lose them, but, if not, they'll suspect something is up when they discover my destination is Whitehall.'

'Then meet Brimley somewhere else,' Tessa said shortly.

'It hardly matters if I go to Whitehall or White's, I'll be followed regardless. I'd rather go in the daylight. If anything is going to happen, I don't want any surprises in the dark.'

Tessa slipped her dress on over her head. 'I don't like this talk, Peyton. You sound as if you're not coming back.' She said the words briskly, but she couldn't keep the tears from forming in her eyes. She swiped at them, angry at herself for being a watering pot at such an inopportune moment. This was a moment for strength. 'Send a message and have Brimley come here. If he wants the list, he can come and get it.'

'That would be a dead giveaway,' Peyton argued softly, moving to take her in his arms. He was fully clothed now and Tessa could see by the set of his jaw that he would not be convinced from his path.

She laid her head against his chest, taking in the warmth of his body, its strength and power, while he laid out his instructions. 'I shouldn't be gone long, no longer than two hours. Hopefully, less. It will depend on traffic. Don't open the door for anyone for any reason. If I don't come back, make a run for the Cotswolds and Dursley Park. With luck, you'll catch up with Crispin on the road. You'll be safe.'

'You'll come back, Peyton,' Tessa said resolutely. 'We'll leave for the Cotswolds together.'

'Yes, we'll have to get out of town until Brimley can send the Russian delegation packing. I don't think Count Androvich will be pleased to discover he's been beaten.'

Tessa didn't wait for Peyton to set her apart from him. She stepped back from their embrace of her own accord, although it took all of her will to do so. All she wanted to do was to keep Peyton in her arms, safe. But Peyton needed her courage now. He didn't need a woman clinging to him. Her worry could prove to be a fatal distraction.

Peyton folded the list and tucked it inside his coat pocket. He slid his customary knife into his boot. 'I'll be back shortly, Tessa,' he said, his hand on the doorknob that would take him out of her bedroom.

'Peyton, I love you,' Tessa called after him as the door shut behind him.

Tessa sat quietly, straining her ears for the sound of the big front door shutting, signalling Peyton's complete exit from the house. She glanced at the clock to check the time. Five o'clock. By seven, this would all be over, she told herself. Perhaps earlier. In the meanwhile, she had to stay busy. She could pack. For them both.

Tessa threw herself into packing and tidying the room. A maid came in to light the evening fire and to offer to help. Tessa let her light the fire, but refused the help.

As the fire caught, Tessa fingered the second list. They'd agreed to burn it. She should do it now. But something held her back. Tessa tucked the list into her chemise. She would wait until Peyton was safe. Should anything happen to him, she might be able to use the list to free him. She had little else to use in place of a ransom. She would not trade these names for water rights, an issue that was volatile and ever changing, but she'd not hesitate to trade these names to save Peyton.

Tessa finished packing at half-past six. Peyton hadn't returned. She fought back the initial desire to panic. He'd said it could take up to two hours. Tessa picked up a book and tried to read, failing miserably. She put the book down and picked up her reticule with her gun inside and sat in the chair next to the fire. Peyton would walk through the door any moment and they would laugh together at her odd vigil, sitting in her chair with her gun.

By half-past seven Tessa had to draw the conclusion she'd avoided for so long. Peyton wasn't coming home.

Something had gone dreadfully wrong. She fingered the shape of her gun inside her reticule. The time for waiting had passed. Tessa scribbled a hasty note to Arthur at Dursley House. The time for action had come.

Peyton's worst fears had come to fruition. He stifled a groan in the darkness as consciousness returned to him, and with it the flood of events that had led to this. He'd left Lily's town house in his coach, alert to anyone who might be following him. Thanks to traffic, his coachman had eluded a couple of the followers, but Count Androvich had grown cleverer over the weeks. He had a network of watchers set up so that there was someone to take over for the others when they fell back. A few hundred yards from Whitehall, Peyton had felt he'd succeeded in losing the last of them. Neither he nor his coachman could see anyone of a suspicious nature in their wake. Peyton had quickly disembarked from the carriage and made his way to Brimley's office, feeling safer once he got inside the building.

As he'd expected, Brimley had been disappointed the list wasn't more detailed. Peyton had to argue far longer than he would have liked to get Brimley to see the merits of what he offered. 'This is the list I have,' Peyton had said. 'I have done what you've required of me.' It wasn't a lie. That was indeed the list he had. If Tessa had another list, well…

'Very well, Dursley. We had been led to believe

there might be something more informative, but this will do, as you've pointed out,' Brimley huffed.

Then chaos had broken out. The door of the little office had burst open and they were set upon by eight masked men. Peyton barely had time to draw his knife. To his horror, Brimley went down immediately, a victim of quiet knife work. It was him against eight. He understood instantly why the trackers had disappeared. Someone had gone directly to Count Androvich. His lengthy argument with Brimley had given Androvich time to put together his forces and make his attack.

Peyton fought them off, satisfied to note that he eliminated a few of them before the inevitable. When it came, it didn't come from the slice of a knife, but from a broken chair leg meeting the back of his head, no doubt courtesy of Sergei Androvich himself who had yet to fight fairly.

Peyton had no idea where he was now or how much time had passed. His head ached, his surroundings were dark, and the stone floor he lay on was cold and uncomfortable. If he had to guess, he was in a secret room in the Russian embassy. According to international law, that meant he was on Russian territory. It would be the safest place the Russians could take him without being caught by the British. He hoped Tessa had the good sense to follow his instructions and not come looking for him.

Peyton did some mental arithmetic in his aching

head. If Tessa got away, she'd reach Crispin on the road within a day and then it would take a day for Crispin to get back. If he could manage to stay alive for two more days, there might be some hope.

The door to his cell opened. Peyton squinted against the light that followed the men in. There were three of them. Peyton pulled himself up into a sitting position, his body protesting at the effort. 'What is the meaning of this? I am a peer of the realm,' he began. There was nothing like a little righteous indignation to get things started, and it was a good reminder to these men as to whom they were dealing with.

One of the men laughed, fingering an ivory-handled blade. As his eyes adjusted to the light, Peyton recognised Sergei Androvich. It was the first time they'd encountered one another since the incident with poisoned champagne.

Androvich sneered. 'This is a most unlooked-for circumstance. You could have saved us all immense amounts of trouble if you'd have drunk the champagne.'

Peyton took immediate measure of the comment. Androvich was a cornered animal. It had been the Count's job to eliminate him and the Count had failed in front of his countrymen. It was clear to Peyton that Androvich now had a personal agenda above and beyond the need to retrieve the list.

'You can't believe you'll get away with this,' Peyton said. 'I'm not an anonymous serf who could disappear without anyone noticing.'

Sergei scoffed at the warning. 'You may be surprised, Dursley. You're nothing here. British influence stops at my doorstep as does your extraordinary amount of luck, I'm afraid.'

That confirmed it. He was definitely in the embassy. 'What do you want with me?'

'We want the list.' Another spoke. Probably Vasilov. 'Your life for the list.'

'I don't have a list. I've given it to Brimley. I haven't any idea what Brimley might have done with it, and, now that Brimley is dead, you don't either.' Peyton hoped he carried off his charade with confidence.

Androvich snarled. 'Your bluff is a poor one. We've got Brimley's list, as useless as it is.'

'Then you've got all that I've got. We're even,' Peyton replied evenly.

'The list has been a wild goose chase the whole time,' Ilanovich said. 'It was never as important as we were led to believe. The list itself was just a bluff to scare the Czar. We should let the Earl go and get home. Our time here has been wasted.'

Vasilov looked ready to agree. Peyton thought he would agree to anything that showed Androvich poorly. He remembered the dissension in the group the night he'd overheard them in the library.

'No!' Androvich said in a forceful tone. 'Don't you see, there's not one list, but two. Ralph Branscombe was no fool. The lists aren't that useful separately. They're only powerful together. He's not telling you everything.'

It was Vasilov's turn to sneer. 'You're spinning fictions out of whole cloth now, Androvich. You're a desperate man. There's no proof there's two lists. Where would the second one be?'

Androvich fixed Peyton with an arrogant stare, daring Peyton to gainsay him. 'The second list is with Tessa Branscombe or on the road to the Cotswolds. She's in bed with the Earl in more ways than one.' Sergei fingered his knife blade maliciously. 'Isn't she, Dursley?'

The words chilled Peyton. He prayed Tessa had burnt the list already. He prayed she was gone from the city. He prayed a thousand things in those first seconds. He tried to think of a subterfuge that Sergei would swallow, that would steer him away from Tessa, that would keep him from tracking down Crispin and the girls. Above all else, Peyton had to keep his family safe. He had only one thing to barter with: his life.

'You're wrong, Androvich. Tessa and the girls don't have the second list. I'm the one who found them both. I had hoped to sell the other list privately on my own.'

'Perhaps you'll consider selling it privately to us in exchange for your life,' Gromsky put in. 'We can be very reasonable.'

'I won't tell you where it is.'

'Because you don't have it, because this is another lie,' Sergei said, stepping closer to Peyton, the knife blade glinting in the shadowed light. Peyton steeled his will not to flinch at the sight of the blade so near his face.

'He's lying to protect Tessa,' Sergei spat.

'I told you he was in love with her,' Vasilov said smugly.

'It hardly matters if this is about love or money. Men have been known to be highly motivated by both.' Gromsky eyed Peyton intently with a cruel glare. 'Shall I call the men and let them get on with it? I find I'm quite curious to see what the Earl of Dursley will do for love or money, aren't you, Androvich?'

Moments later two burly men entered the room. Peyton braced himself. During his time in diplomatic service, he'd been trained for this, although he'd never had to endure it. This would not be pleasant. One of the men ripped his shirt from him, not allowing him the dignity of removing it himself. The other clapped his wrists in iron cuffs and shackled him face-first to the wall.

'Start with twenty lashes and we'll see what he has to say,' he heard Androvich order.

Peyton gathered himself mentally and physically. He had what he wanted. He reminded himself of all his reasons for this sacrifice. The people he loved were protected. The girls were safe. He'd bought Tessa time to get to Crispin. Crispin would come. At last the pain obliterated his thoughts to just one: Tessa loves me. And that thought sustained him.

Chapter Nineteen

Tessa checked the little heart-shaped timepiece she had pinned to her gown. Ten o'clock in the morning. It had seemed an eternity had passed. She'd sat up most of the night, planning, plotting and hoping that at any time Peyton would come home and make her plans unnecessary. She took a final look in the mirror and carefully assessed her appearance.

She'd dressed smartly for this interview in a walking ensemble that had a military cut to it. The dark blue jacket was tapered to her waist and trimmed with braid. Beneath the jacket, she wore a high-collared white linen blouse. The matching dark blue skirt was cut to allow full, comfortable movement, giving the potentially severe outfit a soft, feminine appeal, too. She'd had the maid put her hair up beneath a small jaunty hat to complete the look.

Tessa picked up her reticule. She looked like a

woman paying a social call. She hoped that was what Sergei would see—a friend coming to call. She was betting heavily on the image. She had no idea how much Sergei suspected she knew, or how involved she was in the search for the list. She hoped he suspected her of nothing. It would make the interview easier. Tessa took a final look in the mirror. She was ready to go.

One of the footmen boldly tried to persuade her not to leave the house at the last minute. But she speared him with a silencing look. 'You all have instructions. You're to assist Lord Crispin when he arrives,' she said in a very controlled voice. Then she threw back her shoulders and walked to the waiting carriage and got in. Today she didn't care if anyone was following her. Today, she was going to the Russian embassy, a destination that would surprise anyone assigned to tracking her movements.

The embassy itself was a large, gracious building near Kensington Palace Gardens. The sunshine and the placid beauty of the gardens in full bloom beneath a blue sky made it difficult to believe she was in any real danger. Tessa gave the coachman a brief nod and sent him on his way. She mounted the steps to the columned building. She drew a deep breath and knocked on the door. There was no turning back. Her game was in motion.

'I am here to see Count Androvich,' she said with a sweet smile, extending a calling card to the man who answered the door. He bowed politely and took her card in.

Tessa held her breath. Surely Sergei would not refuse to see her? She waited and rehearsed her story.

The man returned and motioned her inside. 'The Count will see you.'

'Thank you,' Tessa said in Russian, much to the pleasure of the footman who gave off the smug impression that he was tired of hearing the harsh English tongue.

She was shown into a bright sitting room done in yellows and blues. The embassy's interior was quite impressive, extensively decorated with wainscoting and woodwork. Its regal interior fitted Sergei to perfection. He looked quite at home when he entered the room, immaculately dressed, his looks turned out to their best advantage. For a moment, he reminded Tessa of the young man she'd once held an infatuation for. In this bright and sunny room, it was hard to remember the dark game she'd come to play. But perhaps the setting had been orchestrated for just such an effect.

'Tessa! This is a surprise indeed. What brings you here?' Sergei bent gallantly over her hand, a mix of courtly elegance and the intimate informality of a friend. 'I thought you were angry with me after the commotion at the art gallery. I regret I've not had the chance to apologise. I have missed you. This is a big city and I know so few people. What brings you here?' He was her gallant friend of old once more, acting the part to its maximum.

'I am worried about Lord Dursley. He did not return last night,' Tessa began.

'Ah, your erstwhile guardian,' Sergei said with a modicum of regret in his voice. 'Surely, Tessa, you can't expect him to wait on you constantly? I don't mean to be indelicate, but perhaps he's taking a short holiday at his mistress's? I've heard Dursley keeps them.' He waved a hand in an attempt to play Peyton's friend. 'All men do, my dear. It's a fact of life. Do not be alarmed. I am sure he'll be around in a day or two.'

What could she say to that? She knew Sergei was lying. Peyton didn't have a mistress. He'd been with *her*. But she could not call Sergei a liar and tell him otherwise without exposing too much. The realities of the peril she was in at that very moment became very clear to her. Sergei was a smooth pretender. He was lying to her now. People lied to cover things up.

Sergei leaned forward and Tessa fought the urge to cringe. She could hardly stand being in the same room with the snake—a snake she'd once admired. 'Tessa, I am sorry if Dursley has let you down in any way. Perhaps he has led you to believe a certain understanding existed between the two of you? I would not want to see you hurt. But I am gratified that you felt you could come to me.' He reached for her hand but Tessa deftly evaded him, standing up to walk to the window. Her back was to Sergei. She used the moment to open her reticule.

Sergei was still talking. 'Tessa, I confess I still harbour hopes that you will consider my proposal. We have been friends for a long time and I can think of no greater joy than making you my wife.'

She could feel Sergei walking up behind her. Tessa whirled on him, her gun hidden in the folds of her skirt. 'It's time to cut line, Sergei. You've never been my friend or my father's.'

Her anger halted him, his arms spread at his side in supplication. 'Whatever can you mean, Tessa? Has Dursley confused you with his nonsense and jealousy?'

'You did not come to London to woo me. You came because you believed I was in possession of a certain list. You have schemed to have me followed, to have my house broken into and destroyed. In St Petersburg, you stayed close to me to spy on me. I came to you today because I think you've taken Peyton. You've already failed to do away with him twice. He's a menace to you and getting at the list.'

'Tessa, I am wounded by your accusations.' Sergei put a hand over his heart. 'If there have been attacks on Dursley, it is only because of the kind of man that he is.' Sergei gestured to the chair she'd vacated. 'If you would sit down and listen to me, I will tell you about the man Peyton Ramsden really is and then you can decide.'

Tessa eyed Sergei warily and took her seat. A tea

tray appeared on cue. Sergei smiled at her reluctance to accept any food. 'Suit yourself, my dear.' Sergei poured himself a cup. 'Now, as for Ramsden, he's not as perfect as he makes himself out to be. He works occasionally for the Foreign Office. In the 1820s, he spent time in Vienna, not all of it savoury. He's got a quiet reputation for knife work when the occasion arises. But then, we're not all saints. Perhaps we could forgive him for that.' Sergei paused.

'He met my father in Vienna. It's where they were first acquainted,' Tessa said with a touch of steel in her voice. She was not going to let Sergei think she knew nothing of Peyton's past.

Sergei gave a harsh laugh. 'No doubt that's the smallest lie he's told you. Did he actually say he'd *met* your father? He had *encountered* your father on maybe three occasions in Vienna at large state events. The most they'd ever exchanged were polite greetings.'

'My father appointed him as guardian, so surely you're mistaken about the depth of their association,' Tessa rebutted. But doubt was growing inside her. She had not thought of it at the time, but when she'd been looking through her father's papers, there'd been no mention of Peyton, not even as a social acquaintance.

Sergei held up a finger. 'My dear, wait here. I have something to show you.'

He returned in a few minutes and passed her a folder. 'I am not asking you to believe me. Believe the paperwork.' He spoke while Tessa read. She could feel her face paling. This couldn't be true. There had to be a trick. Peyton had been sent to find the list?

'The codicil to your father's will is a forgery, put together by British intelligence in order to place Ramsden into the centre of your lives. The hope being, of course, was that it would allow him access to the list. There is no real guardian, Tess. Your father made no provisions for you beyond the Bloomsbury house and the small dowries.'

'Are you telling me Peyton is a spy?' Tessa's mind reeled with the implications. If Sergei's claim was true, it would reshape the foundations of her relationship with Peyton. How much of their association was a lie? Was the passion a fraud, too? He'd seemed so honest, so upright with his concerns about propriety and her reputation. How could she have misjudged him? What was it Eva had said? It was the perfect ones who had the most to hide.

'Ah, Tess—"Peyton"?' Sergei clicked his tongue in a disappointing sound, picking up on her use of his first name. 'He has trifled with you after all. The man has no morals, insinuating himself into the lives of four girls, using his position and his looks to make promises he doesn't intend to keep.' Sergei shook his head. 'I will call him out for you, Tess. It would give me great pleasure to put a bullet through his black heart, or a sword if you'd prefer. You have only to say the word.'

Tessa's head swam. She put the folder down on the table next to the tea service. She had to be careful and not jump to hasty conclusions. Peyton had *lied*. No, that wasn't fair. He simply hadn't told her the entire truth. Were omissions lies? Why was she suddenly trying to redeem him in her mind? His place in their lives was a fictitious one. She no more knew the man she loved than she knew the truth about Sergei. If Peyton had lied about who he was, who was to say he hadn't also lied about Sergei? How was she to know who was her ally and who was not? Was Sergei the one she should have trusted all along?

Sergei spoke softly. 'That day at the Academy, I was only trying to protect you. I was trying to keep you away from Dursley, but he would not be shaken. I feared you'd be hurt accidentally in all the commotion.'

Tessa stood up. The interview had not gone the way she'd planned. She'd come to fight for Peyton. She'd come to rescue him and she'd ended up betraying herself instead. She'd expected an antagonistic Sergei. She'd been prepared to shoot him if needed. Instead, Sergei had been handsome, apologetic, reconciliatory even. And he'd shared information with her that had changed her plans entirely. 'Thank you, Sergei. I need to go home and think about all this. It comes as a great shock.'

'Are you going back to his aunt's house?' Sergei inquired in gentle tones.

Tessa shook her head. 'No. I think my time there is best ended. I'll go back to the Bloomsbury house. It will do.'

'I hope you don't think I had anything to do with that break-in.'

'I don't know what to think any more, Sergei,' Tessa said non-committally. She was starting to think it hardly mattered. Peyton had betrayed her and she was fast discovering how debilitating a broken heart could be.

They reached the front door of the embassy. Somewhere in the depths of the big building a dog whined. It caught Tessa's attention. 'Sounds like you have a stray dog,' she commented.

'Oh, I've discovered London is full of strays. There's always a bevy of them at the back door, waiting for kitchen scraps,' Sergei said lightly.

The dog yelped again. It was an odd yelp, rather human sounding. Tessa remembered something and shot Sergei a sideways glance. He'd kicked a dog once in her presence. His instinctive brutality had shocked her at the time. 'We had plenty of strays in St Petersburg, too. I don't recall you being so keen on kitchen scraps then.'

Sergei merely shrugged and held the door open for her. 'Thank you for coming, Tessa. I wish I had better news for you. I can see it's something of a blow.'

'I'll manage,' Tessa said, some of her calm and focus returning to her. Something wasn't right. Both Sergei and Peyton had lied to her. Sergei had lied to her that very day and then followed his lies with what Tessa supposed to be at least some truth about Peyton. But she was too intelligent to believe it was the entire truth about Peyton. The man who had made such exquisite love to her, who had worried so thoroughly for her sisters' safety, who had taken his duty to his country so seriously, could not be as corrupted as Sergei made him out to be.

The dog yelped again. Tessa cringed. 'Would you like me to take the mongrel home? I could do with some company in Bloomsbury.'

Sergei favoured her with a smile. 'I think I'll keep this one. Thank you all the same, my dear.'

Tessa started down the steps, preparing to hail a cab for the trip home. For the coachman's safety, she'd instructed him not to come back. If anything had happened to her, the Russians wouldn't allow the coachman to leave.

Sergei called to her, 'Tessa, there's one more thing I should tell you. I thought it best not to, I didn't want to hurt you more than necessary.'

There was concern etched on his face as Tessa retraced her steps. 'Bad news isn't like wine, Sergei. It doesn't get better with age.'

'Your Peyton was here. Yesterday evening. He said he had a list and that he wanted to sell it privately. Frankly, the list wasn't very impressive. I suspect there's another list somewhere that is much more valuable to Russia. I thought you should know, in case you run across anything in your father's papers. I don't know how Dursley found it. I am guessing he found it in the break-in and took it.'

The dog yelped again. Tessa studied Sergei. Her instincts were overriding her mental coolness. Sergei was an excellent liar with his cunning ability to create verisimilitude. But he'd told one lie too many. Peyton had been with her the night of the break-in, waltzing her about the floor, and he was not a man who sent others to do his job. Intuition warred with logic. Intuition won. Sergei was hiding something, wanting to build distrust and hatred. Why? It came to her in a flash: so that she'd turn away from Peyton. She'd not been wrong to come. Peyton was here.

She met Sergei on the top step and pushed him back to the wall. 'That's no dog you've got hidden away, Sergei. Peyton's here. If you value your life, you'll bring him up to me post-haste.'

Sergei's veneer of friendship vanished. His face was cold. 'That's a big threat without anything to back it up, Tessa. You're as poor a bluffer as he is. You forget yourself. Right now you're standing in my country. This is my house.'

'This is my gun.' Tessa pulled the weapon from the folds of her skirts and aimed it at Count Sergei Androvich point blank.

Chapter Twenty

Sergei was at heart a coward, self-preservation being his primary objective in all situations. His capitulation was quick and sure. 'I will take you to him—just put the gun away.'

'No. You weren't listening.' Tessa's hand on the gun never wavered. 'You send for him. I am going nowhere with you. I am not fool enough to let you lead me down into the secret bowels of this place. Let us step inside this door into the hall, you first. You send a footman for Peyton. He comes up alone with the footman only or you die the moment I see any other faces coming to your aid. Who cares if I am eventually overpowered—you're already dead,' she reminded him coldly, quelling any small tendency he might have to play the martyr. 'Do you understand? Are you ready to go inside?'

Sergei nodded, his fear palpable. Tessa prodded

him inside ahead of her, keeping the gun firmly in his back. Tessa hailed the first footman who crossed the hall. 'Tell him what you need, Sergei.'

Sergei did and Tessa added her own instructions in Russian, adding that he had only three minutes to get there and return with the prisoner before she fired on Sergei. The man's eyes widened, but he scampered off to do what he was told.

Tessa wasn't naïve enough to think she'd simply have her demands met and she could walk out with Peyton in tow. So far so good, but she had yet to see Peyton and she knew the Russians would not play fair. In spite of her instructions, they'd attempt to follow Peyton and the footman up. She wasn't convinced they were as enchanted with Sergei's life as he was. They might consider him expendable if it meant keeping Peyton.

Tessa checked her small timepiece. 'Two and a half minutes have elapsed. Is your footman fast? Do you think he cares enough about you to follow orders? Perhaps he's down there right now deciding you're expendable.' She had to keep Sergei on edge, frightened if possible. If she showed any weakness, any reticence to play her part, the ruse was up.

The banging on the door reverberated through Peyton's head with an intensity that caused him to cry out in spite of his intentions not to. He'd been doing a great deal of that lately in his struggle to cling to consciousness. The two big brutes were still in the chamber with him. If he recollected correctly, Gromsky and Vasilov were there, too, drinking tea and issuing instructions while the other two beat him to a bloody pulp. The brutes were resting for the time being, for which Peyton was thankful. His back was on fire from the lashing and the rest of him was chilled from the cold water thrown in his face to keep him awake.

He'd had too much time to take the measure of his captors. Vasilov had proven to be arrogant and quarrelsome. Sergei Androvich had proven to be much the same. It was Gromsky Peyton worried about most. He was the cool-headed one of the lot. There was a cruel streak that ran deep in him, as if he knew exactly how to break a man.

The door opened and Gromsky spoke in Russian to whoever had entered. Peyton couldn't see. Out of deference for his back, he was lying on his stomach. The exchange was short and rapid. The newcomer seemed agitated. Gromsky and Vasilov spoke briefly to one another. Without warning, Peyton felt himself being hoisted to his feet. He wasn't so far gone he couldn't rise on his own and, out of stubbornness, he resisted the assistance, awkwardly getting to his feet with his manacled hands.

'It seems someone is demanding to see you above stairs, Dursley. They promise to shoot Count Androvich if we don't produce you immediately,' Gromsky said, shoving him towards the agitated footman. 'Up you go, although Vasilov and I think it might be rather entertaining to see Androvich get shot. He's not exactly been an exemplary travelling companion.'

Peyton felt woozy from all the sudden movement. He steadied himself against the door jamb, trying to take it all in. Crispin must be here by some miracle. Peyton marshalled his strength. Crispin would need him to be alert and to aid in the fight to come. There were the five Russians, the two brutes and the three ambassadors. Who knew how many servants would come to anyone's aid? If he and Crispin acted fast enough, they might stand a chance. Peyton shivered involuntarily.

Gromsky gave an evil grin. 'Cold? When you get back we'll have a nice fire going that will warm you right up. Whoever is up there has asked that you come alone or they'll shoot Androvich anyway. But Vasilov and I will take our chances with Androvich's life. We'll follow you up shortly to help you back down.'

'We have to go, the clock is running,' the footman said nervously, tugging at Peyton.

Living or dying would happen upstairs, Peyton decided, dragging himself up the long flight of stone steps. He was not going back to that room and whatever fire torture Gromsky was arranging. He had complete faith in Crispin and in his own remaining strength, meagre as it was.

But it wasn't Crispin he saw when he crested the stairs. It was Tessa who held Sergei Androvich at gunpoint. The footman was obviously scared of her and Androvich looked as if he fully believed she'd shoot him without provocation. That was all well and good, but Peyton felt panic rise in his throat. How was he going to protect her in the condition he was in? What would happen when Vasilov and Gromsky came up the stairs and saw that it was her? Oh, God, he couldn't let Gromsky get his hands on Tessa. The foolish woman should have been halfway to the Cotswolds by now.

Peyton saw a glimmer of horror cross her face as she took in his appearance. He was aware how awful he must look, bloodied, bruised, shirtless, dirty from lying on the floor, his hands chained and she couldn't even see his back. *Don't give in to any emotion*, he silently willed her.

'I want to see him close up. Walk him over here to me,' Tessa commanded in her excellent Russian.

Peyton snarled as he neared Androvich. Given the opportunity, he'd not hesitate to wrap the chain of his manacles around the Count's neck. Androvich paled.

'Are you all right, Peyton?' Tessa asked.

'We have to get out of here now. The others won't wait below,' Peyton said in low, hoarse tones, his throat dry.

Tessa had neatly manoeuvred them both close to the front door and Peyton didn't want to lose that advantage. This would be their best chance. Hoping that Tessa would manage Androvich, Peyton turned on the footman with an elbow to the gut that bent him over double, giving Peyton a chance to get the length of chain from his manacles around the footman's neck. The man was tall and he struggled, but Peyton's will was stronger. The man collapsed at Peyton's feet.

'Good lord, you've killed him,' Androvich breathed in disbelief, too frightened at the speed at which it had all happened to do much of anything. 'Gromsky! Vasilov! Help me.'

His foolish cry was all the warning Peyton needed to know the other two had come up the stairs. 'Tessa, run,' Peyton said, bracing himself for a fight.

'They'll just come after us,' Tessa said firmly. 'We can't outrun them in the street.'

'Still, I think we should try,' Peyton advised. In his fear, Androvich made a stupid, sudden move and Tessa was ready for him, bringing the pistol butt down on his head. Androvich slumped to the ground.

'Good girl, we'll need that shot,' Peyton murmured. 'Shoot Gromsky if you have the choice.'

They backed to the door. It was clear now that Gromsky and Vasilov had weapons, guns of their own. They had not come unarmed. 'Put the gun down, Miss Branscombe,' Vasilov urged. 'We wouldn't want anyone being hurt accidentally.'

Peyton wondered what the odds were that they'd actually kill the two of them. There would be no chance of finding the list. Gromsky would lose the chance to torture him if he was dead.

Gromsky and Vasilov edged closer to them. Even if they made the door just two feet behind them, Peyton feared they'd be shot before they reached the street. Peyton wished he had his knife in his boot, but he'd lost the blade back at Brimley's office. He wished he'd taken the gun from Tessa. She had to shoot and he hated thinking that his Tessa had been placed in the position of doing murder, even if it was for a good cause.

Tessa pointed the gun evenly at Gromsky. 'It will be you that goes first,' she said in quite convincing tones.

'And you will go right afterwards,' he retorted.

'Maybe. But what does it matter? You'll be dead. That's all you have to think about.'

Goodness, his Tessa sounded like a professional, Peyton thought with admiration. Suddenly glass shattered to their right. Nervous, Vasilov fired in the direction of the sound. Tessa fired at Gromsky, hitting him in the knee. The man went down, his gun sliding away from him.

'Run!' Peyton flung open the door and pushed Tessa ahead of him, using his body as a shield in case Vasilov came after them.

They pounded down the embassy steps, Peyton stumbling as his strength ebbed. He could hear commotion behind them. Vasilov must be on the move. He heard a shot ring out and waited for the impact. But none came. Peyton turned back and saw Crispin standing over Vasilov's form.

'Where the hell did you come from?'

Crispin gave a cocky grin. 'I heard you were going to need a ride.' He loped up to them and gave a loud whistle.

Within moments, Lily's coach rounded the corner.

Tessa stared up at the coachman. 'I told you not to wait. Doesn't anyone listen to instructions around here?'

The coachman exchanged a glance with Crispin and made a quick nod. 'Just aping my betters, ma'am, just aping my betters.'

Peyton would have laughed at the sight of Tessa getting some of her own impudence back, but he hadn't the strength. 'Crispin…' he managed to choke out and then he was falling. He felt Crispin's arms take his weight, vaguely aware of Crispin and Tessa manoeuvring him inside the coach. He heard Tessa cry out at the sight of his back. 'Crispin, what have they done to him?'

Crispin was murmuring comfort words to Tessa. 'He'll be all right. I know what to do.'

Peyton was shivering again. He tried to cling to consciousness, but this time he couldn't win. The last thing he remembered was Tessa scolding him. 'Don't you leave me now, Peyton Ramsden, you've got some explaining to do.'

Laughter woke him along with the sound of feet running past his door, followed by an ineffectual 'hush'. Sunlight bathed his face. For a moment, Peyton wasn't sure where he was. A baby cried from somewhere in the house and then he knew. Miraculously, he was at Dursley Park in the master's chamber, his chamber. He stretched and groaned. Lucifer's balls, he was sore. His mind felt refreshed, as if he'd slept for ages. But his body did not match the vigour in his brain.

Peyton managed to get himself into an upright position, no mean feat considering he'd been sleeping on his stomach. He took a quick survey of himself. His torso was heavily bandaged and when he looked beneath the covers, he saw that he wore a pair of Paine's loose silk pants from India. Peyton ran a hand across his chin, feeling the stubble. He concluded there was at least four days' worth of beard there. He would have to shave immediately. He pushed a hand through his hair. And bathe.

He glanced around the room. It felt good to be here, but there was certainly a story to tell about how he'd arrived. He remembered none of it. His eyes lit on the chair in the big bay of windows and Peyton smiled. He knew who could tell him, when she woke up.

Tessa slept in the chair, oblivious to the sun on her face. Her head was nestled against one wing of the chair and her hair fell loose over the edge. She looked exquisitely beautiful as she slept. One would never imagine such a delicate beauty had stormed the Russian embassy—an army of one with a gun, all for him.

Peyton pushed himself out of bed and slowly walked towards her, cursing his stiff muscles at every step. He'd be damned if he would play the invalid. It simply wasn't in him. He could be sore in bed as well as out of it.

He hadn't meant to wake her. He'd merely wanted to watch her sleep. But she stirred, perhaps sensing his presence or the shadow his figure cast through the sunbeams. She opened her eyes and screamed in startled surprise.

'Shh, Tessa. It's just me,' Peyton said swiftly. He didn't want a room full of visitors just yet. Right now, he just wanted her. Peyton could feel his member rising at the sight of her lovely eyes. Wonderful, now the only part of his body not stiff was getting in on the act, too.

'What are you doing out of bed?'

'I'm sore, Tessa, not ill,' Peyton said. 'I wanted to see you.'

'I must look a sight,' Tessa said self-consciously, sliding a hand through her hair.

'You look lovely to me,' Peyton said, reaching for her hand to still it. 'You brought us here?'

'We couldn't stay in London. Gromsky was only wounded, not dead. I didn't feel safe in town. Crispin and I thought it was best to get you home, even if it meant three days on the road.' Tessa was up and moving. 'No more questions until you're sitting down.' She urged him back to the bed and Peyton let her. His little sojourn across the room had taken un-expected amounts of energy.

'And my prognosis?' Peyton asked once she had him settled to her satisfaction.

'You'll live. Crispin assures me you were never in danger of doing otherwise, but I had my concerns.' Tessa looked down at the bedspread, suddenly intrigued by its textures. 'I had no idea how badly hurt you were when they brought you upstairs. I have no idea how you managed to fight beside me and get us out of the embassy.'

'There was no other choice, Tessa. When I came up those stairs, I'd already decided I wasn't going back down them. I was expecting Crispin. Then I saw you and I was scared out of my wits at the thought of Gromsky getting to you.' Peyton gave a short laugh. 'It seems irrational now, but at the time all I could think of was how was I going to protect you when I could hardly walk myself.'

'I don't need protection all the time, Peyton. I can take care of myself, you know.'

'I know.' Peyton reached for her hand and laced his fingers between hers. 'Still, when a man loves a woman the way I love you, Tess, it's hard to remember that.' He'd never told a woman he'd loved her before. He didn't expect Tessa to realise the import of his statement. But that was all right. He knew. 'I want to make love with you, Tess. I'm sure we can manage something if we're careful.'

Tessa's reaction wasn't the one he expected. She unlaced her hand and stood up, moving away from the bed. 'No. We can't pretend everything has been restored to normal. I have questions that need answers first. Starting with—why did you lie about being our guardian?'

The peace Peyton had felt vanished. Two thoughts hit him simultaneously: oh, hell, she knew, and, secondly, after all they'd been through, he could still lose her.

Chapter Twenty-One

It seemed he was making a habit of having awkward discussions in bed. First Lydia, and now this. Peyton much preferred to have this discussion in the estate office, behind his big desk, dressed in appropriate clothing.

'Why don't you tell me what you know?' Peyton began carefully. 'Did Count Androvich tell you that?'

'Androvich might be a consummate liar, but that doesn't mean everything he says is untrue,' Tessa countered. 'He says the codicil to the will is a forgery, compiled simply to give you access to our lives.' She fixed him with a sharp stare. 'You were sent to spy on us and you knew it.'

'I was sent to determine if there was a list.'

'You were sent to *get* the list,' Tessa inserted. 'By any means possible, too. Did you think pretty dresses, parties and trips to the zoo would be enough?

You've spent the last month maligning Count Androvich, but you're hardly any different.'

'I never plotted to have you harmed. I did not destroy your home or cause you to live in daily terror of being followed.' Peyton rose to the fight. 'I would say that makes me quite different.'

'You misled me and my sisters. You lied. You were never our guardian.'

'Not legally,' Peyton challenged, knowing Tessa would read between the lines. He'd been their guardian in all but name. He'd protected them. He'd whisked them to the safety of Aunt Lily's when needed. He'd taken them under his tutelage, given her a Season, a chance to make a good match and secure their futures.

'You had secret motives. Why didn't you just tell me?' Tessa retorted.

'Probably for the same reasons you didn't tell me.'

'I had no reason to trust you. I didn't know you and you were so arrogant, sending your servants to my house and re-ordering my life when I had it all under control,' Tessa argued.

'I had no reason to trust you, either, Tessa. You were stubborn and contrary from day one. You fought me over every little thing even when I was being nice. I had not planned to stay in the city very long, just long enough to answer Brimley's summons and break things off with my mistress, if you want to know the truth.'

'Is that why you kissed me at the Broughtons' ball? Because you were getting nowhere in your mission?'

Peyton's jaw worked. If the situation wasn't so dire, he'd politely remind her she had been the one to kiss him first. But this was not the time for humour. He knew what she meant. He'd been the one to prolong the kiss and turn the interaction into something more than what it had been intended to be.

He saw his actions through her eyes and was not pleased with the kind of man that image painted. 'No, Tessa. I never used our passion to manipulate you. I kissed you because I couldn't stand the thought of you kissing Androvich and not me. I wanted you and that complicated my life greatly. I still want you, Tess. But I find I'm a man of pride and I've already been rejected twice.'

Tessa swallowed. 'Then I must advise you not to ask me yet.'

That set off warning bells. What hadn't he done? What else had that blasted Androvich told her that was causing such doubt? Couldn't she see they belonged together?

The door to the bedroom burst open and they were immediately swarmed with family members. Peyton had always thought his chambers rather large, but filled with three girls, two brothers, a baby and sundry relatives, he was starting to reconsider 'large'.

'So much for my privacy,' Peyton joked as they all

pummelled him with questions. 'I'm better, really, I am quite well.' He held up his hands in mock surrender.

Tessa shot him a final look and took a cold form of mercy on him. 'Come on, girls, we have lessons and I think I promised you a treat this afternoon.'

'I'll help.' Julia and Tessa gathered the girls and ushered them from the room. Others took their cues and left Paine and Crispin to play the valets.

Tessa managed to avoid being alone with him for the next two days. It wasn't that hard to manoeuvre. They were constantly surrounded by large groups of people whenever they were together and the others made demands on their time. Not that Peyton begrudged anyone a moment of that time.

Summer was upon them and Dursley Park was showing to best advantage. It was a time for brothers and sisters. As his stamina returned, Peyton strolled the vast gardens of his home, catching sight occasionally of Tessa with her sisters, weaving daisy wreaths beneath the big trees of the parkland, or reading aloud from a book; sometimes he saw her with her head close to Petra's, talking quietly. He wondered if he was the source of their conversation.

He didn't stroll alone. These days, Paine or more often Crispin was with him. Paine was content at Dursley Park, content in his life as a father and husband. When they walked, Paine talked of his plans to return to London and his business ventures in the autumn.

But Crispin was unsettled. Peyton could palpably feel his brother's unrest as they walked. 'You never did tell me how it was that you came to be at the embassy that day,' Peyton asked casually as they strolled one afternoon.

'Tessa had sent Arthur out to find me immediately the evening you didn't return. The rest was luck. I didn't feel right leaving you in London and I had already started back. I was on the main road. It wasn't hard to meet up with Arthur. When I got to town, the coachman told me he'd dropped Tessa at the embassy that morning.'

'I owe you our lives, Crispin. I doubt Vasilov would have missed,' Peyton said, wondering if it was the shooting that weighed heavily on Crispin.

'I was glad to do it. You needn't feel as if you've forced me into taking first blood or any of that noble nonsense you're bound to think. I've killed before.'

'War is different, Crispin—'

'I'm not looking for absolution,' Crispin cut him off sharply.

'Then what's eating at you? We're all so happy here, but you're not.'

'I'll be going soon.'

It was so like Crispin to not say more than that. Peyton would have to drag every last ounce of information out of him. 'Where?'

'I don't know. Somewhere. Anywhere but here. Paine's got Julia and his son now. You'll be settling down with Tessa and all her sisters.' Crispin rolled his eyes at the thought of the Branscombe sisters taking up residence at Dursley Park.

'Well, Tessa has not accepted me yet,' Peyton said lightly.

'Cut up at you over the guardian fraud?'

'We knew it was coming. You warned me.' Peyton shrugged.

'Still, I'll be in the way. I'm not meant for such domesticity.'

'You could go to Farrier Hill. You could go to any of the estates you wanted. You could breed horses,' Peyton offered. 'And you're wrong about the domesticity, Cris. You just haven't found the right woman.'

'I'm a hard man to live with, Peyton. You of all people should know that, after living with me for thirty-five years.' Crispin laughed, his gaze going out to the fountain where Tessa and her sisters sat enjoying the warm weather.

Peyton divined his brother's thoughts. 'Is that another reason you're leaving?' He nodded in the direction of Petra Branscombe.

'She's too young for me,' was all Crispin would offer on the subject. 'I'm not nearly refined enough for her. What's your excuse? Surely you're refined enough for Tessa, intelligent enough, wealthy enough?'

Peyton studied the tableau at the fountain and shook his head. 'I wish I knew.'

'Why do you hesitate, Tess?' Petra asked as Eva and Annie drifted off to gather flowers. 'He's done nothing but follow you with his eyes all week. You cannot doubt his affections for you are real.'

Tessa scoffed at the statement. 'Real is something of a sticking point between us. I don't know what is real any more.'

Petra sighed and trailed her hand in the fountain basin. 'Are you still upset about the forged codicil? If it hadn't been for that, you never would have met him. Surely that's worth some forgiveness.' They had been discussing Peyton's perfidy all week, arguing the merits of the lies against the truths. Tessa was no closer to any answers.

'That's just it. I never would have met him. Girls like me aren't supposed to meet earls. The Earl of Dursley should marry someone of consequence.'

'You are someone of consequence, Tess. How could you believe otherwise? You speak three languages, you've given parties for diplomats from all over the world. You've run large households before. You'll be a perfect Countess.'

Tessa smiled wryly at her sister's assessment. 'You forget a few things. I have no title, no titled connections, and I come with the attendant scandal of being Ralph Branscombe's daughter.' The gossip had been bad enough before with the little criticisms of her behaviour. Now, she was at the heart of the Russian issue circulating through society.

Thanks to Sergei's petty-minded idea of revenge, she was being forced to wait and see how the rumours would affect her, and how they would affect Peyton. Tessa hesitated for Peyton's sake. In the absence of Dursley's power in town, Sergei and Gromsky had had free rein to do what they pleased. The scandal could be of monumental proportions.

Tessa could imagine how Sergei might construct his lies around the truth to shield the Russians from blame. Ralph Branscombe had concocted a list in the hopes of selling it to the highest bidder in hopes of fomenting rebellion in Russia. Put that way, her father's actions reeked of privateerism, not patriotism. She didn't want Peyton tied to such a scandal by marriage. He was too honourable a man. It would be the height of irony to see him brought low by such a scandal.

In her heart, she'd forgiven him for the initial deception. She might not have liked being the recipient, but she could understand the reasons for it and she respected his motives. Regardless of his deception, he'd never misrepresented his true character in their association. Inside his assumed role, he'd behaved with honour and treated her with respect and courtesy, even if that couldn't have been easy at times.

'You should let Dursley be the judge of that, Tess.

It's not fair for you to decide that the scandal super-sedes his happiness,' Petra said.

'Then I'll wait and let him see what becomes of the issue. I wouldn't want him to decide too precipitately.'

Petra stood up and brushed her skirts. 'Sometimes you're too stubborn for your own good, Tess.'

Tessa's resistance was driving Peyton mad. After two weeks of polite meetings and family dinners, he had to do something. He needed an activity to take his mind off waiting for Tessa. He appreciated she needed time. He appreciated how her stubborn nature must be working through everything. But in the meanwhile, he lived with the mental torture of having her near and not being able to touch her. During the day he fantasised about catching her in an empty room, taking her up against a wall and kissing her senseless. At night, his fantasies took a far more erotic track. Day or night, the result was the same. He spent hours in a frustrating state of unrelieved arousal. He would settle for a fight if that was all he could have. Just anything but this polite aloofness she favoured him with.

He was drinking port with Crispin when a perfect outlet for his frustration offered itself. 'Did you see the post today?' Crispin asked casually.

'Only briefly.' He had been finding it hard to con-centrate on anything for long except Tessa.

'Count Androvich has been spreading unsavoury

rumours around the *ton* about the Branscombes. He's been suggesting that Tessa's father also possessed a list of Russian revolutionaries he intended to sell. The way Androvich tells it, Branscombe is a double-dealing bastard of the lowest order.'

Peyton fingered the stem of his glass. He didn't need Crispin to spell out the consequences. The deceased Ralph Branscombe didn't care what anyone did or said about his reputation, but the rumours could ruin Tessa and her sisters. Who would want to marry into a family tainted by a scandal of such a dis-honourable nature? If he did not go up to London per-sonally and put paid to those rumours, Sergei Androvich would have some modicum of revenge against Tessa. He probably hoped it would be enough to drive her from society's good graces.

Peyton stretched, testing his back. He would bear the scars from that horrible night the rest of his life. He'd be damned if Tessa would, too, although her scars would be of a different nature. He looked mean-ingfully at Crispin. 'It's time for retribution. How do you feel about a trip up to town?'

Tessa cursed her own stubborn pride for the hun-dredth time. She'd waited too long. She'd hesitated and Peyton was gone. She'd let him dangle without a word from her for two weeks and then he'd simply left. She'd woken up one morning to the news he had gone to London. When she'd asked how long he'd be gone, Julia had softly said, 'He didn't say.' That meant indefinitely. When she asked what he'd gone to town for, Julia and Paine had looked at each other and said again, 'He didn't say.'

But they knew. Tessa could sense it. He'd gone to town and she wasn't supposed to know why. She could imagine a myriad of things. Some of them were harmless explanations—he had business in Parliament. Other explanations were less so—he was bored in the country, he was picking out a new mistress, he was tired of waiting for her to decide. He'd said himself that he wouldn't ask a third time unless he was sure of her response. She'd done nothing to encourage that third time.

The irony was that she wanted to say yes. She'd decided that life without Peyton was not worth contemplating. If he was willing to live down the scandal, she would, too. Nothing mattered more than being together. In hindsight, she recognised she'd known that for a while now. She'd known it since the day she'd gone to the embassy and fought for Peyton in spite of Sergei's revelations. The revelations were a mixture of truths and lies, designed to drive her away from Peyton and into Sergei's confidence. But her heart had known a deeper truth that could not be thwarted that day, and Sergei's ploy had failed.

Tessa approached the big Dursley house, signalling the end of her afternoon walk. She screened her eyes against the sun, searching for a sign as she did every day, that Peyton had returned. It had been three weeks, and she needed him, wanted him.

There was no sign. She hadn't expected there to be. She told herself she couldn't realistically expect him back until after Parliament rose. She couldn't expect him for two more weeks at best. Perhaps she could write to him. Her pride was not greater than her need these days or her desire.

Tessa entered the wide hall. The big house was quiet. Her sisters were out with Lily. Tessa started up the stairs to her own room, surprised to meet Julia coming down the hallway. Julia usually rested this time of day while the baby slept.

'He's back,' Julia whispered in hushed tones. 'He's in the nursery.' She motioned to the stairs leading to the third floor.

Tessa shot her a look of gratitude. She didn't have to ask who Julia meant. She had not said much to Julia about her situation with Peyton, but the other woman seemed to divine much of her feelings.

Tessa hurried up the steps to the nursery, her heart in her throat. She had so much to tell him. At the nursery door all the thoughts, all the conversations she'd held with him in her head over the weeks, fled. The sight before her brought tears to her eyes in its simplicity and beauty. Of all the facets of Peyton Ramsden she'd seen, she'd yet to see this one.

Peyton stood at the nursery window dressed only

in his shirtsleeves, Julia's baby cradled confidently in his arms while he crooned a soft lullaby. The baby fussed a bit and he readjusted the little bundle, holding the baby up to the window. He began a recitation of all the things to be seen out of the window. 'There's the rose garden. There's the fountain. You'll like splashing in it when you're older. Maybe next summer, your mama will let you dangle your toes in it…'

She shouldn't be surprised. Peyton had been quite good with Annie. But a ten-year-old was different from an infant. He was going on about pony rides now and Tessa wiped quickly at her tears.

He turned from the window and caught her at it. 'Tessa?'

'Julia told me you were home. That you have news?' she said, ignoring the fact that he'd caught her at her tears. She'd forgotten how handsome he was. How had she managed to do that? There was something intoxicating about Peyton in a simple shirt and tight breeches.

'Yes, I do. It came to my attention that there were certain loose ends with the Russian issue that needed to be dealt with. I am happy to report that Count Androvich and Gromsky have been escorted off British soil with strict commands never to return. A letter regarding their conduct, which outlines their attempts to coerce a peer of the realm and terrorise an upstanding young lady, has been sent to the Czar. The Czar may have commissioned them. He may even have given them permission to act as they saw fit, but he cannot publicly ignore an outraged letter from a fellow monarch. Suffice it to say, they will not trouble us again.'

'And the rest of London society?' Tessa queried.

'Scandalised that the Count could behave in such a fashion,' Peyton affirmed. 'Your father's reputation and yours remain intact.'

Recognition dawned for Tessa. 'That is what you've spent three weeks doing? Fighting my dragons?'

'Our dragons,' Peyton corrected. The baby had dozed off and he moved to put him in the crib. 'It occurred to me that perhaps you feared the scandal, that it might be the reason you held yourself apart from me these last weeks. Has it, Tessa?' He wagged a finger at her. 'You should have told me. These last weeks have been torture, not knowing, always wanting you.'

'I know.' Tessa said simply. 'I had all these things I wanted to say to you, but now that you're here, all I want to do is kiss you.'

Peyton reached for her and pulled her close. 'That's all right with me.'

She sank into his embrace, her mouth easily finding his. She drank in all of him, the feel of his body hard against hers, the smell of his shirt, starch mixed with the sweet grassy smell of a man who'd ridden in the summer air.

The baby fussed in his cradle. Peyton broke the

kiss and went to tuck a blanket around it more securely. The child settled immediately with a coo.

'You're awfully good at that,' Tessa whispered, coming to stand behind him at the cradle. 'You'll make a wonderful father.'

Peyton turned slowly. 'Do I have reason to hope that will come to pass?'

Tessa took a steadying breath, unnerved by the devotion she saw in his eyes. Was ever a woman loved as much as she? In her stubbornness she had almost thrown this away. 'Yes.'

Peyton grinned. 'Then I guess the special licence I procured in London won't go to waste.'

'No, it won't, neither will a single minute of the rest of our lives.'

Dinner that night was a celebration both of Peyton's return and the announcement of their marriage. Afterwards, in Peyton's chamber was a celebration of a more private nature.

'I can see the babe already,' Peyton whispered huskily, kneeling before her chair as he undressed her, his hands rolling down her stockings.

'How?' Tessa said, knowing full well at six weeks her stomach was as flat as it had ever been.

Peyton's hands moved to her thin chemise and pushed it up over her breasts. He palmed them gently. 'Here. I can see it here in their fullness.' He leaned forward and stole a soft kiss. 'The prospect of my child suckling at the breast of the woman I love quite unmans me.' He slid his hand up the side of one breast.

Tessa gasped. She'd forgotten it was there.

'What is this?' Peyton asked, drawing back his hand. 'You carry paper in your chemise?' He unfolded the paper, his brows knitted together.

'I couldn't burn it until I knew you were safe,' Tessa said quickly.

'You had this with you at the embassy,' Peyton said, pieces starting to fit together. 'I thought you didn't want to risk these men.'

'Not for waterways. But I would have gladly given them up for you that day. And later, when it became clear Sergei would make a scandal of it, I thought crazily that I might sell the list to him as hush money if it would just get him to go home.'

'And now? Is there a reason to keep this list now?' Peyton asked huskily.

'No, the dragons are slain and by much nobler means.' Tessa reached for the paper and tossed it on to the grate where a little fire burned. It felt good to watch the slip of paper that had caused her so much trouble burn into oblivion. It could trouble them no more.

'Come to bed, Tessa,' Peyton whispered after a while. Later, as she climaxed in his arms, she knew with a certainty that the past was gone. With Peyton, everything had become fresh and new. The world was clean again.

Epilogue

A year and a half later

Peyton Ramsden, the fourth Earl of Dursley, was doing what he did best these days, juggling his twin boys on his legs while he attempted to eat. Already they'd managed to smear cake on his shirt, but he didn't care. Today was his fortieth birthday.

Beside him, Tessa laughed as the boys landed another forkful of icing on his lap. She dabbed at him with a napkin to no effect, but he appreciated the effort none the less.

Near him, Paine and Julia kept an eye on their son, now a strapping two-year-old, too squirmy for sitting on laps for long these days.

Further down the table, the Branscombe girls enjoyed the al fresco picnic with a few of their new friends from the area. Petra seemed quite taken with the squire's son, a nice boy who liked horses. Eva had been allowed to pin her hair up for the occasion. Annie was twelve now and chatting gaily to some girl friends her age.

Peyton knew he was blessed to be surrounded by so many family members. Only Crispin was absent, but he'd remembered the occasion with a letter, assuring Peyton he was doing well and a nebulous promise that he'd return later in the year.

Beneath the cloth covering the table, Peyton squeezed Tessa's hand, hoping the simple gesture conveyed all the joy he felt when he looked at her and their family.

Her eyes danced with mischief as she discreetly lifted his hand beneath the cloth to her stomach and leaned forward just for him to hear. 'I have a birthday present for you.'

Peyton smiled. 'Another? I thought I'd already got my present earlier today.' That morning, they'd locked the bedroom door and Peyton had engaged in something else he did well, making passionate love to his wife with every fibre of his being.

Tessa blushed. 'Well, this one won't arrive for another seven months.'

'It will give me time to put an extra order in for shirts.' Peyton reached around his messy boys and kissed her soundly on the mouth, not caring who might chance to see them. It was no secret he loved his wife. Neither was it a secret that, in his fortieth year, Peyton Ramsden had all he wanted and more. His life was complete.

* * * * *